THE
FUTURE

THE
FUTURE

RAIBEART MACDOUGALL

First published in Great Britain
in November 2011
by Inform & Enlighten Ltd

ISBN: 978-1-4709-7812-9

Designed and edited by Peter F May

INFORM & ENLIGHTEN LTD
47 FONTMELL CLOSE
ST ALBANS AL3 5HU

WAR DAY + 546

THE BORDER CONTROL POINT AT SWIECKO
ON THE RIVER ODER
AT THE EASTERN EXTREME OF GERMANY

"Alfa is closing," the quiet American voice was calm. John Horne pressed the small red button on his console. Thirty metres away, in a small office, Lieutenant James swivelled in his chair and viewed his bank of television screens. Alfa was closing. He leaned forward.

Horne's eyes were pressed to his glasses. From his viewpoint, some twenty metres off the ground, he had a perfect view of the checkpoint. About five hundred metres away a steel shutter was sliding slowly across the narrow road. He murmured into his throat microphone:

"Prepare for runner."

At ground level, just metres inside the line, Peters— with the handset held close to his ear— relayed Horne's message to his group leader. Lieutenant James, watching the heavy steel shutter move on his screen, picked up the blue 'phone and pressed three buttons. It was answered after less than two rings.

"Allison."

"Action on Alfa, sir".

"Is it live?"

The lieutenant opened his mouth to express doubt. At that moment the six video cameras covering the approach to the heavy steel shutter picked up the fast moving Mercedes.

"Jesus," Horne murmured, forgetting for a moment that all sound and vision was being taped. "We have a live one. We have a live one".

"Confirmed live. Confirmed live," Peters shouted. The six men were moving before he'd finished speaking.

"She's live," the lieutenant said into the 'phone. "Live," he repeated. He watched fascinated as the Mercedes tore towards the moving barrier. His finger found and depressed the 'Preserve Tapes' button on his console without his eyes leaving the screens. All sound and vision picked up by the video cameras and transmitted through their communications equipment would be saved—not only future action, but also the last thirty minutes.

It was an old model, cream coloured Mercedes saloon, low slung and spacious. It swayed slightly as the driver came out of the gentle 'S' bend necessary to straighten-up for the bridge as he crested the gentle rise after leaving the customs and immigration sheds. The sheds themselves were hidden from view. The Merc was smoking badly as the driver held his foot flat on the floor.

"Understood," Allison's voice in his ear piece. It was moving fast, very fast. It might just make it.

John Horne swore. It was going to be close. The Mercedes was really moving, but the barrier was solid. It would stop almost anything once it was locked into position in the concrete bunkers on both sides of the road. But the barrier wouldn't make it all the way across the road before the Merc got there. Would it?

He struggled to see how many people the car held. He wondered what the playbacks would show later. If the car hit the barrier it would be wrecked. 'Move, man, move, move, move,' he found that he was almost speaking aloud.

"Floods," a voice said in his ear. He flicked a switch and the whole border area was lit up brighter than day.

"We'll want the dazzlers in a few moments, Sergeant" the lieutenant added, "when I give the word".

"Understood, sir". His fingers hovered over the power relays.

If the Mercedes was wrecked the occupants would have to cover the three hundred metre bridge on foot. Almost impossible. Both sides had it floodlit and the other side would be shooting. The dazzlers might help, but they could confuse the runners badly.

"Medics on station, sir. Fire tender alert."

"Bring it on station".

"Understood, sir".

The Mercedes was mere metres from the barrier, but it wasn't going to make it. The driver wasn't letting up, though. He was going for broke. He was keeping to the outer edge towards the bridge. The river itself was lit one hundred metres in each direction. There was no provision for pedestrians and the bridge was barely wide enough for two juggernauts to pass each other without considerable difficulty. Not many juggernauts passed this way nowadays.

The Merc seemed, quite impossibly, to flounder in the gap for a moment—trapped. Close-up North showed the driver being badly shaken as the car tried to ram itself through a gap that was too small and growing smaller.

And suddenly, with a scream of ruined steel, it was through.

"Survived impact," Horne intoned. Another amplified voice roared out from across the bridge, "Second verbal warning. Runner still moving. Fences will be live," he pressed a large green button on his console. All around the point at which the road met the line a series of small green lights began to flash to indicate that hostile defences were activated.

"Defences live," Peters intoned needlessly. The ground crew were surrounded by flashing green lights.

"Runner under fire".

"Runner under fire," Peters repeated. This was a dangerous spot to be in right now. If the marksmen at the far end of the bridge were shooting at a moving object on the bridge, it took little imagination to wonder where the projectiles would go if they failed to find their intended target. The ground crew adopted an uncomfortable crouch.

Horne was grinding the glasses into his face in attempt to see as much as the lieutenant could see from his comfortable leather swivel chair in his office. The Merc was still travelling at about thirty miles an hour, but it was very badly damaged. The right hand side was torn and jagged, the left hand side pummelled flat, but this was merely cosmetic. Far more important, the left hand front wheel assembly was collapsing. The wheel seemed to have developed a mind of its own and had adopted a crazy angle. The tyre itself had disintegrated in the impact.

The driver was struggling.

Two of the marksmen were firing. The ground crew were as low as they could be while keeping on their feet.

Suddenly, the rear of the car became a ball of flame. A spiral of acrid smoke rose above the snaking Merc.

"Fuel tank ignited," why didn't people ever learn?   Protect the weak points; people, tyres, and fuel. This runner had lost two out of three already.

And still the car came on, the driver battling with the wheel.

Two hundred metres to go to home.

A head bobbed into Horne's view. Oh, no! "Second runner; female; white; twenties".

"Two up," Peters yelled. Group leader nodded.

The female head showed up in startling clarity on close up South. She was young, very young. The lieutenant doubted that Horne's estimation was actually wrong, but the girl can't have been much above the low twenties. She appeared to be shouting something to the driver.

The rear of the car was still burning, the thick, dark smoke pouring out and filling the air and effectively preventing the marksmen from doing their job properly.

With a final lurch, the Merc veered to the left with too much violence for the driver to combat. The left hand front wing caught the bridge and the car swung through a violent arc, spinning through 180 degrees and slamming the right hand rear wing against the bridge. Soft steel crumpled, the suspension collapsed and the car sagged. The bonnet seemed to loosen itself and the boot flapped open. A small cloud of dust and mud hung in the air for an instant. And still it hadn't stopped moving.

"Runner disabled. One hundred metres. Watch that line!" Horne's word of caution was for any of the ground crew who felt tempted to step over the line.

Slowly, oh so slowly, the Merc was still spinning. The violent blow against the bridge, taken by the whole of the right hand side, had absorbed most of its velocity, but it was still moving, sliding gently in an arc on its wrecked wheels, its belly scraping the tarmac and leaving a trail of sparks and gouges.

It swung slowly, or so it seemed to those who watched, although what sort of a nightmare was going on inside the car was anybody's guess.

In moments it had stopped, smoke and flames pouring from its half opened boot, broadside on, blocking the bridge. It rocked slightly and settled.

"Runner stationary; disabled; vehicle burning".

Camera three showed the lieutenant the female runner ramming her shoulder repeatedly against the inside of the passenger door of the burning car.

It wouldn't open.

A second figure, shadowy in the smoke, was visible moving in the car behind her.

It wouldn't open.

The camera showed her shouting, her head shaking, her wide eyes, the hang of her hair.

It wouldn't open.

Horne was praying. The glasses were grinding marks around his eyes that wouldn't disappear for three days. He hadn't prayed for years. Very many years. She was going to burn.

It wouldn't open. She couldn't open the door!

"Jesus, Groupie," Peters yelled at the ground crew's leader.

"Get the fire team in," the lieutenant yelled into his mike, "kill that fire, now". His eyes didn't leave the screen. She was still ramming her body against the door.

"Affirmative. We're moving".

"Let me go," Peters yelled. It would take them minutes to put out the fire at one hundred metres. They would have burned in half the time. The whole rear end of the car was alight. The passenger compartment was full of smoke.

"Stay there," group leader yelled. "Stay put," he yelled again, handing his weapon to Waugh. He was one step over the line and then running fast, zigging slightly, but relying on his crouch and the cover of the smoke to protect him.

There was a sudden burst of heavy fire from the bank just south of the bridge, and he was down. Just like that. He slumped to the ground and lay, unmoving.

"Jesus," Peters forgot himself for a moment "Medics, medics," he recovered, yelling into his handset, "one down, one down".

The lieutenant swore.

The rear door of the car burst open. A moment later a young man tumbled out onto the tarmac.

"Get the girl, the girl, the girl, get the girl," Horne muttered loud enough for his mike to pick up.

The young man picked himself up, reached back into the car and pulled her out. A dark bundle on the tarmac, filthy, coughing, retching, wide-eyed, but alive.

For the moment.

Together, they crouched, protected from hostile fire by the wreck of their car. Their clothes were a mess; torn and stained. Their faces were blackened with filth, perhaps the acrid smoke or perhaps the dust from the impact. They looked around wildly, but there was only one direction to run. They seemed to be coughing a lot.

Understandable, thought the lieutenant, but they'd better start to move while they've got the cover of the smoke.

Two shots rang out.

The man was pulling something from inside his shirt. He held it up for a moment. It was, unbelievably, a British passport.

"Runner appears to be carrying a British passport," Horne. That would explain the right-hand drive Merc. But what the hell was he doing out there? The lieutenant was already leaning forward to examine the close-up more carefully. His left hand was reaching for the blue 'phone..

"Come on," Peters yelled, "run. Run!"

The two half-stood. The man reached for the woman's hand and, without looking back, they began the hundred metre run.

It would have taken a schoolboy athlete under fifteen seconds. It could take them the rest of their lives. The further they ran from the car the less protection the smoke gave them from the marksmen.

"Allison," the voice at the other end of the line was unhurried.

"I think you'd better come down here, sir. This looks…difficult."

Chapter One

WAR DAY

LUBLIN, SOUTH EASTERN POLAND

The telephone woke him. He struggled up through layers of cotton wool, not certain where he was, his mind painfully heavy. He managed to haul his head off the pillow. There was a long pause. The 'phone rang again. That was the trouble with these foreign 'phones, he thought, there was such a long gap between rings that one always thought for a moment that the caller had hung up.

His hand scrabbled in the darkness for the handset. Beside him he could feel the warmth of Marzena. He wanted to find the 'phone before it woke her. He found it before it had rung for a third time. His hand grasped the plastic, began to lift it, fumbled and dropped it. It clattered to the floor.

Marzena stirred, turning in his direction and mumbling, "What is it?"

"Nothing," he responded automatically. He found the hand piece and held it to his ear.

"Hello?" a male voice was asking. It sounded doubtful.

"Hello," responded Jamie.

"James Ingram?"

"Yes," he was still fumbling to make sense out of this. It was the middle of the night. Where was his watch? What time was it?

He remembered his digital alarm clock. He turned towards its reassuring glow, only it wasn't glowing.

"British Embassy, Warsaw," the voice was in a hurry now that he'd identified Jamie. Jamie grunted, but the voice went on without a pause, "Time to get out. Fast. The balloon's gone up. They're moving in from the East."

"They?" but he knew the answer, already. There'd been a lot of news recently about the New Russian Confederation's imminent collapse. Overspill was the word that had become popular in this respect. Overspill. They meant the westward movement from the impoverished NRC. The New Russian Confederation that had been a disaster of varying degrees since its inception.

"The NRC's on the move. The Eastern borders are closed both ways, but we're expecting some heavy movement very soon."

Heavy movement Jamie thought. That's what they called the armed forces when they didn't want to say what they meant.

"Right," he said, uncertain what response was actually required. He rubbed the back of his head.

"You must move now. Immediately. This is the last warning you'll get."

"Things are that bad?" He could feel that Marzena was awake.

"That bad. Yes. You'll be lucky to get out; it's too far from Lublin to the border. The southern borders are closed, so you'd have to make for Germany. About four hundred miles. Really," he was about to continue, but Jamie interrupted.

"Airports?"

Marzena was getting out of bed.

"Hardly, old fellow. Even if they're still flying they won't be in hours. And any that go out will be chocca."

He was wide awake, now. He heard Marzena flick the light switch. The room remained dark. He heard her mouth something.

"What about the children? Aren't you arranging flights for them?"

"The children?"

"We can't take them by road. It's too far. It'll be far too dangerous."

"What children?"

"Shouldn't we have had more warning?"

"The FO finalled all parents four days ago. The last children left over 30 hours ago."

"Finalled?" his head was spinning. Marszena left the room. He heard another switch being flicked. Nothing! No power.

"Four days ago."

"But," he paused, trying to make himself think, "you didn't final us."

"No need, no children," the voice was brisk, firm and confident.

Jamie swore, "We have. Two," he paused for breath. An obscenity, hardly discernible, but grossly obscene came down the line from the British Embassy.

"Just how serious is all this. Surely, there's no real problem."

"Get those kids out. This is really most unfortunate. We have a full crisis alert here. All non-essential Embassy personnel are leaving Warsaw now. We're expecting thousands of hungry, armed men to cross from the NRC in a matter of hours. There has even been talk—nothing official, of course, mere conjecture, you understand—that the army moving west has a nuclear capacity. Field arms only, but we're talking the real thing."

"How?"

"How, what?"

"Are they getting out?"

"What? Who?"

"The embassy staff?"

"Flight."

"From where? When?"

"Now look...no."

"Two kids. They're tiny. They'd weigh less than two suitcases. When?"

"I can't."

"When?"

"Eight fifteen."

"What time is it now?"

"What time...?" he began, "five fifty-six."

"Where? From where?"

"No, I really..."

"Tiny kids. From where?"

"Okecie."

"Ace! Who are you?"

"Me? What...? Charteris."

"Thanks. I won't forget this, thanks."

He slammed the 'phone down and yelled, "We leave in five minutes."

Marzena ran in the dark, one small child in her arms, the other scampering behind her.

"Tom," Jamie knelt down to his son's level, "I want you to get dressed quickly. Jeans, warm clothes, outside boots, okay?"

"Wrap'em up warm," she nodded. His eyes were growing more used to the light. He slipped on jeans himself, put his briefcase by the small flat's front door as he slipped on a shirt. Thermal underwear?

"Thermals, bring them," he was trying to remember how much fuel they had in the car. It was almost exactly one hundred miles from Lublin to Warsaw. Shouldn't be a problem.

He raced into the kitchen, grabbed a handful of large bin bags and ran around the flat filling them. Food, clothes, anything that looked handy. Not so easy in the dark.

Two hours. It wasn't long enough.

It was possible, though, he knew. He'd spoken to one or two people who reckoned they'd done it in less than ninety minutes. Complete loonies, every one of them, but it was possible. Especially at this time of night. The roads would be clear. But would he find Okecie? He'd never driven to Warsaw airport before.

Socks, jersey, jacket, coat, keys and papers.

"I'll get the car," he left the flat, running evenly down the forty steps from the second floor. Outside the outer door the air was crisp. Must be about minus ten, he thought. Could have been an awful lot worse. Last year in February it had dropped to minus twenty five for a couple of days. No joke. You have to treat temperatures like that with respect.

The Volvo started on the second turn. Thank you, Volvo, he thought. In the four minutes that it had taken him to walk briskly to the car pound he had felt the cold. Even in just minus ten it was important to stay well wrapped.

He scraped the ice off the windscreen, side windows and mirrors. It was all very well having heated windows and mirrors, but in this kind of weather they took a while to do the job. The heated seat was nice too, although it always reminded him uncomfortably of peeing in his trousers. Not that he'd done that for a while.

Outside the flat, he left the car locked and running and ran back up the forty steps. How many times had he climbed them? How many times had he counted them? He didn't know. Millions?

Two adults, two kids, one suitcase, one briefcase and four overfilled bin bags and they were off. He glanced at the clock.

Six fifteen. Blast!

"Map of Warsaw?"

"Yes, it's here," she waved it.

"We've got to find the airport."

With his foot down they were already on the road out of Lublin. The car could cruise at speeds far greater than the roads would allow. Most of the road to Warsaw was single carriageway, nearly all of it with a generous hard shoulder on each side. This encouraged the extraordinarily dangerous habits that the Polish had established on their roads.

"Passports?"

"Yes."

"Money?"

"Yes."

They flashed out of Lublin at just under eighty miles an hour. The limit in built up areas was forty odd, and in other areas almost exactly sixty. It seemed very black once they had left the street lights.

He put his foot down.

"Is this really necessary," Marzena had her head down over his briefcase which she had opened on her lap.

"I hope not."

She grimaced, "I haven't washed my teeth."

"Nor me."

There was laughter from the back of the car. Marzena turned, "What's up, Trix?"

"You're naughty," the tiny blonde grinned at her mother in the dark.

"Why am I naughty?" Marzena reached back and rested her hand on the side of Trix's head.

"You must wash your teeth," she found this very amusing. Her voice was laughing, "you know you must."

"Yes, you're quite right."

"Is it the NRC? Are they coming?" Tom asked. They couldn't see his small face in the dark, but there were times when he looked so young and so serious that Marzena hadn't been able to prevent herself from wrapping her arms all around him—which wasn't always considered suitable by a boisterous six year old boy. There was just a moments silence as his parents each deliberated on whether the truth was a reasonable or a dangerous response.

"We think so..., " Jamie started, but Tom had already continued.

"Their tanks can cruise at over fifty miles an hour, Dad, on a ploughed field. How far are we from the border, Dad?"

"A hundred miles, maybe, maybe less."

"Wow," Tom paused, "Wowie!" Even a six year old could cope with maths like that.

So, Marzena was thinking, Lublin could be full of NRC tanks by breakfast. Which reminded her that none of them had eaten yet. She began to pull a loaf to pieces.

+

They hit the edge of Warsaw at seven forty. The place was unusually deserted for a weekday morning. Jamie was driving far too fast, but so long as he didn't hit anything he didn't care. They sped over the series of lumps placed on the approaches to the roundabouts and lights, their stomachs shaking like jellies in moulds. He jumped the lights as they were changing. But it all made little difference. There was so little traffic that they would have arrived only moments later if he'd driven with his normal caution.

It was well before eight and they were only a few hundred yards from the airport when they found the road blocked by a road block. It looked official. For a ridiculous moment he considered jumping it, but this was no American movie, this was real life and he had Trix and Tom in the back. There were a handful of armed men in uniform standing idly around the block. He slowed, opening his window, hoping that they would wave him through. The Volvo had the green number plates that showed that he was a foreigner. They didn't, so he stopped.

It was the Policja. Warsaw traffic police. One of the policja ambled over after a moments delay. He was middle-aged, running very slightly to fat and, sporting a fine black moustache on his rather plump face.

"Officer," Jamie leaned out of the window and spoke in his appalling Polish.

"Ah," the policeman smiled, "English?" He, too, spoke in Polish.

"Yes," Jamie raised a smile. It wasn't easy. "We're in a bit of a rush. We're running a bit late."

"The 8.15 London flight?"

"Yes."

"You have tickets?"

"Yes," he was no good at lying, but perhaps his appalling Polish would hide the otherwise obvious lie.

"Yes, yes," he indicated with a waving motion that they were to pass through, but nonetheless he continued, "It is late. It will be delayed for some time, I think."

"Thank you, officer," he hoped that his look of relief wouldn't be too apparent, but perhaps it was okay to look relieved when you professed to have a ticket to flee a sinking country.

The car park was a mess of poorly abandoned cars. Little regard had been paid to normal Polish motoring conventions, which were themselves often compared unfavourably with British habits.

They found a quiet spot, not far from the entrance. Not too far, anyway.

"Money and passports. Nothing else," he looked over his shoulder at the two kids. "Nothing, okay."

Trix simply nodded, her bright eyes pinned to her father's face. Her beautiful blond hair swung with her enthusiastic nodding. Jamie smiled. She was clutching a small stuffed bear.

"Okay," he relented, "We can't leave Fangs behind, can we." He looked at Tom, "anything you need, kid?" He called him 'kid' when they were being men together. Tom shook his head. He was still wearing a solemn face. Far too solemn for a six year old.

They wrapped the kids in outdoor coats, scarves and gloves and tightened their outdoor shoes, wrapped themselves up and strode out towards Departures.

With the kids a few metres in front of them, Jamie explained in response to Marzena's query that if there was time and if they got places they would come back for some luggage. Bin bags, he reminded her, not luggage. But, in the meantime he would feel a lot better if they weren't cluttered up with luggage. Anyway, they wanted to look as compact as possible if they hoped to squeeze onto the plane.

Departures was a nightmare. Every spare space was cluttered with people or luggage. A lot of the luggage had obviously been thrown together very quickly, and quite a bit was of the bin bag variety like their own. It was years since he had been there. The whole interior was far more modern than it had been when he was last there.

They each grabbed a little hand and waded into the crowd, headed for the BA desk which was showing a departure time—delayed—of 8.15. Expected departure time now 9.00.

Getting to the desk itself proved to be impossible. It seemed to be the very centre of the whole mob. The cluster of people, in a totally disorganised melee, was thick, hard and tight around the three sides from which the desk could be approached.

Jamie turned to Marzena, "We can't do it. Not all of us." She nodded. They were separated by two solid looking couples. He lifted Trix above his head and passed her across to her mother.

"Wait here, I'll dig in and see what I can do," he smiled. He was worn already. She looked good, though. Always had. Always did.

"Love you," she mouthed at him. He smiled.

On his own, he made better progress. Realising that he was battling through mainly Polish speakers queuing for a British Airways desk, he began to murmur in his own awful Polish, "Excuse me. I'm British," each time that he found himself unable to squeeze past a solid body.

At last, he was one layer behind the front line. He pulled out his British passport and held it above the heads of the people at the front. It took only moments for the girl behind the counter— who was being assisted by a more than averagely beefy young man— to register the fact that he was there.

"British national?" she asked.

"Yes," he said. He supposed that he was. He was British, he had a home in Britain, a family in Britain, a British passport. What did the word 'national' mean? He was British. This was no time for a language lesson.

"Yes," he repeated, afraid that his momentary doubt might show.

She took the passport from him, flicked through, and looked up.

"BA 106 to London?"

"Is that this one?" he indicated the screen above the desk.

She smiled, "It's the only one."

"The only one?" her meaning wasn't clear. They simply wanted the next one.

"Ours is the only non-military transport on the ground here. Warsaw is refusing clearance for incoming commercial flights." Her smile was very sad. "That makes this the only flight out of Warsaw. If it wasn't a British 'plane it would have been impounded last night."

"I'll have four, please."

"Smoking or non-smoking?" Was this relevant?

"Non smoking, please."

"The flight's boarding now. Hand luggage only."

"Okay."

"How will you pay?" His hand fumbled in his pocket. Even at this hour, the eleventh hour, it was a question of cash.

"Cash or plastic," he offered her. He hadn't used his cards for months.

She smiled, "You can pay with all normal credit cards." She took the one he offered her and began the brief paperwork. He was still separated from the counter by one layer of people. A very solid layer. Behind him the crush was growing even greater. He could feel more and more pressure on his back. He tried to turn to signal to Marzena that all was well, but the girl was speaking again as she completed the docket.

"You'll have to be quick. They're boarding now," she repeated. He glanced at his watch. It was past nine. He glanced at the board above his head: departure time delayed to 9.00.

"We may be refused clearance to leave," she added, "in which case your account will be credited with a full refund."

"Refused?" he repeated, confused.

She gave him a very old fashioned look. What she was thinking was, doesn't this guy listen to the news, or what? What she said was, naturally, more polite.

"The NRC army is less than eighty kilometres east of Warsaw, and moving. Anything could happen." She shoved a form towards him, "Please sign this." He began to read it.

"You've no time to read it. I'll give you a copy."

"What is it?" He never liked to sign anything unread. But ...prioritise, he told himself. Get things into perspective.

"Release. Releases British Airways from civil liability. From any liability. Disengages the Warsaw convention. Meaning you travel at your own risk," her sad smile was back. He paused. She shook her head very slightly.

"No sign, no go," she said it very gently. She took the sting from the words, but the meaning was clear. She softened, "If it's any help, I can tell you that Captain Morgan wouldn't take her up unless he knew he could get her home." She made it sound like a bomber in a war film.

"Jesus Christ," he was shaking his head. I don't believe this, he was thinking.

"Passports," she was holding her hand out.

He was aghast. He only had his own. His mouth opened. Marzena had the others. How incredibly stupid!

"They're..." he indicated backwards, across the thick crowd.

"One for each traveller," she explained.

He could feel his mouth hanging open. He closed it.

"I must see a passport for each ticket."

"Surely..." he began. She was shaking her head.

He turned, wide-eyed, to the crowd behind him, and then back again. His mouth closed and opened again. The pressure of the crowd was quite intense. He could never do it. He couldn't reach Marzena and fight his way through this crowd again, not if the 'plane was already boarding. Hc looked back at the crowd. Miles of blank faces.

Oh Jesus.

"The kids," he said, the despair clear on his face.

"I can't do it," she sounded really sorry, "not without an EC passport. One for each traveller."

"Jesus," he muttered, as another thought hit him. Marzena had a Polish passport. Again he turned wildly back to the crowd. Suddenly, in the distance, Trix appeared. Impossible, but true. Sitting on Marzena's shoulders.

"Marzena," he yelled. People turned, "Trix," he yelled even louder, overcoming his normal

British reserve. What was it that Graham Greene had said? About the British. And their reserve.

Trix waved happily, Fangs held tight in her tiny fist. She bashed her mum's head with the bear, waving and grinning. Marzena began to try to move towards him, or maybe it was just his imagination.

"Marzena," he yelled as loud as he could. But there was a lot of noise, an awful lot of noise all around them, "Passports," surely he was screaming now. Any moment he expected to hear that the departure gate had closed.

Jesus, Jesus, he was praying. Don't let us be incarcerated here for the sake of a formality.

She was struggling forwards. He stood on the tips of his toes. For a moment she did the same. He yelled,

"Passports," deliberately mouthing the word for her lips. She responded by disappearing for a moment— how was she coping with both the kids?—and re-appearing with the three documents in her hand.

She was only thirty feet away."Look," he said to the girl behind the counter, waving at the passports in the distance. She looked.

"Two minutes," the beefy guy spoke quietly.

"One's Polish," she said accusingly. She looked as if he had deliberately attempted to mislead her.

"My wife," it wasn't enough, he could see that.

"Can't you...we're married?" he was struggling. He didn't know what to say, which way to turn.

"Please," he was desperate, "Please."

30

"I can't. I need an EC passport for each ticket I issue. I'm very sorry, truly I am." Jamie suddenly realised why there was such an enormous crowd at the desk, yet there were still seats on the plane.

"Four tickets, please," he was begging. He knew that he was begging, but somehow the part of him that was British knew, just knew, that everything would work out all right. Hadn't it always before? In the end everything was always all right, wasn't it?

She just looked at him.

"Oh, Jesus."

If there was one thing that the Polish knew how to deal with, in Jamie's opinion, it was paperwork and related regulations. Unless you knew someone, someone 'higher', someone with clout, the only thing that could change a regulation concerning paperwork was cash. Hard cash. Would that still work?

He pulled out a handful of notes, mainly deutschmarks and possibly amounting to several month's salary, even nowadays, for a bilingual Polish ticket clerk.

"Four?" he asked, the handful of notes held out.

"I can't," she indicated the crowd, "even if I'd wanted to. It's more than my life's worth. I can do three. One for each EC passport"

He nodded, beaten, and stuffed the money back into his pocket.

Moments later he was struggling back through the crowd. It seemed to have grown even more solid and the people more numerous.

"Three," he said in answer to Marzena's unasked question.

"Three?"

"Move, we must move. They've almost finished boarding," he had taken Tom's hand. They were moving at a slow run towards the check-in point.

"EC passports only," he explained, "but you three go and I'll drive. I'll be home in two days."

"No," she was shocked. Horrified. Blind terror on her face. You can't stay here. I've heard what they've been saying," she indicated the crowd. She shook her head. "Terrible things," she was close to tears.

"Got to," he smiled, "got no choice." They were at the gate. The clock showed 9.15.

"Get another ticket," she pleaded.

"I can't. She won't sell me one, and even if I could there's no time."

"Tickets," a voice said. Jamie handed over the three tickets without really looking.

"You've got no choice," he said again, "Kids can't go on their own and I'm certainly not going to leave you here."

"Three to travel?" the voice said with an element of surprise or doubt.

"Yep," Jamie answered.

"Passports," Jamie took Marzena's and the kids' two passports from Marzena and handed them over the counter.

She was crying, "No, no, no, you can't..."

"EC Nationals only," the man was handing back Marzena's passport.

"My wife has a ticket," Jamie stated.

"Tickets are issued against EC passports only," he said accusingly. Jamie was suddenly aware of the four large, uniformed men lounging in the near distance. They looked like a mixture between airline personnel and policemen.

Was that a refusal or an acceptance? A moments silence.

"EC Nationals only," he repeated. One of the four large men stirred.

"Shit."

"Gate's closing," he stated as though addressing somebody else. He wasn't looking any of them in the eye.

"Shit."

"Go," she said, "go."

"No," he gave the check-in clerk two tickets and the kids' passports.

"Quick," he said, already tears were appearing in his eyes.

She was pushing him, "Go, go, go, go..." He stood his ground.

"Aren't you coming?" Tom's face was a picture of horror. He looked from his mother to his father. Trix let out a moan.

"Who'll..." he began, looking helplessly at his two tiny children. One of the large men had sauntered up.

"Grzegorz?" he was addressing the man at the gate.

"Two," the man asked Jamie, "or three?"

"Two," he had no choice. He couldn't leave Marzena alone, not here, not with the NRC just miles away. Not with...but what about the kids?

"Two unaccompanied children," the gate man stated to the uniform.

Trix was screaming, clinging to her Dad's leg.

"Why do we have to go?" Tom was crying.

"You have to leave," Jamie had bent down and now found that he was kneeling on the solid plastic flooring talking face to face with Tom and Trix, "We'll be with you very soon. Granny and Grandpa will meet you at the other end. And we'll see you in a couple of days."

"I want Mummy to come," Trix's face was a mess of tears. Her tiny fist was clenched around Fangs, the muscles squeezing tight. The terror clear on her face.

"We'll have to go," the uniform was saying kindly to Tom and Trix.

"No, no," they wailed back in unison. He took one of Tom's hands, "Come along now, young man. Let's go have a look at the airplane."

With a scream, Tom pulled free and flung himself at his mother.

"No, no, no, no," he was screaming. His little eyes wide with terror. His lips white and taut.

The uniform looked questioningly at Marzena. She nodded. He waved one of his colleagues over, bent and picked up Tom. The six year old kicked, thrashed and tore at the man.

"I don't want to go," he was screaming, his tiny voice already becoming hoarse from the effort, "I don't want to go." The man reached out and took two tickets and passports from the desk, and walked slowly away as the second guy lifted Trix gently from the ground. Jamie watched as Marzena prized her daughter's grip loose from the child's last desperate attempt to remain with her mother, finger by tiny loving finger.

Oh, Jesus.

For a moment they watched, aghast, as the two large men walked slowly away. The two tiny faces screaming over their shoulders, the tiny bodies wrestling uselessly against the strength of the two large men. Beside him, Jamie could hear Marzena sobbing. He didn't recall standing up, but he was standing now. With a final howl of despair, terror and anger, frustration and fear the two children disappeared through the swing gates, around the screens, and out of sight.

"Oh, God," Marzena was looking at the ticket man. Looking daggers, looking death. Jamie put out his hands and held her gently. He was afraid she was about to spring on the bloke. She pulled against his hold, but he gripped tighter.

She said something that Jamie didn't catch. The man paled. She had probably been speaking in Polish, and not very pleasant Polish either if the man's reaction was anything to go by.

"Come on, come on," he soothed.

"And you're bloody useless, too," she turned on him with a scream. Her left hand lifted, he raised his right hand in surprised defence and the palm of her right hand slammed into his face. He put his arms around her and held her wrapped up in his love. For a moment she struggled, whimpering, and then seemed to lose energy. She sagged gently in his arms, weeping.

"Oh, I'm sorry, I'm so sorry, so awfully sorry..."

Chapter Two

WAR DAY

WARSAW

Their first thought was to find a 'phone. The bank of 'phone in Departures was surrounded by crowds almost as intense as that around the BA desk. They had seen the plane leave at just before nine-thirty, which meant that it should arrive at about 10.30 British time.

"We'll head into the city, find a Telekom centre and "phone from there," he had said as he steered the distraught Marzena through the lounge. It was a beautiful day outside. The sun was shining; there wasn't a cloud to be seen. The snow was soft underfoot, the landscape white. It was lovely. It was also still about ten degrees below. The road block had gone. No need, he supposed, now that the last flight had left. He pointed the car back towards the city centre. It wasn't far, and the roads were still largely deserted.

Once at the centre, she directed him to a large Telekom centre. He parked the car on the pavement, Polish style, and they walked the few yards to the entrance only to find it locked.

"What now?" He wasn't sure. They stood in silence for a moment. She was wiping her eyes with a sodden tissue.

"The Marriott?" They'd stayed there recently whilst he'd attended a two day seminar. It was a very nice place.

"Brilliant," he glanced at his watch nervously. It was going to be close to impossible to get through to his parents in time for them to get down to Heathrow. He wasn't sure how long it took from Bishops Stortford to Heathrow, but it had to be well over an hour. And that assumed that they were at home, and that they would have no traffic problems. With a sinking heart he realised that today would be a normal morning on the M25. It would take them ages to get from home to Heathrow.

"Come on," he took her arm gently, and they walked back to the car. He wasn't sure who had suffered most at the airport, Marzena or the children. Marzena, of course would get over it fairly quickly once they were all reunited. It would only be a couple of days, three at the outside. But how would the kids take it? What sort of harm would a parting like that cause? What would happen to the trust? He remembered his fear as a small boy that his mother might leave him on a London bus by mistake. How would that compare with being forcibly parted from your parents and put on a thousand mile flight?

And then, he thought, to have no one to meet you at the other end. This was far worse than anything he'd ever feared as a child, and his fears had seemed so very real then. It was only a short ride to the Marriott. They dumped the Volvo outside, and made straight for the bank of 'phones.

"Book a call," he said, "Through reception. I'll use a box." That way they had twice the chance of getting through. He pulled out a couple of phone cards and dialled out. For some years now the 'phone system in Poland had been comparable to the rest of Europe, but if the NRC was really only fifty odd miles from Warsaw it seemed likely that the lines would be busy and possible that they might be damaged.

He punched the numbers into the keyboard; 00 44 27894 5093, for his parents' home in the small village near to Bishop's Stortford, Hertfordshire. A series of short beeps told him that the number or the line was engaged. He punched the re-dial button.

Marzena was opening the cubicle door.

"They won't do it," she was crying as she squeezed in. This might be a multiple star hotel, but there still wasn't room for more than one in their 'phone cubicles without a squeeze.

"What?" She'd been only moments.

"Place the call," the tears were streaming down her cheeks.

"Why not, for..." he stopped himself. He realised that he was shouting, "Why not?" he repeated in a more reasonable tone of voice.

A series of short bleeps. Engaged.

He punched the re-dial button as she said, "Residents only."

"Book in, Kochana," he replied without a thought. She smiled at his Polish endearment.

"But," he knew that look. It meant that something was expensive, but not only expensive. It meant that in her view the price was a gross misjustice. He touched her face. It was wet, blotchy and puffy. He loved her. He loved this woman, the mother of his children.

"Do it," he said softly.

"Use a card," he replied to her unasked question. She hadn't got her bag. He fumbled, and with one hand pulled out his pouch containing cards, "Any one will do."

As he watched her slight form, fifty kilos of pretty woman in jeans and duck-down coat, walk away he heard the short bleeps again.

He punched in the whole number this time, misdialled, managed not to swear, and began again. He turned back to the cubicle door as the telephone did its electronic whirrings and clankings. She was out of sight, presumably at the desk around the corner. He hummed a slight tune. Deliberately, he forced the picture of his two children being carried away screaming out of his mind.

There was a distant thump, like a large and rather solid door slamming upstairs.

Upstairs?

He watched idly through the window in the door.

Bleep, bleep, bleep...still engaged. He punched the re-dial button, again.

Marzena appeared, running. She's got through, he thought, and turned to replace the handset. She pulled harshly at the door.

"Bombs, they're bombing."

"They are? What is? What?" he was struggling to grasp her words.

"Bombs. They're firing rockets. I don't know." her eyes were wide, "Oh Jamie, I do hope that they're all right."

He wrapped his arms around her, the telephone still in his left hand, "They've got to be better off than if they were here." There were two distant, but nonetheless quite distinct, crumping noises in the distance. Thump. Thump.

"Jesus," he was trying to think. Prioritise, prioritise he said to himself. But this isn't real. It can't be. Can't be. Prioritise! While we're under fire? Bombs! Where do I...how can I?

It was ringing! The telephone in his hand was ringing.

WAR DAY

HERTFORDSHIRE
GREAT BRITAIN

The television was too loud. "Turn it down," she yelled from the kitchen. There was no response. Outside a lorry rumbled past. She didn't notice it. She wandered to the door, her hands held away from her apron. They were covered in dough. She wiped a few strands of hair away from her face.

"Miriam," she yelled, "turn that thing down." In the living room the television was on its own. She sighed. She'd been shouting at an empty room for the last five minutes. Automatically, she headed for the remote control, but using it was a different matter. She'd get dough all over it. She got onto her knees and tried to turn off the set with her elbow.

"What on earth are you doing, Mum?" her astounded eight year old asked as she trudged in from the garden.

"Don't," her mother yelled, but immediately moderated her voice, "come into this room with those shoes on." Miriam stopped dead. Tears began to well up in her eyes.

"What, what is it little one," she went over to her daughter and put her arms around her. The television was still far too loud.

"It was Isabel," she sobbed. The television really was too loud. She kept her arms around her daughter while the tiny voice recounted the latest problem she and her 'best friend' had encountered. Most of Sylvia's mind was on keeping her doughy hands off her daughter's clothes and her daughter's muddy shoes off her carpet. It wasn't easy. She rocked Miriam gently, the television catching the corner of her eye as she swung to her left. It was a news flash. More problems. Always problems.

The 'phone. began to ring. Oh no! Doughy hands and a daughter with muddy shoes. She let Miriam go, whipped off her shoes with her doughy hands and ran through into the kitchen to wash her hands. Dough wasn't easy to get off.

"Get that, would you," she yelled at Miriam, running her hands under the tap. Another air crash, the news flash was saying. Somewhere abroad. Part of the NRC problem. Possibly shot down. No information on casualties. More reports later. Miriam walked in.

"Well?" she'd got most of the dough off.

"It's a man."

"Who is it, love," she smiled at her daughter.

"I don't know."

"Well, ask him."

"Who he is?"

"Yes." Miriam returned to the 'phone.

"Who are you?" she asked, holding the handset awkwardly to her small face.

"Can I speak to your father?" a voice was saying.

"He's not here," she replied simply, and added for her mum's sake, "He wants to speak to Daddy."

"Daddy's not here, love," she wasn't interested in Rob's calls.

"Or your mother," the voice continued at the same moment that her mother had spoken.

"I told him," she paused for a moment, confused. "Oh," she said into the mouthpiece. She held the 'phone away from her ear, no longer sure who she was speaking to.

"He wants you, Mummy," she placed the handset carefully onto the carpet and walked away from it.

"Who is it, love," she asked again coming into the room.

"I already asked him," she sounded exasperated.

Her mother laughed, "Well, who is it then?"

"I don't know," suddenly she was upset, fed up, annoyed.

"Hello, hello," the voice was saying from the carpet. Sylvia picked it up.

"Hello?" she asked.

"Is that Much Hadham 5093?" he knew by now that it wasn't, but he had to ask.

"No," already she was moving the handset from her ear, preparing to replace it on the receiver, "you have a wrong number."

"Please," he almost shouted. He recognised that tone. The woman was about to hang up on him, "please listen." Her hand paused.

He didn't know where to start. His mind was alive with thoughts. The woman had a child. There was an enormous thump, followed by a rushing sound. Shit!

"I have children," he shouted, not sure whether she was, at that very moment, hanging up. "On a plane. On their own," he tried to organise his thoughts. She hadn't hung up. That meant that he had a few moments to get his message across.

"I'm calling from Poland," he said firmly and clearly, "from a pay phone." The screen was telling him that he had finished his first 'phone card. He whipped it out and slid in his other card. The screen said that it was virtually finished. Less than half full, anyway, and the units were disappearing at a truly alarming rate.

"I want to contact my parents," he deliberately avoided using the imperative 'must', "in Much Hadham, Hertfordshire. I am having a lot of trouble getting through," he paused.

Just a few units left. Maybe good for thirty or forty seconds, yet. He pointed desperately at the tiny telephone screen, and then at Marzena's bag. She shook her head, but began to look, anyway.

"Please," he paused again, "please could you 'phone Mr Ingram on Much Hadham 5093. Do you have something to write with?" he cursed himself for asking. If the woman disappeared now, his card would run out before she'd come back.

"No," she replied, "but carry on."

"Please tell him that Tom and Trix are on flight BA 106, due into Heathrow at about 10.30. Can you remember that?"

"Yes", she said. Just because she had a couple of children and seemed to spend half her life in the kitchen, half her life cleaning up after her family, and the other half...didn't mean that she was an idiot. "You want me to 'phone. Much Hadham 5093 to tell Mr Ingram that Tom and Trix are on flight BA 106, due into Heathrow at

10.30, okay?... but how do I know that this isn't a wind up?"

"Please," the sound of his voice alone was enough, "please just 'phone... They're two little kids on their own. They're very frightened..." the line went dead.

"Don't worry," she said into the dead phone. "And good luck." She had no trouble remembering the number. The caller had misdialled by just one digit. Her own number was 5083. She put her finger on the toggle for an instant to clear the line, and dialled 5093.

WAR DAY

WARSAW
POLAND

They left the Marriott at a run. When they had emerged from the 'phone cubicle the enormous lobby area was empty. Even the staff seemed to have disappeared.

Eerie! An abandoned hotel. Well, reception area, anyway. The bar area was empty as well. Most unusual, to Jamie's mind. Outside, no one was visible.

"Where IS everyone?" he looked around.

"I don't know. Let's just get out of here. This place gives me the creeps."

They headed towards the car. A car tore past. That was something, at least. They weren't the only people in Warsaw. Maybe the Marriott simply wasn't the place to be at a time like this. It was a truly enormous building, maybe forty or fifty floors. Air Lot, the Polish airline used to have their head office there. It was a landmark that a visitor to Warsaw would find difficult to miss, and perhaps that also applied to visiting armies from the East. A large white building, taller than most, in the centre of Warsaw.

They headed West. With the roads almost empty travelling at a reasonable speed was no problem. The trams were still running, but they were mostly empty.

They had enough fuel for about another hundred miles. From Warsaw to the German border at Swiecko was about three hundred miles. As they approached the outskirts of Warsaw it was almost ten thirty. Although the Polish roads had improved massively over the years, it was still possibly six or seven hours to Swiecko. They could be in Berlin in time to 'phone Tom and Trix and to go out for a hot meal.

"Keep your eyes open for a fuel station," he said, "When we've filled up we'll just keep going until we hit Berlin."

"What about the border?"

"There's rarely any delay there, now."

"There wasn't, you mean. Today might be different," her tone suggested that half of Poland would be fleeing west, and that crossing the border would certainly involve a lot of waiting.

"We'll see," he said, "Anyway, fuel is our number one priority right now."

"How much have we got?"

"Enough to do us about a hundred miles."

"What's that in kilometres?" she had never made any effort to understand miles, yards, or feet and inches etc., feeling that they were a nonsense. The rest of the world, it seemed, agreed with her so he wasn't about to argue. Anyway, she had learnt to speak English and was now fluent. She would normally pass for English in England, except for the occasional vowel. Or perhaps he was biased. Anyway, as he had never really learnt her language, but had instead learnt a sort of pigeon Polish that allowed him to get through life in Poland, it would have seemed churlish to criticise her for not learning an isolated and archaic system of measurement.

"About a hundred and sixty."

They were in open countryside now, separated from the frozen, snow covered fields by a shallow ditch and a thin, bedraggled line of trees. The countryside was mainly flat and very beautiful. The trees glistened with a fine layer of snow or ice. Most of the trees were occupied by one or more large black birds. Crows? He didn't know.

"They'll be halfway there, now," the children, "Bless their little hearts." He could hear the smile in her voice.

There was a sudden roar. An explosion. Before it had really finished, there was another explosion. Jamie slammed on the brakes. He didn't know what was happening. The noises were louder than he could ever have imagined possible. The car rocked, their ears hurt. Marzena was covering hers with her hands.

Another terrific noise, a third tearing explosion, ripped through the car. They were stopped. He held his hands tight over his ears.

As a fourth explosion ripped through the car Jamie began to perceive that horrifying though the noise was, it wasn't actually anything to do with them. And nor did it offer an immediate threat.

The four small, silver airplanes were out of sight before either Marzena or Jamie had had time to fully understand what the noise was.

"What the …?" Jamie began.

Marzena was shaking her head, gingerly feeling around her ears. She turned, and looked at him, perplexed.

"Sonic boom," I suppose. He thought his voice sounded strange.

She shook her head, pointing at her ears and apparently mouthing something. He smiled.

He put the car into gear and they moved off. How terrifying. And that was without the Migs firing a shot. And they must have been Migs, because there wasn't anything else in this part of the world. They can't have been more than a few feet above the ground! Although he knew that his estimate would probably be laughed out of court by an airman, he really did feel that they had been flying just feet above the ground.

They came around a long, gentle bend. On each side there were the open fields, white with snow, and the occasional stark, icy tree. On each side of the road there was the shallow drainage ditch.

"There, Jamie," she said, pointing across him to the right. A fuel station. It was just as well that she had pointed, his ears were still ringing.

"Great." He indicated and slowed. There was no traffic behind them. He pulled off the road to right, slowing to just a few miles an hour.

"Holy shit!"

They were committed; he couldn't veer back onto the road without driving through the forecourt. He put his foot down, dropping the car into second. The turbo cut in, power surged through to the back wheels, the rear end snaked and suddenly they were almost flying.

The two armed men filling the ancient lorry turned in surprise as the Volvo sped through the small gap. Two other men lay on the forecourt. The one in blue jeans was unmoving in a small puddle of blood. The older one was gripping his thigh, rocking gently. His fingers were stained red. He was mouthing something.

"Jesus," Marzena breathed.

He nearly lost the car as they came out of the forecourt at almost fifty miles an hour. There was a small patch of gravelly surface before they hit the road proper. The rear swung, putting the fear of God into him, but in a moment they were on tarmac and he was back in control.

He heard a swoosh noise, then two more.

He regained control, straightening out and keeping his foot flat on the floor changing gear only when he couldn't stand the sound of the screaming engine anymore.

"Jesus," Marzena breathed again.

"That was nasty," he agreed.

Things didn't look too good, he was thinking. It might well be possible to get to Swiecko in a few hours, but it would have been very nice to have been able to do it without stopping. Why hadn't he kept the wretched thing full? He always had in the old days, in the days of shortages, when periodically there were long queues for fuel.

He could hear Marzena breathing. He smiled.

"It'll be okay," he said gently. Would it?

"Jesus, Jamie," she sounded very frightened. He didn't want to stop, not until they were a fair distance from those armed men and their lorry. He put out his hand, found hers and held it.

"It'll be okay, love. Things will be just fine," he could hear the lie in his voice.

Her hand gripped his.

He drove on steadily and fast. There was very little traffic so they were covering the ground fairly quickly.

WAR DAY

GREAT BRITAIN

She dialled the number again. No answer. There'd been no answer for over fifteen minutes. She sent Miriam outside while she looked up the name in the directory. There it was, only ten minutes walk away. 154 High Street. Sylvia shrugged on her coat as she left the house. She checked for keys and purse the moment before she pulled the door closed. Good.

"Miriam, love," she yelled at her daughter, "Come with Mummy."

"Where're we going," the little girl scrambled after her mum, caught up with her near the front gate, and grabbed her hand. Sylvia could feel the softness of warm mud in her hand.

"What have you been doing?" she released her hand from her daughter's grip.

"Yuch!!" her right hand was all muddy, "What have you been doing?" she repeated.

"Nuthin'," came the sweet reply.

"Well, nothing or nothing, it was muddy," her mother complained, wiping her hand on a tissue.

"Where're we going?"

She looked down at her daughter's beautiful face. Despite the grubbiness, despite the mud, despite the recent crying, even despite the scratches, she was beautiful. 'My little heartbreaker' Rob called her. She smiled at her.

"Where're we going, Mum?" More demanding this time.

"Just down to the High Street, maybe pop into the shop." Miriam's eyes lit up. That was all she needed to hear. The shop meant sweets, or at least it normally meant something sweet. She hopped and skipped to keep up with her mother's fast pace.

After a few more breathless moments, she demanded, "Why're we goin' so fast? Mum. Why're we runnin'?"

"We're not running, love," as Sylvia said the words, she glanced down at Miriam and realised that although she, Sylvia, was not running, they were moving at quite a fair pace for someone as small as Miriam. She laughed.

"I'm sorry, love," she slowed her pace, but not much, "I want to pop in to see someone for a moment, before we go to the shop."

"Ohh. Mum," a disappointed whine. She had learnt just how long her mum could spend 'popping in', "Why before?"

"I'm afraid we have to."

"Mummy!"

"Because I say so, okay?"

"Okay," defeat. You can't win when someone else holds all the cards. Miriam knew when it was time to quit. 'You quit before you get hit', Isabel would say, but then Isabel had bruises an eight year old oughtened to have had. Isabel's parents sometimes got very angry. She didn't like Isabel very much, which was a problem, because Isabel was her best friend. It was all very confusing.

Like Daddy and Mummy. Daddy and Mummy loved each other very much, but sometimes Daddy would get very angry and Mummy would scream at him. Sometimes Miriam heard words that she knew were bad, because Jimmy had said them once at school and had had to go and see the head teacher. He'd nearly been sent home. Jimmy was her boyfriend, although Isabel said that he wasn't. How would she know? Sometimes Miriam thought Isabel knew nothing. But, in fact, she knew that Isabel was probably the brainiest, apart from grown-ups. But most grown-ups hardly knew anything, anyway.

Once, Mummy had thrown a plate at Daddy. It had missed him. But the food hadn't. The food had gone on his face, and on his shirt. She had thought that it was funny, but he hadn't. When he'd stood up the food'd fallen down his trousers and onto the floor. It'd looked very funny on the floor. She hadn't dared to laugh though, because Daddy had looked so very wild. He'd looked like he was going to explode.

At last. They were there. She sighed. At last. Her mum rang the door bell. It was quite a nice day, Miriam thought. A good day for playing in the park.

"Mummy, can we go to the park?"

No response. Her Mum didn't seem to realise that she was talking.

"Mummy?"

Sylvia rang the bell again.

"Mummy!" almost a shout.

"What?"

"Can we?"

"Can we what?"

"Mummy," exasperated, "I already said!"

"What, love," what if there was no answer? She was beginning to feel that no one was going to answer the door. What then?

"Can we go to the park?" she spoke patiently, slowly and clearly as though speaking to someone hard of hearing and rather stupid to boot.

"Don't you talk to me like that, young lady," she looked sternly at her daughter. Perhaps rather more sternly than she had intended. She wasn't too happy about this door not being answered. She rang the bell for the third time. She gave it a good healthy press. If this didn't work they'd have to go around the back. She didn't really want to do that.

BA 106, she repeated to herself. Heathrow 10.30. That was the one on the M4, wasn't it. Yes. She knew that it was. She glanced at her watch. It was 9.35 already! She rang the bell again. Hard and long. Suddenly frightened for two small children on an airplane on their own. She peered around the side of the house. She could see an empty garage and part of the garden.

"Come on, love," for one wild moment Miriam thought that her mum had abandoned this visit and was about to head straight down to the shop. But, no such luck. She should have known.

They walked, hand in hand, down the narrow driveway beside the house. Nice place, Sylvia was thinking. A few bob's gone into this place. Inside it was all fitted carpets, quality stuff, and antiques. Beautiful tables covered in small and rather lovely odds and ends. Any one of them would have kept their family in food and warmth for a week—at least. There was no one visible through any of the windows down the side of the house. They stopped at the back door. No bell. She tapped on the door. From here they could see straight into the kitchen. It was empty. Beautiful, too. Fitted pine. But empty.

She banged on the door. And waited. Ten minutes later she realised what she'd known for some time. There really wasn't going to be an answer. She and Miriam walked slowly down the driveway. What now?

Beside her Miriam skipped lightly. She thought she might have Maltesers today.

At the end of the drive, Sylvia turned left, towards home.

"Mum!" Miriam squealed, pulling to the right. To the shop.

+

Deep in the heart of Wales, in an old stone farmhouse, five people had sat down to a very late breakfast. More like an elevenses, Lucy felt. In the fireplace a modern wood-burning stove radiated heat. It was nice to sit down and enjoy the warmth.

"It's really nice to sit down and enjoy the warmth," she said. Tom raised his eyebrows meaningfully at Jack. Jack ignored him.

Helen was concentrating on her coffee. She needed her coffee first thing in the morning, and this morning it was far from first thing. Lucy's help hadn't arrived and they'd had to feed the animals themselves. Or at least, Lucy had had too. John looked approvingly at his daughter. Lucy was looking well, and fit. She looked good. She looked up and caught his eye.

"You look good," he said with a smile.

"Thank you," but she didn't believe him. She was aware of sagging skin, greying hair and aching muscles. At the age of thirty six, with two young children and forty seven monkeys, it was lovely to be told that you looked good, but believing it was another matter.

Jack was balancing his bowl at an impossible angle.

"Mummy," Tom suddenly yelled, "look what Jack's doing." She looked. The bowl toppled slowly, the remainder of the cereals and milk spilling onto the plastic table cover. That's why she had a plastic table cover. The bowl fell and, with a guiding hand from Jack, slid off the table onto the floor. That's why they had plastic bowls. The kids.

Jack looked at her in defiance. His big, bold blue eyes issuing a wild challenge.

"Oh, Jack," she smiled gently, "You are a little messer, aren't you." It wasn't a question. He grinned.

It was a pain that Iris hadn't turned up to help with the monkeys. It took a long time to feed them, especially with two kids in tow and her parents. It was almost ten o'clock and she hadn't done anything yet. They hadn't even had breakfast. She shivered. She'd have to go down later and chop some wood.

"Is it cold outside," John asked.

"'Course it is," Tom responded abruptly.

Helen looked startled, and glanced at Lucy to see what she would do.

"Tom, you shouldn't talk to your grandfather like that," Lucy offered. Tom looked perplexed.

"Like what, mum?"

"Be more polite. Grandpa hasn't been outside yet, so he doesn't know how cold it is."

"Why not?"

"What?"

"Why not?"

"Why not what?"

"Why doesn't he know?"

"Oh, Tom," she said gently, "do be quiet."

"Why not, why not," chanted Jack, Tom's three year old younger brother.

"Stop it," Tom yelled, turning to his mum for assistance, "Mum he's..." but she was taking no notice, and he could tell from the way that she was taking no notice that she wasn't going to take any notice. He banged his spoon on the table and shouted, "Stop it, Jack."

"I think you're wonderful with them," Helen smiled. She felt that, with the aid of the coffee, she was beginning to surface.

Lucy grimaced. Her mother meant that the two boys were behaving badly.

"I don't mean that they're being naughty," Helen said with a smile. She could read her daughter's face, "I think that you cope with them so well."

"A pair of rascals," their grandfather said with great fondness. He reached over to ruffle Jack's head. Jack ducked sideways, wriggled madly and disappeared under the table.

"Tom," Lucy cautioned, catching the look on his face. He had begun to swing his legs viciously under the table in the hope of catching his little brother as he passed.

"Stop that," she commanded.

He stopped, a look of enormous innocence passing across his face.

"What?" he asked.

"You know."

John glanced at his watch, "Anyone heard the news today?" There was no immediate response. Obviously not.

"I'd like to see what's happening," they knew what he meant.

"There's nothing to be worried about," Helen reassured him, "Nothing's going to happen out there."

"I'd just like to see it, anyway. You never know."

"You're just a pessimist, Dad," Lucy was getting up to make some more toast, "Or maybe you just want to sit down in the living room with the television while we clear up."

"No," he protested, secure in the knowledge that he wouldn't be required to help with the clearing up whether he chose to watch the news or not.

"Anyway," she continued, "I haven't lit the fire in the living room, yet."

"Oh," it would be freezing in there.

"It'll be freezing in there," she added.

Just what I was thinking, he thought.

+

Chapter Three

WAR DAY

THE M25
GREAT BRITAIN

He was about seventy, with a lean face and fine head of silver-grey hair. Beside him, wide awake, her piercing blue eyes missing nothing, sat his wife. He didn't like his wife, not any more. Sometimes he wondered if he ever had. Liked her. He'd loved her, yes. And lust. Yes, he'd lusted for her, a lust that had taken years to sate. He'd loved her, he'd lusted for her, but like her? He thought not. He thought perhaps not.

His face remained motionless. He'd learnt years ago that she had an uncanny knack of discerning the train of his thoughts. It would be wrong, quite wrong, to imply that she could read his mind, but there were times when she had come startlingly close to it. He shivered. Too late he remembered himself.

"Cold, dear?" she asked kindly.

Shut up you old windbag, he thought. One day he would slip. One day he would say it. And then what would happen? Would the world end? Would his world end? Or would her world end? He shook his head. He was afraid, afraid of hurting her. This woman who had turned his life into a misery. A nightmare. He didn't want to hurt her. But he hated her!

Or loved her? Which?

She reached forward to the heater control. It was cold outside, but the temperature was just fine in the car. He sat in his light trousers and jacket in the large, modern Vauxhall.

"Leave it, dear," he started kindly, "Unless you want to change it?" a sort of a question, he supposed. To show his concern, a concern that he no longer felt. A concern that had outwardly grown whilst the inner feelings that it implied had grown smaller and harder in his shrunken heart. He felt no concern.

She began to adjust the heater control. It was a complex piece of equipment. To his mind it offered too many choices. He'd have been happy with something simple. Something that would blow hot or cold, something that could be directed at windscreen or passengers. Or both, he thought. That's all he needed

He sighed. Inaudibly. He'd just made one mistake. He wasn't about to make another.

"All right dear," he wasn't sure if she was asking a question, and if so whether it related to the temperature in the car, (which didn't appear to have changed, yet), or to his inaudible sigh. Inaudible? Well, it was difficult to tell from the inside whether the sigh was actually inaudible, and it was important not to lose sight of the fact that the old witch could practically read his mind.

He said nothing. Silence was often the best defence. Stupid old witch. He kept his face straight. He wondered what she thought. It didn't really matter. He'd never liked her...he wasn't sure. But he was sure of his feelings now.

Her eyes caught sight of a small car, an Escort?   She was never certain with the little cars. An Escort or an Astra?   It was overtaking them. It must have been going extremely fast. She leant towards her right slightly. Yes. They were doing seventy—she didn't like Ronald to drive any faster, and after all that was the speed limit—so the small car, which was travelling significantly faster than they were, must have been going very fast.

She frowned. "What's wrong, dear?" sometimes she wondered if he could read her mind!

"Nothing," she replied, "just looking at that little Escort. The one in the fast lane."

He hated it when she called it the fast lane. She hadn't got a clue. It was a good thing that she didn't like to drive.

They both watched the Ford Escort. It was an old model, ten years old judging by the registration, and it looked its age. Just like her, he thought. It was travelling at about eighty miles an hour. It looked well worn, tired, dented and rusty. In the back a peculiarly attractive young girl was making faces out of the window, the side window. No doubt, she considered her efforts were transforming her otherwise pretty face into something horrendous. If so, her efforts were wasted. She looked like a very pretty little girl making horrid faces.

Ronald laughed. That made him feel a little better. The murmur of the radio changed. The news.

"Twenty years ago you'd have seen to those two young ladies."   What two young ladies, he thought? He realised that she was referring to the driver and the front seat passenger of the Escort. Would she never realise that he'd left the force for ever. There would be people retiring from the Met. who had joined after he'd left! That was all practically a lifetime ago. And she'd never stopped being a copper's wife.

"Shhh," he said gently, turning up the radio slightly for the news. He liked to know what was going on. He always had, but more especially so now. Now that there was so much tension within the NRC. He knew things must be bad, they wouldn't have flown Jeannie back unless they were.

+

"Stop that, now," Sylvia instructed.

"Oh, Mum," she whined, and then brightened, "What? I wasn't doing anything."

"Just stop, okay love."

Sylvia grinned at the driver. Petra was clinging to the rattling wheel with a grim determination.

"How far, now?"

"I don't know," she paused, "How far have we gone?"

"I don't know."

"Useless."

"What?"

"We are."

"Why? We're doing something, aren't we?" Petra took her eyes off the road.

"If you're going to drive so fast for heaven's sake keep your eyes on the road," she paused, "well, one eye at least."

Petra laughed, "You could have just stayed at home, instead of dragging me out on this wild goose chase."

"I'm sure that we could have 'phoned somebody, done something better."

"Like who?" she pulled into the middle lane, "or what?"

"International Aunts, or somebody."

"Who???"

"I'm not sure. International Aunts? They collect people, well children, young girls, at airports and things. They make sure that they're okay, take them home etc."

"Do you know these people?"

"No."

"So, how do you find them?"

"I don't know."

"Well then."

"Or perhaps the airport?"

"The airport?"

"Would they just let a couple of kids off a plane, or would they look after them?"

"I doubt they'd look after them, I don't know."

"But we could have 'phoned and told them."

"Maybe," with a sudden swing of the wheel she was back into the right hand lane, "but when?"

"When?"

"Yes, 'When?'"

"Well..." she paused, "then?"

"Then?"

"Yeah. Then, when I called you?"

"And if there'd been no answer? If they couldn't help? And, anyway, WHO would you 'phone? How would you find them? You're talking nonsense, Sylvie, you're doing the best thing you can do: you're meeting them from the plane. If you'd done anything else you may not have found anyone to help. Then they'd have arrived on their own. No one to meet them."

"I suppose so. I just feel that I could have done something better."

"Time?"

"Just on eleven. Oh, do hurry Petra."

"If I go any faster this old thing's going to fall apart. And if we get pulled it'll delay us no end."

"How far?"

"Don't know. Not far. We should be okay. They're due in at, what, ten thirty? If they're a bit late, they're always late, and you can add a bit of time for customs and things, perhaps an hour or maybe thirty minutes, so we've got what?" she paused while she did the maths, "until say almost, well perhaps eleven thirty. No sweat."

"M4," Sylvia read, "Here. One mile."

"Got you," Petra was still weaving in and out of the traffic. There had been a welcome silence from the back seat for a little while, now.

"Here," Sylvia yelled, "here," waving to the left.

"Shit, that was quick," Petra made a desperate lunge for the exit, leaving a small trail of panic and anger in her wake.

"No problem," she breathed.

"Daddy doesn't drive like that" came the small and apparently rather disapproving voice from the back. Petra raised her eyebrows and glanced sideways at Sylvia.

"Daddy doesn't drive at all at the moment," Sylvia leaned over into the back. Miriam was settling back onto the seat.

Petra shot another sideways glance at Sylvia.

"Two years," she said, "two years."

"Two?"

"Yeah."

"Why two?"

"Dunno. He won't talk about it. I read about it in the newspaper."

"You read about Rob in the paper?"

"Well, he wouldn't tell me."

"Shit."

Sylvia frowned at her language, but for once Petra had her eyes on the road.

"Fan-tas-tic," she laughed, "we're here. Which Terminal?"

"What?"

"Which terminal?"

"Terminal?"

"You don't know?"

+

The Vauxhall veered across from the centre into the near side lane. There was a sudden squeal of rubber on tarmac as two cars and a lorry carrying rather more glass than it ought, did their best to avoid it and each other.

Two seconds later and it was all over. Everybody swore, breathed a sigh of relief and continued on their way. Everybody except the Vauxhall, its driver and passenger.

"Silly old bugger," the lorry driver thought as he accelerated away from near disaster. Three hundred yards behind this near miss a police motorway patrol car watched with interest, indicated left, pulled into the near side lane, activated his roof lights and hazards and slowed down.

"Ronald," she was nearly shouting, "What are you doing?"

Shut up you old bitch, he wanted shout.

"Listen," he said firmly, in a voice that was barely raised. She took it that he was referring to the radio. This was not like Ronald. She listened.

Thank heavens the bitch had shut up. He guided the car over the hard shoulder so that it rolled to a halt with two wheels in the deep gravel. "....over the coast of Poland. Unconfirmed reports suggest that the passenger aircraft may have been brought down by enemy fire. There are no details on survivors. We'll bring you more news as reports come in..."

"Oh, Christ," he was sitting, motionless, staring ahead.

"Oh, Christ." This was most unlike Ronald.

"Ronald!" She looked at him, amazed. At a slight sound, she turned. Behind them, lights ablaze, parked horribly close, was a police car. "Ronald!" He didn't hear. He was sitting, motionless. She turned back to the police car. A young man, an extremely young man, was getting out. He pushed his door closed. For a moment he paused, adjusting his trousers and putting on his cap, before moving slowly towards the driver's door of their car. He exuded an air of extreme confidence.

She looked at Ronald. He was sitting quite still, still staring ahead. "Ronald?" she said, rather more quietly than a moment ago. He didn't seem to notice. She looked back. The young man had paused to look at something on the side of their car. Their wheel? The other one was still seated in the police car, talking on the radio. She noted that it looked more like a telephone

WAR DAY
ROUTE E8
TRAVELLING WEST FROM WARSAW
POLAND

By half past twelve the fuel situation had become critical. They had made incredibly good time, covering the best part of a hundred miles since leaving Warsaw and now the needle was hovering above the red line. He had lost count of the number of fuel stations they had passed. Two had been in flames; another four had been completely destroyed. And, he thought to himself, I mean completely. They had been barely recognisable. He wondered if the Migs had played a role in their destruction, it had been so complete. And he simply hadn't dared to try the others, each time putting it off until the next.

The next one, he promised himself. Again. We'll fill up at the next one. We must be safe by now. He wondered what on earth was going on in Warsaw. Would the NRC simply overrun the city, or would there be fighting? He had seen no sign of any Polish defence.

He needed a pee, anyway, so they had to stop. A few minutes later he pulled gingerly into a modern forecourt. His eyes wide open, looking for signs of trouble. He wasn't a fighting man but every nerve, every sense seemed to be wide awake. The quest for survival, he was thinking, with a wry smile at himself. It looked okay.

He came to a halt at the diesel pump. By his reckoning they had covered about two hundred miles since leaving Lublin, which meant that they were almost exactly half way to the border.

Yes. The filling station looked normal. One man at the till in the small shop. No other people or vehicles around.

Good. Was it self-service? Yes, it looked like it. This was not a day to make mistakes. It was bad enough under normal circumstances helping yourself to fuel by mistake in a filling station that was not self-service, but on a day like today it could be a fatal mistake. For that matter, it could be a fatal mistake just being in a fuel station. There was no room for misunderstandings today. He lifted the pump handle carefully, watching the man at the till. There didn't seem to be a problem. He put the nozzle into position and squeezed the trigger.

A moment later he jumped in fright as a voice yelled something. Even as he turned he had the presence of mind to keep his fingers wrapped around the trigger so that the precious diesel kept on pouring into the car. A second man had appeared. He didn't look like he belonged. He was dressed altogether too smartly. Who was he shouting at?

He was wearing a blue suit and looked altogether more formal than was normal in Poland where suits were a relative rarity. Most Poles who might have worn a suit had they lived further west preferred to wear sports jacket and trousers. Added to which, it dawned on Jamie, if he wasn't wearing a coat he couldn't have come far.

Twenty five litres would get them to the border, Jamie reckoned, although he'd like more. No point in cutting it too fine, they had to consider spending a lot of time at the border and getting to Berlin.

Seven, eight, nine...

His eyes flicked from the man in the suit to the man in the shop and back to the pump.

Eleven, twelve...

The man in the suit was getting very excited. The guy behind the till was being very cool about it all. He appeared to be ignoring...

The man in the suit produced a small gun.

Jamie didn't stop to think. In one fluid movement his hand released the pump handle, he took two steps, slid into the driver's seat and rammed the car into first without shutting his door. As the rear wheels spun his door slammed.

He didn't look back. He just drove, keeping his eyes on the road. It crossed his mind a moment later that perhaps the man in the suit had been a sort of security guard for the fuel station, in which case he and Marzena were now guilty of theft. And they had been seen doing it.

But they could hardly have hung around to find out, could they?

He realised with dismay that he still hadn't had a pee.

WAR DAY
GREAT BRITAIN

The Escort screamed to a halt. The van behind veered around them, its horn blaring. The driver appeared to be yelling something. Mouthing something, anyway. It didn't look as though he was wishing them a good day.

"Which way?"

"I don't know," she hadn't had any idea that the place was so big. It was enormous. You could drive around for a week and probably not notice that you were going around in circles. Would it matter?

"It's enormous."

"Are we lost?"

"Of course not," she paused, "We know where we are, don't we?"

"I'm not sure that that's the point."

"No, you're right, of course."

"So, we're lost?"

"Guess so."

"Shit!"

"Over there," she indicated a policeman, "ask him."

Petra rammed the car into first. As she pulled away a blue saloon thundered past, its horn blaring.

+

He looked into the traffic policeman's eyes. He knew that look. The young copper was going to nick him. And so he should. Ronald sat, stunned. He hardly moved. He had reached into his pocket and produced his driver's licence without a word. She was leaning forward, fussing, being a bloody nuisance.

The last plane out of Poland. That's what the news flash had said. The last plane out of Poland had been brought down by hostile action. Hostile fire. Something. Brought down. No survivors.

His daughter was on that plane. Jeannie was on that plane. Dear God. His beautiful Jeannie! He sat quite still, looking straight ahead.

"Are you all right, sir?" the young copper's voice held just a hint of concern. Genuine concern—the old codger looked quite ill. He ignored the young man's voice. It was as though he were somewhere else. Hostile action. Jeannie. Sightlessly, he stared ahead. Oh Jesus. Oh dear Jesus. Jeannie.

"Ronald." What did she care? The old witch.

"Ronald!" she repeated more urgently. What was wrong with him? Stupid old fart. She looked at the young policeman. He looked at her. Oh shit, he thought.

Marzena was awake.

"I've got to stop for a pee," he said. They hadn't seen another vehicle for over ten minutes. He wasn't sure whether to stop in open view on an open stretch of road, or to choose somewhere secluded.

"What time is it?" she was sleepy.

"Coming up to one," he glanced at the dash. Yes.

"Where are we?"

"Just over a hundred miles out of Warsaw."

"Kilometres?" she smiled. He could hear it in her voice.

"One sixty, about," multiply by one point six. That way was easy. It was more difficult being accurate when converting the kilometres on the signposts into miles. Multiplying by point six did it, more or less. Or halving it and adding one eighth was more accurate, but not always easy. Still, while driving he hadn't much else to do. Not normally. He still thought in miles. He supposed that he should have changed to kilometres, but his mind was happy in miles. And the car was a British model, the speedo was calibrated in miles per hour. He'd always bought his cars in England, despite having been resident in Poland for several years.

Yes, he thought, several years. He reached out and put his hand on Marzena's slim leg. She was the reason. He'd fallen for a Polish girl years ago, and was still with her. Always would be. She rested her hand on his.

"They'll be with your parents by now."

"I hope so," he couldn't help the note of caution. He'd have felt a lot better if he'd been able to get through to his parents himself.

"Maybe we could stop and 'phone."

"I think I'd just rather get out of this place. It'll be easy to call from Berlin." He pulled over into a small lay-by. It offered no protection from passing traffic, but neither were they obvious to traffic until it was almost upon them. He got out and undid his zip while still standing close to the open car door.

"Are you going to do it there?" She was amazed.

"I'm going no further from the car than I have to," she could hear the relief in his voice. I don't believe that I've had a pee since I got up, he realised, and that was a while ago. He grinned. That was better.

"I want to go, too," she was getting out and moving away from the car.

"Stay by the car."

She looked surprised, "Don't look."

"Don't be ridiculous," he snorted.

"What does that mean?" she retorted, her grin taking away the bite.

"How long have we been together?" he laughed, "How many babies have I watched you have? What have you got to hide?"

"Just stay over there," she instructed.

"Right you are, ma'am." He stood there looking up and down the road. Nothing.

"Golly, its cold," she was standing in a hurry, doing up her jeans, "Get in quick and get it warmed up." They got back into the car.

"You all right for driving?" she asked.

"Yep."

"I'll make some sandwiches."

"Great." She began to rout around in the back, discarding a couple of bin bags before she found what she was looking for.

"Can you feel a draft?" she asked.

"No."

"Well, there's a small hole beside the window."

"What sort of hole?"

"Small," she repeated. Her tone suggested that he hadn't been paying attention.

"Okay," he grinned, "What sort of small hole?"

"Just a hole. How many kinds of small hole are there?" A pause for thought.

"Okay. How small?"

"About the same size as my little finger."

"Does it go right through?"

"Right through?" she was kneeling on the front seat leaning into the back.

"To the outside?"

"Yep."

"Beside the window? Which window?"

"Beside the back window. Not a side window, the back window," she repeated.

"But there isn't a 'beside' the back window. The back window goes all the way across."

"Bullet hole, I 'spect," she continued. This was a conclusion that Jamie had already reached but had been hesitant to put into words. He said nothing. Just thought for a moment. Those whooshing noises when they had stumbled upon the armed men in the fuel station?

"Well," she was impatient, "Whatcha reckon?"

"If that's your gangster voice," he laughed, "it's pathetic."

"Oh," she clambered back into position in the front seat and began to concentrate on sandwiches, "'pathetic' is it?" She laughed.

"Tell me, Mrs Ingram," she went on, "What was it like being under fire in a hostile country? Did you find a new closeness, an even greater bond perhaps, forming with your husband? Did the fear of death, imminent and sudden, bring you closer together?"

She paused, poked him in the ribs, and continued, "Pathetic! I'll pathetic you, my man, by golly I will."

"What are you talking about?" He laughed as a thought occurred to him, "It probably happened while you were asleep."

"Why?" she asked, "What happened?"

"Well, nothing actually, although I did meet a man with a gun," he exaggerated, "and stole...We stole, you and I stole fourteen litres of diesel."

"Stole?" she was incredulous. There was a moment's silence.

"Why?"

"And why fourteen litres? Was that all that they had?" He said nothing.

"You stole it?" she asked, again.

"We stole it," he repeated.

"We?? I was asleep. It's not possible to steal something when you're asleep."

"Who says?"

"I do."

"Well, you did."

 "I did not."

"How do you know?"

"You're talking nonsense, Ingram."

"I saw you."

"Saw me?"

"Steal it."

"Oh, yeah. Tell me about it..." she had stopped making the sandwiches.

"I'm starving," he looked sideways at her lap and the food spread out on it.

"The road! Keep your eyes on the road. And tell me"

"Will you make the sandwiches if I tell you?"

"Yeah," reluctant, "okay."

So he told her.

WAR DAY

HEATHROW AIRPORT
GREAT BRITAIN

They ran into the terminal, Miriam's tiny legs barely touching the ground. It was a big place.

Arrivals. They stood, for just a moment.

"Where?"

"There," Sylvia pointed. Miriam's legs left the ground, almost, and they were off. There it was, on the screen; Flight number BA 106, due 09.25. Delayed. ETA now 11.50. She glanced at her watch, 11.45. Ace. She grinned.

"Ace!"

Petra grinned, "We made it? We made it!" Her shoulders, her whole body seemed to sag in relief.

"Thank you, oh thank you, Petra."

"No prob. I'll go sit in the car." They'd left it in the tow-away zone. She gave Miriam a grin and turned back. There was a fair crowd at arrivals. Sylvia found a seat set back from the crowd and waited. It would be a while. They weren't due to land for a few more minutes, and then there was customs and so on to deal with. Maybe she should try to 'phone Mr Ingram again. She didn't move. She was exhausted. Mentally, physically, everythingly. She just sat. And enjoyed just sitting. What a day.

For a few minutes Miriam just sat, too, which was a lovely bonus.

"What do they look like, Mum?"

What, indeed?

"I don't know, love."

"How will we know who they are?"

How, indeed?

"I don't know."

Perhaps there was a passenger list, or something. But how would that help her? It wouldn't show her what they looked like. But...there couldn't be many unaccompanied small children on the plane. Could there?

"Well, Mum?"

"What, love?"

"What shall we do?"

"What shall we do about what?" Such a pretty girl, she thought. She knew that she was biased, but she knew that she wasn't wrong. Miriam was beautiful. Even more so with that gorgeous look of concern all over her sweet little face.

"How will we know its them?" the pretty little face demanded, almost stamping its foot. Almost, but not quite. She knew the limits. Making demands was one thing, experience had shown her, but making a scene was another.

"I expect we'll manage. You just keep your eyes open for two children on their own. About your age." Were they? She realised that she actually had no real idea how old they were. Somehow, she had simply pictured Tom and Trix as being about Miriam's age.

"Both of them?"

"What?"

"Both of them?"

"Both of them what?"

"Are both of them my age?" Sylvia grinned.

"No," she corrected herself. How easy it was to forget how much difference every year made when you were tiny. She carried on grinning.

"Mummy?" She began to giggle. "Mummmmmmy!" The giggle became more solid.

"Mummmy, stop it!" Miriam was embarrassed. Being eight can be difficult, but having a mother who insists on that kind of behaviour in public...she couldn't express her dismay, her horror, her mortifying embarrassment. Thank heavens Isabel wasn't here. She sat perfectly still in her seat, looking away from her mother, hoping against hope that no one would realise that they were together. No one had noticed them. No one would.

The giggle became a soft laugh, then died away. She found a tissue and wiped her eyes. Glancing at her watch, seeing that it was just past 11.50, she glanced back at the screen.

ETA now 12.05. 12.05?

Another fourteen minutes. So what? I expect this happens all the time. It's just as well that it's so late, otherwise those poor kids would have been on their own for a while.

Chapter Four

WAR DAY
ROUTE E8
TRAVELLING WEST FROM WARSAW
POLAND

"I reckon we'll get to Poznan on the fuel we've got," he was saying. Fuel was turning into a major problem, and would probably be even worse in the cities. Even if there had been fuel in the cities, it would almost certainly have run out by the end of a day like today.

Who really knew? After so many years he still didn't understand the Polish mind, let alone predict how they would behave. However, he was fairly confident that if there was a shortage of fuel—or the fear of a shortage, or even the rumour of a shortage—the Poles would immediately form queues for the stuff. This would strengthen the fear of a fuel shortage, which would lengthen the queues, which would, in turn, create a real shortage. Which would, he supposed, justify the fear that had caused the queues. It was a strange world that they lived in, and Poland was no exception. Just around the long and gentle bend there was a long straight stretch. Halfway down the straight there was a road block. He began to slow.

"What is it?"

"Not sure," he was trying to see what was happening before he got too close. Was it manned by men in uniforms, and if so what sort of uniforms? As it seemed impossible that the NRC could have overtaken them, it seemed to follow that any uniform should be...should be...friendly.

The block was made up from a barrier across the road and four vehicles parked across the road so that one was forced to slow down and weave through the gap. It didn't look so good. He couldn't see any uniforms. He had slowed to little more than a crawl.

"What are we doing?"

"Not sure. What do you reckon?"

"Don't know. It should be all right, shouldn't it?"

He considered the alternatives. Although they were on the main road leading west out of Warsaw to Berlin and the rest of Europe, they hadn't yet reached the long autostrada section that led into Poznan. The road was rather narrow here, especially if one was considering a speedy three point turn.

"Yeah," he paused, again, "I guess so." They continued forward at a snail's pace. Jamie touched a switch and a buzz and a click told them that all the doors were locked. I wish we had a weapon, he thought. But there were those who said that having a weapon would simply make things worse if you didn't know how to use it. And he certainly didn't know how to use a weapon. Marzena had done a self-defence course, once. That was all the experience that they could muster between them.

As they drew to a halt at the barrier, waved down by a young man in jeans and short sheepskin coat, Jamie realised that now that they had reached the barrier there was nothing except the barrier itself to prevent them ignoring the block. All the strategically positioned vehicles had been to the east of the barrier - the direction from which they had come. Perhaps the idea of the block was to stop people moving east? Perhaps?

The barrier itself was a piece of steel piping painted red and white. One end was resting on an oil drum. The other end was out of sight.

"Where're you going?" The man shouted through the closed passenger window. He indicated that he wanted Marzena to wind down her window with an exaggerated winding motion of his hand.

"Don't," Jamie said, at the same time waving at the man to indicate that he, the driver, was on the other side. The 'wrong side'. The man looked exasperated for a moment and then walked carefully round in front of the car.

"I think he's got a gun in his pocket," Marzena sounded very cool. Jamie looked carefully; he certainly had something heavy in his right hand coat pocket.

Another man sat on the bonnet of a lorry, swinging his legs. He must be cold, Jamie thought, unless the bonnet's hot. With a start Jamie noticed the third man. He was leaning against a tree watching them. In his hands he held what looked like a modern rifle. It looked rather fatter and more metallic than Jamie would have expected, but its purpose was obvious.

"Shit," he muttered, wondering whether to let up the clutch and simply go instead of waiting for the man wandering around the front of the car. For a moment his eye wandered back to the man with the gun. He, too, was dressed in jeans. Jeans, shabby boots and worn coat. No, this didn't look good.

Not good at all. The man looked rough. He hadn't shaved for a day or two. There was, Jamie noticed with a start, the top of a bottle of vodka protruding from one of his coat pockets.

"Jamie!" her shouted warning jerked his eyes back to the man closer to the car. In one swift and apparently well practised movement he had removed a knife from his pocket and was bending towards the front near side tyre. His right arm, the one with the knife, was drawn slightly back, as though to plunge...

Jamie didn't wait to finish the thought. Marzena was still uttering his name as he lifted his foot off the clutch and stamped on the throttle. The man leapt back shouting in anger or fear as the Volvo leapt forward.

The make-shift barrier rolled up the bonnet, clattered noisily but harmlessly against the windscreen and fell out of sight, and they were in the open.

The open.

About three hundred metres of open road. Straight road. There was shouting. He heard shouting.

Foot on the clutch, ram it into second, right foot flat on the floor as left foot lifts from the clutch. A jerk as the power reaches the rear wheels and they surge forward.

Second gear...and moving. Fast. For just a moment the rear end had snaked as they had pulled away. For just a moment. Now they were thundering away, true and fast.

He rammed it into third. And glanced into the mirror. The man on the truck bonnet was sitting there, swinging his legs. The man with the knife was picking himself up from the road. He may have been shouting. With a sudden smack the rear windscreen disintegrated.

Shooting! They were shooting.

A moment later he heard the crack of the gun above the sound of the engine. Something thumped into the back of his seat. A hole appeared in the windscreen in front of him. A tiny hole, or so it seemed. Something was happening to the roof-lining. Bits seemed to be coming off? Dust was appearing from nowhere. There was the constant sound of the gun, rather muted but nonetheless definite even to the untrained ear.

What was the range of a weapon like that? He had no idea. He kept his foot down, in third. Probably a kilometre, something ridiculous like that. How could a man AIM a weapon at a target so far away? Most of the shots were coming in through the back window and ending up in the roof lining.

Two more. A sort of whining sound. The rear near side door window shattered with a crack and disappeared...how? It didn't matter. His mind was empty. A blank. There was only one thing to do, only one thing a normal healthy man with a wife and family—or without for that matter—would want. To get out. To get away. To get away from the madman with the gun.

A man he didn't know, a man he hadn't even met was trying to destroy Marzena, him, their lives...why? For their fuel? Their car? Their jewellery, money, or what? Thank God the kids were out of this.

And still the bullets came. Two more holes appeared in the windscreen...why hadn't it shattered? Or split, or something?

It didn't matter why the bastard was shooting. It was too late to ask, anyway. Thank God he hadn't disabled the car. Without wheels they'd have been defenceless against three men with guns. Yet, he corrected himself. Thank God he hadn't disabled the car yet.

Only a hundred metres to go now...he was thinking like Marzena, now. Metres, yards, so what?

In truth, he wasn't thinking at all. He was fleeing, and while he fled his mind was a blank. Pictures, thoughts, and impressions raced across his mind, but they were nothing. He was running.

They were running, running from a pointless death at the hands of a killer with a gun.

Dear God. Nearly there. They were almost at the bend at the end of the straight. He felt himself breathe. How long was it since he had breathed, since he had drawn breath? It felt like it had been a while.

Dear God...they were there. The longest three hundred metres of his life!

He entered the bend with his foot still flat on the throttle, without any thought about surviving the bend itself. He hadn't considered that it might be sharp, dangerous, or anything. The bend in the road had been his goal. His sole goal. Nothing else had mattered. Now that they were there he had to get the Volvo around it...

It was a nasty bend and they were travelling fast in third gear. Very fast. At the last moment he stomped on the brakes, realising at the same instant that that was a mistake. Even with ABS it would have been relatively easy to put her into a spin on that bend in these conditions. He lifted his foot off the pedal, clung to the wheel and prayed. An awful thought entered his mind...would the bend protect them from the gun? It better had! And if he wrapped the car around a tree where would that leave them? Up shit alley, that's where.

Jesus, Jesus, he was muttering. Or maybe just thinking. The Volvo didn't want to do it. He'd pulled the wheel around to the right and was hugging the near side kerb, only it wasn't a kerb. The rear end was beginning to slip. He could feel it beginning to hang out...

Holy fuck, he thought. Shit, shit...am I going to die with an obscenity on my lips? It looked nasty. It WAS nasty.

The rear wheels held onto tarmac for longer than he could have hoped for, but with a sudden flip they gave up, and the back was swinging. He had no idea how fast they were travelling, but it was fast. Far too fast.

Dear God, no!

They were sideways on and moving fast. He struggled with the wheel, trying to steer into his impossible slide...this isn't a skid, he was thinking, this is a disaster, this is death...dear God...

...he could hear the scream of rubber on the tarmac...all it needed was a nudge and she'd roll...dear God...these roads were rough...a pothole would turn her...

...traffic? A car or something bigger coming the other way? It didn't bear thinking about...

...he'd lost it completely...if his senses were anything to go by they were travelling backwards...

...dear God...

...nothing to do now, but pray.

A sudden cloud of dust. A part of the car...the front wheels?...were on mud and dirt. That meant that they were over the hard shoulder and heading into field.

Slowly, the car swung around. He realised with a shock that his foot was rammed down hard on the brake. They were almost stopped! And they hadn't hit anything. They weren't actually out of trouble, yet, but things didn't look nearly as grim as they had a few moments ago.

As the Volvo slowed he was able to correct what had now become a relatively gentle slide, and pulled into the side of the road. He wasn't sure which way they were facing or how many times they had spun. All that mattered was that they were still alive...and the car was still the right way up.

"Thank you, God," he breathed. He turned to Marzena, an apology on his lips...

...and his world ended...

...She sat, unmoving, unseeing, leaning forward against her seat belt. Her head drooped, her hair swinging gently. He knew immediately.

But he didn't believe what he saw, he didn't believe what he knew.

"Marzena," he shouted. Perhaps he screamed, perhaps it was a whisper. He didn't know that he had spoken. It didn't matter, she didn't hear him. She would never hear him.

She would never ever...

He seized her shoulders, pulled her around to face him. She was limp. Her face hung down.

"Jesus," he prayed.

He pushed her face up. Her eyes were open. Sightless. She looked at him. Sightless. The face that he loved, the face that he'd looked at more often than any other. The face that had always reflected his love...sightless.

"Jesus!" he screamed. He wanted her back. This wasn't to happen.

Suddenly, remembering himself he pushed her back into her seat, and stared intently at her to ascertain if she was breathing.

Nothing.

Pulse? He drew his finger in a line down from her ear. About three inches. And then halfway around to the front of her neck. And felt for pulse.

Nothing.

For two minutes he desperately searched for a pulse...no pulse, no pulse. Nothing. Nothing.

Nothing.

Tears were streaming down his face. She was too young. He stopped searching...there was no pulse.

She sat there...just like a few minutes ago....but she was gone. The self that was Marzena had gone. She wasn't there. Some bastard had...he screamed. He screamed as loud as he could. He screamed until there was no breath left in his body.

Why? Oh God.

He was filled with an enormous sense of...nothing.

He sat there. He did nothing.

He thought nothing. The tears fell, but he was unaware of them.

Marzena...they'd been together for a long time...and the kids? ...dear Jesus...how would...oh, no. No, no, no...he looked back at his wife. She sat still...at rest? Oh Jesus. Her sightless eyes in her drooping head. Oh Jesus. He remembered those eyes, how they had shone...when Tom had been born...when she had held Trix for the first time...before she was even Trix...she'd been Tricks first, but Marzena wouldn't let him register her as Tricks...when they'd first met, so long ago...was it so long? ...it was nothing...in a lifetime their lifetime together was nothing...nothing, but everything...

Oh Jesus.

+

After he didn't know how long he put the car gently into gear and drove West. He still had a fair way to go. He didn't know quite what to do, but neither did he care very much. He drove more slowly, not wanting to disturb Marzena, who sat in the front seat supported by the seat belt. It was cold in the car with the two windows missing, but he didn't notice. His mind was blank. He felt strangely calm.

At the next road block he drove gently to a halt. A man approached the offside front door. A scruffy looking fellow, quite obviously not policja, and apparently not armed although it wasn't really possible to tell. He took one look at Marzena, realised that the car was right hand drive, gave Jamie a startled look, lifted the barrier, and waved the car through.

After a while Jamie turned on the radio. It was Polish, of course. He rarely listened to Polish radio because the Polish was too fast for him to understand with any clarity. He scanned through the wavebands to see if there was anything in English. It was always possible. He could pick up BBC Radio on the long wave as far East as Berlin, although reception was fairly poor. Unfortunately most broadcasts, including the ones that used to be aimed at British troops in Berlin—he wasn't sure if they still had them; the troops or the broadcasts—seemed to be on FM, which meant that their range was virtually only 'line of sight'. Which meant, in turn, that East of Berlin he had never managed to receive English radio in the car.

Of course, if he'd had short-wave in the car...but he hadn't. He left the radio tuned into a Polish station. It was comforting to hear the human voice. Understanding wasn't so important. He drove on slowly. There seemed little reason for rush. Whether he got to Berlin tonight or not now seemed to depend upon fuel. There was no need to rush. He was well ahead of any invading army. In any case, the army had probably been stopped—or at least slowed—by Warsaw.

After a while the nature of the radio programme began to dawn on him. As he should have expected from a country that was being overrun it was a news broadcast. A constant broadcast of news with frequent summaries. It was the third news summary that finally got through to him. He slowed the car to a halt at the edge of the road. His mind refusing to accept what he was hearing. He stared straight ahead...

...the fields were white with snow, the road was stained white with snow and salt, the trees were a stark black covered in part with frozen snow or ice. It was beautiful, stark, and meaningless...

...he didn't notice the cold...it was well below freezing outside the car...the wind blowing in through the glassless windows...

He sat perfectly still for a very long time. Long enough to hear two more summaries and a little more detail...

...he hadn't thought that he could lose more...

...but he'd been wrong...

He'd heard it three times, now.

The last scheduled commercial flight out of Poland had been destroyed in the air.

Dear God. Tom and Trix.

WAR DAY

HEATHROW AIRPORT, LONDON
GREAT BRITAIN

She was bored. Bored stiff. And hungry. Very hungry. "Mummy," she enquired politely and perhaps a little timidly, "when will we have something to eat?" All around them the gentle chatter and bustle of an efficiently run international airport hummed away.

"I'm not sure, darling," the problem was, her problem was that she hadn't brought very much money with her, and it hadn't occurred to her to bring food. It hadn't crossed her mind that they might have to wait at the airport. At the time it had seemed all-important to get to the airport fast. To rush to arrive. The possibility of having to wait for any time at all simply hadn't crossed her mind.

She glanced at her watch. Again. Miriam didn't understand what the problem was. Why couldn't she have something to eat? She wanted something to eat. She always ate now. In fact, food was very overdue. So, what was the problem? Where was the food? She was starving.

"Mummy," she began again, her little tummy rumbling quietly, making demands that were normally met fairly promptly.

Sylvia looked at her with a gentle smile. What were they going to do? It was almost two. The plane should have been here hours ago. How could it be so late? I mean, how could it? What was happening? A plane can't be that late...where is it while it's being late?

"I've got to go, love," it was Petra. She had to pick up the kids from school. Sylvia hadn't noticed her coming over. What were they going to do?

"What are you going to do?" Petra asked.

She didn't know.

"I don't know," she felt hopeless. Stupid and hopeless. She probably hadn't even got enough money to get home by train. In fact, she was sure that she hadn't. She couldn't stay, because if she did she couldn't get home. What good would she be to the kids if she couldn't take them home? She felt the tears well up behind her eyes. Anger, frustration, she wasn't sure what, but it was burning. Maybe it was just being broke. "Shit!" she muttered, almost inaudibly...

"Mummy!" she didn't know her mum could say such words. Just wait until she told Isabel!

"I'm sorry, love," her mum was very unhappy, she could see that.

"You all right for money?"

Sylvia paused, absent-mindedly wiping her nose with the back of her hand. Miriam watched in stunned amazement. She was not allowed...she was forbidden to do that. Her eyes popped wide. What a day!

"Can you give me a tenner?"

"Will that be enough?" Petra looked doubtful. They'd been through a lot together, but on the other hand money was tight.

"Not really, I don't know. How much can you spare? What will the train cost me?" Petra grinned at this barrage of questions.

"I can give you twenty," could she really? She wasn't sure that that was wise, but this was an emergency, wasn't it? She pulled the notes out of her purse and handed them across.

"Thanks, Petra, you're an angel," she smiled through her tearful face. She felt terrible.

+

After Petra had gone she sat down in the hard chair and tried to work out what on earth could be going on. It was past two. The plane was due at around ten thirty and it wasn't here, yet? It didn't seem possible.

"Are you waiting for BA 106?" a quiet voice asked.

She turned. An elderly man was leaning gently towards her, a look of concern on his face.

"Yes?"

"May I?" he indicated the chair next to her.

"Yes, yes, of course," she said, taken aback. Where she came from you just sat if you wanted a seat.

"Are you, then?"

"I beg your pardon?"

"Waiting for BA 106?"

"Oh. Yes, yes I am." She noticed his eyes. They were deep eyes. Very deep, very concerned.

He leaned forward in his chair, resting his chin on his hands in which he clasped a smashing looking cane. He looked away from her, staring across the concourse.

"What's happening?"

"It's late," he laughed. A dry sound. Without humour. He turned back to her.

"I think perhaps there might have been an accident."

"An accident?" Her mind had gone blank. Babies! It was having kids that had done that to her!

"They've been delaying ETA since nine fifteen," he glanced at his watch, "it's two fifteen, now," he paused.

"Five hours," she said.

"Exactly."

There was a pause.

"It's a two hour flight," he stated.

"But it wasn't due until about ten thirty, was it?" was it? She was confused.

"It was scheduled to arrive at nine fifteen..."

"I thought," she interrupted. He frowned. She stopped speaking.

A moment's silence.

"I'm sorry," she said with a smile.

He returned her smile, "No, no. You were saying."

"I thought it was due in at..." she realised that it didn't really matter. It was very late whether it was due in at ten thirty or nine fifteen. There was a few moments' pause. She really had nothing to say. She didn't know what was happening. She had to wait. She had very little choice. No choice, she corrected herself. I hope the little blighters have got enough for their train fares, she thought. If I have to pay for them I'll never be able to pay Petra back.

Twice she had 'phoned Mr Ingram's number in the village. They'd obviously gone somewhere for the day, or—she shuddered—for longer. Information had been worse than useless. What was the girl paid for? She'd been no help at all; simply referred her back to the Arrivals Information display, or whatever she had called it.

He looked at her face. She was young, pretty and quite obviously poor. He glanced involuntarily at her left hand—a move which would have embarrassed him acutely had he thought that she had noticed—and which would have annoyed his wife intensely.

"At your age!" she would have stormed. He smiled to himself, half smiled anyway. A tired smile.

"What can we do?" she asked.

"I'm not sure," his smile died, "Information hasn't been very informative."

She smiled her agreement. "It's difficult to imagine that they can have lost the airplane. They must know where it is."

He paused, considering the alternatives to an airline knowing where one of its airplanes was. Judging by the look on the young woman's face the same thoughts were growing in her mind. They both looked up, in that special sightless way, as the tannoy opened and a well trained voice asked all those awaiting flight BA 106 to go to the VIP lounge. Sylvia looked at her new companion and was about to speak but, seeing the fear in his eyes her heart sank and she closed her mouth. They stood up.

"Where is it?"

"Follow me."

WAR DAY

ROUTE E8
TRAVELLING WEST FROM WARSAW
POLAND

It was freezing cold. He was driving slowly, not far from Poznan. He was empty. His mind, his heart...empty. No thought, no feelings, no emotions. Just a pit. A sort of a gap where his feelings should have been. He had cried a bit. Not much. He didn't seem to have it in him. He didn't seem to have the energy. He felt dry. Dry inside.

Around him, the world continued. A crazy world, a world turned upside down. A world of strangers, most of them dangerous. He'd passed through a half a dozen road blocks, all of them manned by men with guns and no uniforms. What was happening? He didn't really care.

All the fuel stations were either closed or destroyed. There was no fuel to be had. Nothing. Maybe he could buy some in Poznan, on the black market. Maybe not. He wouldn't need much, just a few litres. Enough to get him to Swiecko.

He didn't really care.

The kids.

Was that really just a few hours ago?

Maybe it wasn't their plane he caught himself thinking time and time again. But he knew the facts; their plane had been the last out.

Was it really less than twenty four hours ago, that he and Marzena had put the kids to bed and had spent the evening watching television, eating a curry and drinking Polish beer? A normal evening.

And now? Nothing.

No Marzena, no Tricks, no Tom...he breathed deeply. The passenger seat was empty. Marzena lay in the back under a rug. On the edge of Poznan, the last major Polish city before Germany, he pulled over to the edge of the road.

The fuel needle had been in the red sector for some time and had been on the pin for several miles. He'd be lucky to get into the city at all. He sat for a while, in the freezing cold, pulling a loaf of stale bread into pieces, some of which he absently put into his mouth. He chewed the hard bread thoughtlessly. Above him, in the fading light, the sky was filled with hundreds of large airplanes.

He sat there, oblivious. As his mouth chewed on the tasteless bread he stared sightlessly out of the windscreen. The radio was turned on, but he wasn't listening.

Thousands of feet above him hundreds of NRC airplanes headed West, destination Poznan.

He brushed the crumbs off his lap with only limited success, opened the driver's door and got out for a pee. His snow boots crunched in the snow. Moving only a couple of metres from the car he unzipped his fly and began to pee.

He looked up.

"Jesus," he whispered. The sky was black. There must have been a hundred planes up there. More. He had no idea. The sky was full of them. He got back into the car and headed West. He was no longer ahead of the NRC.

+

It was dark when he reached the edge of Poznan, and there was no road block on the edge of the city, which rather surprised him. He still wasn't sure what purpose the road blocks served, and to whom they served this purpose, but he would have expected one on the edge of a major city like Poznan.

He ignored the new by-pass and headed into the city itself. Without fuel there was no point in going any further.

For some time now he had seen virtually no traffic, and Poznan was no different. There was nothing on the roads and no one on the pavements. The place could have been empty. The only sign of life was the lighted windows in the blocks of flats - at least there's electricity here, he thought - so presumably that's where everyone is.

To his astonishment he found an open fuel station a couple of miles beyond the turnoff for the by-pass. It was brightly lit and normal. He drove towards it very cautiously, and, not daring to drive in, went past it, turned and drove back.

It looked normal. Normal by yesterday's standards. Extraordinary by today's.

He didn't believe it. He pulled in slowly...

...it would be ace, really ace, to fill up and get out of this place, he thought. A moment later he was wondering why, for what? What was the point?

Maybe the kids...

...no, he told himself. You know! There's no chance. You're just clinging to straws, threads...

...and as he pulled in, a pump attendant walked towards him rubbing his hands on a cloth. Like every other pump attendant in Poland, Jamie thought, they all look the same. He almost smiled, but it died on the way to his lips. It would take more than a pump attendant to bring a smile to his face.

"Dollars?" the man asked, reminding Jamie very much of the days prior to the big changes in 1990. He paused.

"Deutschmarks?" Jamie offered.

"Good," the attendant beamed. So, the zloty was no good, again. The attendant stood, stationary.

"Diesel, please" Jamie prompted, in his appalling Polish.

"How much?" the man was moving towards the pump.

"Thirty litres, please," that would be more than enough to get him into Berlin, he reckoned. He hadn't yet considered that there might be a problem at the border...not merely crossing the border, but crossing the border with Marzena in the car...

"Deutschmarks," the man was holding out his hand, obviously requesting payment in advance. Not unreasonable, Jamie felt, given today's extraordinary circumstances.

"Yes," he responded, "How many?"

The man named a sum far in excess of the going rate. Jamie, who had once been a keen haggler, didn't bat an eyelid as he reached into his pocket, pulled out the notes and handed them over without a word.

The man smiled, counted the notes with great care, and began to put the precious diesel into the tank. Jamie couldn't believe his luck.

...27, 28, 29....and 30 litres. He felt that glow inside peculiar to the motorist in third world or similar countries when he has just filled his fuel tank. He was wondering whether he should have actually filled the tank—but that would have been greedy wouldn't it?—when something cold, hard and unmistakably a gun was pressed against his neck.

"And the rest," a voice said in his ear.

He could smell the man's sweat. Not the sweat of a few moments fear, but the stale sweat of a body that doesn't get washed as often as it should. He could feel the man's body lightly behind him...he could hear his breath...but most of all he could feel the cold steel on his neck, pushing at his scarf. It had been a long day...and he had nothing left to lose...he had nothing...he'd lost everything already...nothing. He stood...quite still...thinking...

He'd never done anything violent in his life. He'd always avoided even the most minor of confrontations. But there comes a time...there comes a time. And was now such a time, he asked himself?

It was.

"Now," the voice demanded, the steel of the gun pressing harder into his neck.

Now indeed, Jamie thought.

Jamie lifted his elbow and rammed it into the gunman's stomach area...he hoped. He'd seen it done in a few films. Generally, it worked.

He heard a sort of 'ooommpphh', which was encouraging, and began to turn. At that moment there was the most terrific bang and for a moment he wondered if the world was coming to an end...and if so, so what? a part of him asked...most of its already ended...the crashing bang of the explosion seemed to go on for ever...well, for a long time, anyway...and everything seemed to be happening in slow motion...

He turned slowly, his hands reaching up to where the gun was...to where he thought it was...to where it had been...reaching into empty space...the noise of the explosion still bouncing back and forth inside his head, making any thought impossible...

His assailant with his right arm back...his right arm in a slow arc...swinging towards him...towards his face...the heavy steel of the gun...moving gently, slowly...and Jamie frozen to the spot, not moving, hardly breathing...no time for breathing, he thought...no time for thought, he thought, realising how incongruous...the arm reached his face...the heavy steel of the slow moving gun against the side of his face...

...the pain...the impression that he was going to have to sit down for a moment...the sudden thump as he collapsed to the ground...the oily forecourt...raising his hands to his face as the man...the man reached for him, his arm swinging back again...the cold of the ground...a sudden pain as one of the man's boots thumped against him...not my day, the ridiculous thought sailed gently across the forecourt of his mind, confused with the oily concrete surface, the dirt around the base of the fuel pumps and the man's boot raised again...not really my day...for a brief moment a confused vision of Marzena and his mother floated into his mind...Freud, he thought, Freud would like that one...

...things seemed to fade...

+

And then he was sitting up on the forecourt, aware of the filth, trying to stand, his gloved hands pushing at the greasy concrete, a severe pain in his back and his face. He wanted to touch his face, but he was still on the ground and anyway he was wearing gloves, thick skiing gloves.

He wanted to laugh...so, he thought, the worm has turned...he grinned, but judging by the way the attendant was looking at him it didn't look much like a grin from the outside.

Oh dear. He could taste blood...and there was something loose inside his mouth...a tooth?...he felt carefully with his tongue...realising at the same time that he hadn't made any progress with getting to his feet. He was still sitting on the oily fuel station forecourt.

"Oh, shit!" he spat, noticing that the Volvo had gone. He got to his hands and knees, giving up all attempt at decorum...he paused, looking down at the concrete...blood and saliva dribbled and splattered lightly.

Mine? he thought.

Must be.

With a sudden shaft of pain he realised that with the car he had lost Marzena!

He remained on all fours for a few moments, tears pricking his eyes. The attendant was saying something but it wasn't sinking in. With a monumental struggle he forced himself to kneel...and, facing one of the pumps began to pull himself upright...it was greasy, oily...his head was spinning and he felt nauseous. He clung to the pump, desperately willing himself not to be violently sick...

...but why? he asked himself...

The attendant was helping him, holding him...still talking, still saying something, although it was unintelligible. He was concentrating on survival, on keeping body and soul together, and on not bloody sliding down the greasy pump... and on keeping his body off the concrete...the oily concrete...he hated oil.

And, at last...he was standing.

He grinned, shakily, to himself.

He felt like...like someone had wapped him across the head with a gun, knocked him to the ground and kicked him...several times...bloody hell...he hurt...

...trying to look like Eastwood, he spat out a tooth...only it turned out not to be a tooth...it was saliva and blood...he failed to spit cleanly, the bloody saliva slid down his chin...

...he felt a wreck...a mess...

...and he looked worse...

...he looked around, still clinging to the pump...

...bloody hell...he hurt...he hurt all over, now that he came to think about it...the attendant was still speaking...offering him coffee...

...coffee?...

...what good?...

...coffee, he thought, yes I'd love...I'd love a coffee...

Weakly, ever so carefully, he nodded, opened his mouth to speak, pausing to see if he was going to dribble, wiping his chin with the back of his hand, looking at his hand...blood and saliva smeared...oh, bloody hell!...

Very carefully, and with the attendant's assistance, he made his way slowly to the small shop and cash desk, slumping down in the spare bright red plastic chair.

Once seated it took him only moments to realise that not only had his assailant taken the car, together with Marzena, he had also taken his money - all his money! —and his passport. All he had left was his Dowod Osobisty, his Polish ID

"Oh, shit," he muttered without enthusiasm. No money, no real papers, no car...no family...

...his head drooped. It was difficult to imagine how things could get worse...

+

It was snowing when he left the filling station, hoping to find a hotel that would let him book in while he sorted out some money and papers. It would have to be one of the big ones, an international hotel. No one else would take him looking like this without money or papers. It must be late, he thought vaguely.

It was still a mile or two into the centre of the city, he reckoned, and it would take him a while to walk. There was no traffic and he didn't believe that he'd seen more than one bus since they'd left Warsaw.

The snow on the ground had formed the brown sandy appearance that was so common in Polish cities, and which he assumed was the result of adding sand or salt to the snow in an environment where the temperature didn't rise to above freezing for weeks at a time. It wasn't at all icy, and appeared to have the texture of a thick brown sugar.

He walked with his collars turned up against the falling snow. There was a slight wind, driving the falling snow against the side of his face. It was very cold. As well as his coat he was wearing a balaclava, a woollen hat and a long scarf wound around his neck. On his feet he was wearing his snow boots which gave wonderful insulation against the cold and offered fabulous grip on almost any surface except actual sheets of ice.

There was no one else walking in the street. He hadn't seen a single pedestrian...and, it dawned on him, not a single vehicle since he'd left the fuel station.

He turned at a sudden roaring clatter...

"Oh, Jesus," he flung himself towards the ditch, half running, sliding crawling...clawing the ground, slithering, face covered in freezing snow, his hands grappling for a grip where there was none...

...it was a tank. A fucking tank!...

"Jesus, Jesus," he was praying. This was all a bit difficult to cope with...

Two tanks, he realised, abreast...simply sweeping vehicles aside. rushing them, squashing them like...like...what? The vehicles were simply being swept to one side...

...he crawled deeper into the ditch...

"Oh Jesus, Oh Jesus..." he hadn't stopped praying. What am I doing here? Has the whole world gone mad? Or is it just me?

The tanks were moving fast, very fast. What was it that Tom had said? "Fifty miles an hour over a ploughed field"? Well, these things were moving, that was for sure...

Behind the tanks, more!....

...no, not more tanks, he realised...vehicles, other vehicles...loads of them...bright lights shining everywhere, sideways, forwards, up, down, everywhere...

...he pressed himself deeper into the ditch...why? Because it seemed the most reasonable thing to do when faced with an advancing army!

He could feel the snow melting against his face, and between his scarf and his neck from his initial scrabble into the ditch. He lay still, head down in the ditch, his hands over his head. He couldn't help wishing that he wasn't wearing a bright green coat.

The tanks crashed past, how far... how close to his feet he couldn't tell...didn't want to know. He was praying...

...for several minutes the convey of vehicles roared past. When all seemed still he lay unmoving for another...how long?...he had no idea...half a lifetime?

Eventually, he risked a gentle movement. Nothing happened.

Slowly, oh so slowly, he moved so that he could face the road. He was still lying flat in the snow.

Someone nudged his back gently. He jumped, and turned slowly. Above him stood a soldier...at least he's a soldier, he thought, before realising that he didn't recognise the uniform...

"Up," the soldier said in very bad Polish, waving his rifle. Was it a rifle? A machine pistol?

Jamie stood. Behind the soldier there were literally dozens more, apparently combing the streets.

"Papers," he requested. Jamie reached for his inside coat pocket. He'd seen enough films to know to keep the movement nice and slow. The young soldier looked as nervous as he felt.

He handed him the Dowod Osobisty.

"Curfew," the soldier stated flatly in his atrocious Polish, without attempting to examine the document. He simply held it loosely in his hand.

"I'm going to my hotel," Jamie offered.

"Curfew," this time it was a shout. His weapon waved erratically and—it seemed to Jamie—dangerously.

An officer came over.

"Curfew," he repeated in Polish that was just as bad as the enlisted man's.

"I was just going back to my hotel," Jamie explained again.

"Curfew," the officer repeated, shaking his head, and drawing his finger across his throat.

"Holy Jesus," Jamie watched horrified as the soldier raised his gun. His heart was pounding in his ears. Can it really have come to this? But, of course it could. The rest of his family had died in the last few hours, so why not him?

Why not indeed? He looked the soldier calmly in the face...do it, he found himself thinking, do it you bastard...

The soldier waved the pointing weapon,
"Come."

Chapter Five

WAR DAY

HEATHROW AIRPORT
LONDON
GREAT BRITAIN

The elderly man had a grin on his face that spread from ear to ear. Miriam had never seen a grown up with such a large grin. It hadn't budged for half an hour, either. It had just sat there on the old man's face.

Miriam was happy, too, because she'd had two puddings. She'd had to eat firsts first, as usual, but it had been okay—apart from the brown sauce with bits in it. She hadn't been able to eat that, and thank heavens mum hadn't made a fuss. She'd just scraped it off the food and put it on the edge of the plate.

Anyway, she liked the old man, because he'd given her his pudding. And that had been good. He'd said that he didn't like it, but how would he know? He hadn't even tried it. That's what mum always said when she didn't want to eat something. But Miriam hadn't told him, because then he might have tried it and found that he did like it.

Miriam had found it all rather puzzling. One minute they'd been waiting for the plane, the next minute they'd all been taken to this big lounge, which mum kept calling the vee-aye-pee lounge. Then they'd been told that the plane that they were all waiting for was in Germany.

Well, that didn't seem like very good news, but everyone seemed to think that it was. In fact, everyone seemed over the moon. They were wandering around chatting, laughing and even slapping each other on the back. A lot of them were drinking. Everything seemed to be free in the vee-aye-pee lounge. Miriam wondered why they hadn't come here in the first place. It was far nicer than that other place they'd had to wait in. There was food, Pepsi and comfortable chairs. It even smelled nicer.

Anyway, when they'd come in a man in a uniform had stood up and had told them all about the airplane. He had said that it had landed in Germany because it had had a problem. Miriam wasn't sure what this problem had been, but the man had said that it hadn't been nearly as bad as some people had seemed to think. He said that news reports had greatly exaggerated the problem. They'd all got out in Germany and they'd be given another 'plane as soon as there was a spare one. Miriam wasn't sure what germany was, but he didn't explain that bit.

And now they had to wait. He'd said that it'd be about three hours. And in the meantime, food and drink in the vee-aye-pee lounge was free.

Also, mum had said that the old man was going to give them a lift home. Quite what Dad would say when he heard that they'd been given a lift by a stranger Miriam simply couldn't guess.

WAR DAY

HEATHROW AIRPORT
LONDON
Late evening

Well, it seemed that they'd found a new airplane, at last. Miriam grinned. Soon they could go home. She wondered why it had taken so long to find another airplane. You only had to look out of the window to see that there were loads of them hanging around not doing very much. She was very bored and very much looking forward to getting home.

Beside her, she was shocked to see that her mum was asleep. She was slumped in the comfy chair her head resting on the back of the chair, her mouth very slightly open. She'd only turned her back for a few moments and her mum had fallen asleep! She looked very tired. Poor mum.

A man in a uniform had just come over and had told the old man something. The old man had grinned and had said to Miriam,

"They'll be here in a few moments." His eyes had been bright and his face had looked funny.

"Oh, good," she had responded. She hadn't known what to say. Adults could be so difficult.

"Mum," she pulled at Sylvia's arm. Her mum stirred for a moment and then came awake suddenly, looking startled. She looked first at Miriam and then around the lounge, comprehension dawning.

"What time is...?" she began.

The old man hardly glanced at his watch. "They're clearing immigration and customs, now," he looked as though he'd just won a gold or something, Miriam was thinking. The last time that she'd seen that look on someone's face was when Helen had got three gold stars at school. Three!

"Oh, fantastic," mum seemed to shake herself awake. She wondered if the Ingrams were in yet. What time was it? She glanced at the old man's watch, a sort of sideways peer. Nearly nine. The plane was about eleven hours late. Well, still a chance to get everyone home in time for a decent night's sleep.

"...another ten minutes," he was saying.

Ten minutes, she thought, that'd give her time to telephone the Ingrams. They must be back by now. They must be. She didn't allow herself to consider the alternatives.

There was a 'phone within sight, she'd already used it several times.

"Could you?" she asked the elderly gent, indicating Miriam.

"Of course, it's a pleasure", he grinned happily. More accurately, he simply continued to grin. He hadn't stopped since the airways rep had told him that the 'plane was on the ground and that it was disembarking. He had just sat there and grinned.

There was still no answer! She couldn't believe this. What was she going to do with these two kids if Mr and Mrs Ingram didn't show up? They could be anywhere. She closed her mind to the thought that they might be on holiday. They must, surely they must, have seen or heard the news about Poland. They wouldn't stay away. Would they? Oh shit! She couldn't keep the thought out of her mind. What would she do...?

She dialled again. Still no answer. No bloody answer. Where were they and what the hell were they doing? Oh shit. Shit.

She put the receiver back with exaggerated care. It was all that she could do to stop herself from slamming it, and slamming it hard.

There was a sudden bustle of activity at the end of the room. Human noises of relief, the sound of bodies hugging each other, laughter. She turned from the 'phone.

People were standing. Nearly everyone was on their feet. Passengers were beginning to come into the room. They looked very tired indeed, but all their faces wore enormous smiles. Big tired grins all over the place.

She made her way back to Miriam. The elderly gent was still grinning. She couldn't help grinning, too. He looked like a great big, happy Cheshire cat. Miriam reached for her hand. She sat down in the comfortable chair, but immediately realised that she couldn't see anything now that everyone was standing. She sighed, and stood up, peering at the door at the end of the room through which the passengers were emerging.

"Mummy!" Miriam was pulling at her arm.

"Yes," she said, looking down softly at her daughter. Goodness, she was tired.

"Mummy," Miriam said plaintively, indicating a uniformed figure who had apparently been addressing Sylvia.

"Oh," she started, taken aback. She'd been staring intently at the arriving passengers.

"Mrs Wallis?"

"Yes?"

"You're meeting Thomas and Patricia Ingram?"

Thomas and Patricia?

"Yes," she felt like a fraud. Like a child-stealer. What right had she to meet these children? Two children who...

"They're very tired," she continued, "and very upset. It's been a difficult journey. For everyone, but particularly for the children," she paused, "I believe that they had to leave their parents in Warsaw?"

Sylvia found herself nodding, although to be honest she wasn't quite sure if it had been a question. Her nod slowed to a halt. They'd all seen the news reports during the afternoon. What the bombs, shelling and rockets had done to Warsaw. She wondered why the parents hadn't travelled with the two kids. The city was flat. A pile of rubble. There'd been more damage in one afternoon than in the whole of the second world war...or so the news programmes would have one believe. Why had they stayed behind? But she could hardly ask this person.

"So, we've got them in a side room," the airline official continued, "they're waiting for you". She began to lead Sylvia away. Sylvia turned and gave the elderly gent a small wave and a tight, rather frightened smile, and followed, gripping Miriam's tiny hand in hers.

"I understand from our cabin staff that Thomas and Patricia had a fairly traumatic time in Warsaw. They were very unhappy when they boarded, although they seemed to brighten up after a while. The young lad, apparently, actually enjoyed the mid-air incident," she looked ruefully at Sylvia, "the only person to do so, I suspect."

They were approaching a small door, a small blue door. Sylvia was feeling sick. What would these poor kids think, what would they say? Oh, the poor things would be so horribly disappointed. And after such an awful day. Through the door, her heart in her mouth, and into a narrow corridor. And, what on earth was she to do with them?

Oh, shit! She felt sick.

And down the narrow corridor the three of them walked. There were three salmon doors to the left and two to the right, and then the corridor disappeared around a corner. More of a bend, actually, she noticed with surprise. Corridors normally had corners, didn't they, not bends.

She felt sick. Bend or corner, she still felt sick. The airline official stopped at the third door on the left, turned the handle and pushed it open for Sylvia and Miriam.

Two tiny children sat slumped in waiting room chairs. They were motionless. They barely glanced up as the three walked into the room.

"Hello," said Miriam brightly, "We've come to take you home."

A moment's pause as they all viewed each other.

"Yes," Sylvia dropped to her haunches, "your grandparents were unable to meet you, so we're going to take you home. My name's Sylvia," she smiled.

"Where's Granny?" the little girl, Trix asked.

"Daddy said that they'd be here," the boy added.

Goodness, Sylvia thought, they're tired.

"My Mum spoke to your Daddy on the 'phone," Miriam spoke proudly, "he dialled the number wrong. I spoke to him, too. He was in a hurry," she added after a pause. She was wondering why they were wearing such funny boots.

Sylvia reached out for Trix, lifting the tiny body into her arms. The poor, dear face was tear stained and grubby. She was gripping a small bear in both her hands.

"Shall we?" she held out her spare hand for the boy.

"Mummy!" demanded Miriam, holding out a hand. Sylvia changed her mind, lowering herself into a chair. The little girl in her arms was concentrating on her own hands and avoiding Sylvia's gaze.

"You're Tom," she said, looking at the young lad.

He nodded. "Where's Granny?" he repeated his sister's question.

"I'm not sure, Tom, but I expect they'll be at home when we get home," she smiled a reassuring smile. She looked down at Trix, who was still concentrating on her motionless hands.

"You've got funny boots," Miriam addressed the pair of them. They both looked surprised for a moment, glancing at their own feet and then at Miriam. There was a moment's silence.

"We saw a Mig. It was an NRC Mig. It attacked our plane," Tom stated with evident pride.

"Well," began the airline official with a sideways look at Sylvia, "it didn't actually attack your plane did it?"

"I saw rockets," he responded, "it fired rockets. And it came so close that I could see the pilot," he took a breath, "Ruskie bastard."

There was a moment's stunned silence. Both the airline official and Sylvia looked as though they'd never heard the words before, Trix was ignoring the conversation, and Miriam was singularly impressed. That was a bad word, she knew that. It was bad.

Tom, aware of the unexpected effect that his words had had and not wishing to take the blame himself, added,

"That's what the man in the plane said."

"He did?" responded the airline official, feeling silly.

"And we went to Germany," he continued quickly, the pride still evident. It was clear that he was keen to remove himself as far as possible from his last remark.

"What's germany?" Miriam asked.

"Sshh," Sylvia was horrified. The girl was eight, surely she ought to know where Germany was...let alone what it was.

"I want to go home," Trix said quietly.

"What? What was that, Trix?"

Sylvia hadn't understood what the little girl had said, she had spoken in Polish, but she didn't repeat it. She just shook her head, her eyes not leaving her hands.

"Where's your luggage?" Sylvia asked brightly.

"We left it all behind," Tom said, "we couldn't bring anything with us. Only Fangs."

"Fangs?"

"Yes," Trix waved the bear in front of Sylvia's face, speaking in English this time, "this is Fangs. He's a bear. We left everything else behind. Daddy and Mummy have it in the car. They'll be here soon. They said."

A small smile appeared briefly on the young face.

WAR DAY

ROUTE E8
TRAVELLING EAST FROM POZNAN
POLAND
A few minutes before midnight

The third shot killed the driver and the car plunged off the road into the bushes. It had been travelling fast when the driver had failed to stop at the makeshift roadblock.

With the driver slumped sideways into the passenger seat the car simply drifted to the road's edge and, when the near side wheels touched the unevenness of the slight bank beyond the hard shoulder, the car veered off the road, its headlights picking out the small, bare bushes moments before the car flattened them. The car's velocity was such that it didn't settle to a halt until it had hit a small tree some twenty five metres off the road. A few moments later the power in the shattered battery faded and the car's lights were reduced to a glimmer.

Two of the four men on the roadblock ran towards the spot where the car had left the road, but a sudden and unexpected clatter from above stopped them in their tracks. As if from nowhere two immensely powerful floodlights began searching for movement on the ground. The four men flung themselves to the ground for cover. The two still on the roadblock were almost instantly caught in the light—a fact confirmed by two very brief bursts of gunfire from the helicopter. Three minutes later the gunship had found and killed the other two, satisfied itself that it had effectively destroyed the roadblock, and left.

Five hundred yards from the nearest of the four bodies, the glimmer of lights on the Volvo faded and died. Marzena lay, undisturbed on the back seat. The dead driver lay uncomfortably across the front seats, Jamie's wallet and papers in his jacket pocket.

WAR DAY + 1

POZNAN
POLAND

It was after midnight. That made it tomorrow. Jamie sat on the wooden bench, his head hanging low, his elbows on his knees.

His head was empty. He'd had the stuffing knocked out of him. He was lost. He was as lost as if he'd been dumped in the middle of nowhere. He'd been plucked out of his ordered life, seen it destroyed, and found himself removed to a reality that he didn't understand.

His sense of direction, his sense of self had gone. It had slipped from his grasp over the last twenty four hours. Too much reality had been removed. He was having trouble, big trouble, accepting that where he was now was reality.

He stared at his boots, unseeing. He was in some kind of a shed. It was not very big, but it was warm Every now and then the door at the end was opened and more people would enter. They were all civilians, mostly in family groups. They arrived in fits and starts, being quickly searched by the soldiers at the door and then being ushered towards the centre of the shed.

There were several soldiers outside and four just inside the door. They were all armed.

Jamie had been there a while. He wasn't sure how long. It didn't seem critical right then. The bastards had destroyed his family and locked him in a shed. The passage of time could take second place to the boiling rage.

He stared at his boots.

There was a wooden bench down three sides of the shed. The centre of the shed was bare of furniture. A few people were standing, a few had chosen to sit in groups on the wooden floor and the rest were sitting on the wooden benches, their backs against the walls. There was a great deal of sobbing. Jamie had long ago decided that Polish women were more easily moved to audible signs of distress than their British counterparts. For their part, the Poles were inclined to regard the British as cold and unemotional. This had been one of their jokes, he found himself thinking. Marzena had often called him her cold Englishman—with a broad smile on her face. This was often as she used him to warm her in bed. She'd had the most unbearably cold feet at times.

He almost smiled, but at the same time he could feel the tears in his eyes.

He continued to stare at his boots.

Oh shit!

+

Some time later the door opened yet again and a single man entered. Even while being searched his face seemed to be smiling. Not his mouth. His mouth was expressionless. It was the rest of his face. It carried a sense of humour, a sense of humour bubbling away just under the surface.

He glanced around the room while being searched, nodding gently to the soldiers when they indicated that they'd finished and that he should move along into the shed. He walked slowly, calmly. He looked relaxed. He looked as though he was used to this sort of thing. He chose to sit next to Jamie.

Before sitting he glanced briefly at the bench itself as though to ensure that it was clean. Apparently satisfied, he sat, leaning carefully against the wall.

"Cigarette?" he asked Jamie, holding out an opened pack.

"No, thanks," Jamie didn't look up. Nor did he take in the fact that they had both spoken in English. There was a pause as the new arrival lit a cigarette and proceeded to smoke it with obvious pleasure.

"Been here long?"

Jamie shook his head, "Nope."

Over the next few seconds it dawned on him that they had both been speaking English and, more importantly, that the other man's English was the English of a native English speaker. English was his first language.

He looked up.

"No, no I haven't been here long," he repeated.

"Paul Flowers," the other man said, sticking out his hand.

"Jamie, Jamie Ingram," Jamie said, gripping the proffered hand.

"Hello, Jamie," Paul said, the smile spreading to his mouth, "I guess you've been through the wars, eh?"

Jamie looked at the man's face. 'Through the wars?' Well, he felt that that probably summed it up fairly well.

He nodded. He didn't dare speak. Thinking about the last twenty four hours was painful enough. Speaking about it would be unbearable. He couldn't help wondering, though, how Paul had arrived at that conclusion so quickly. If he'd looked in a mirror, though, he wouldn't have wondered. You couldn't live through a day like the last one without picking up a few rough edges.

"What're you doing here?"

Jamie wondered what exactly Paul meant. He was very tired. He'd been up for the best part of twenty four hours. His mind didn't seem to be operating at quite 100%.

"Leaving," he said, "Leaving Poland."

Paul nodded.

"Me, too," he took a long and what appeared to be a rather satisfying pull on the cigarette, "Foul habit," he continued, eyeing the cigarette with distaste. He went on,

"They'll let us out tomorrow. We'll be in Germany by lunch time."

Jamie looked at him with renewed interest, "You reckon?"

"Yep, they'll throw us all out tomorrow morning. First thing. They don't want us; they just want to clear the streets. Enforce the curfew."

"Why?"

"Who knows? They're soldiers," he laughed. Jamie looked at him in astonishment. One or two people turned and stared. Paul ignored them, "It's their job."

"Excuse me," they both turned. The voice had been an almost silent whisper. The speaker was a young man with very blond hair. He was with a group sitting on the floor about a metre away.

"You are English?" he continued in that same whisper.

Paul and Jamie nodded.

"I think it is best if you don't speak in English," he said in slow and imperfect English, his eyes moving fast between their faces and the soldiers at the door.

Jamie opened his mouth to speak, startled.

"Do you speak Polish?" the young man continued.

"A little," Jamie nodded, speaking in his awful Polish.

Paul nodded slightly, "A very little," a grimace passing across his face.

"These Russians," the word 'Russians' came out of the man's mouth as an insult, "These Russians, they do not speak Polish. They will not realise that you are not Polish if you speak your Polish. Of course, we Poles will know that you are not Polish, but this is not important."

"But why is it important that they don't know that we are British?"

"One hears things. One hears many stories. Maybe, they are not true, maybe they are. But I think that it is better for you. They will not notice you if you are Polish."

"Thank you," Paul said rather doubtfully.

"Yes, thank you."

"It's nothing. Remember, we have been here before. This is not new for Poland."

"Stories," Paul asked, "What stories have you heard?" Jamie grinned. Paul's Polish was bad, very bad. The young man smiled gently. Jamie recognised the look. It meant that the foreigner, who was normally Jamie in Jamie's experience, was speaking Polish abysmally but that the Pole had probably understood the meaning...or thought that he had, anyway.

"Bad stories. The Embassy in Warszawa...it was not good," he didn't go on.

There was a moment's silence.

"Slawek," the young man held out his hand. One of those difficult names, Jamie thought. Spelled quite differently from its sound. To the English ear it sounded more like Swar-vek.

"Jamie," he said, grabbing the man's hand.

"Paul," Paul said.

"The Embassy?" Paul prompted after another moment's pause. He pulled out his pack of cigarettes and offered them around. The two other men shook their heads.

"D'you mind?"

The two men shook their heads, again.

"You heard about Warszawa?" Slawek asked. As he talked a stunningly attractive girl from his group turned and took his arm.

Paul and Jamie shook their heads.

"I was there this morning," Jamie said.

"Now it is gone," Slawek shook his head, "Now the city is gone."

"What?" Paul began. He looked stunned. Jamie was sitting with his mouth wide open.

"They say that every building has been damaged. I have seen the pictures."

How he had seen the pictures, Jamie wondered.

"Satellite TV," he continued, as though reading Jamie's mind.

"What did he say?" Paul murmured in English. Slawek frowned.

"Satellite TV," Slawek repeated in English, his voice dropping back to an almost silent whisper.

"Thank you."

"They even have cameras in the missiles," his voice contained a mixture of astonishment and horror. "The Russians destroyed the Palace of Culture," Jamie knew the building. It was one of Warsaw's landmarks. "Stupid bastards. They gave us the building at the end of the last war. An awful place. Stupid bastards."

"Slawek," the girl soothed.

"Ah," he turned to her, "This is Paul and this is Jamie."

She held out her hand.

"Renata," she smiled.

"My wife," he smiled.

They shook her hand.

"So, what are you doing here?" Paul asked Slawek and Renata.

"We were in Poznan for a few days," he grimaced, "we just chose the wrong days. We came for the festival."

"The festival?"

"The festival, yes," his eyes twinkled with amusement. It was easy to forget about things like festivals in a corner like this, "of modern art," he continued. He grimaced, and then grinned at his wife, "It's not really my thing, but Renata's something of an expert on the 'American Influence'."

She was grinning, too, but shaking her head.

"It's just a hobby."

130

"Hobby!" he raised his eyebrows and laughed. A silent laugh.

"We were due to return earlier today, but there weren't a lot of trains heading East today."

"No, I suppose not," Jamie wasn't surprised. You'd have to have had a few buttons missing to drive a train East into the teeth of an invading Russian army. He wondered vaguely and inconsequentially if that meant that all the trains were now at the Western extreme of the country.

"We got picked up as they were sweeping the northern quarter. It's annoying, but we'll be out tomorrow. I expect the trains'll be running in a day or two."

He glanced at his watch.

"We'll be out in an hour or so."

Chapter Six

WARDAY + 1
POZNAN
POLAND

"This'll do." They were shattered. Absolutely wiped out. They'd been let out of the shed in small groups at short intervals just after dawn. Fresh snow had fallen during the night and it was very cold. Neither of them had slept at all.

Paul and Jamie had decided that their first priority was the railway station. There weren't any buses and there were no taxis so they were walking. Neither of them had a map of Poznan so they were relying on the advice of strangers. The only trouble was that there weren't many around.

They were quite obviously some distance from the centre of Poznan and it was going to take a while. They couldn't even hitch-hike. The only vehicles that they had seen on the road were NRC military vehicles—and they didn't fancy another ride in one of those.

"This'll do," Paul repeated. It was a grubby looking, single floored Novotel Hotel.

"We need to get warm," Paul continued, looking at his watch, "we've been out for over two hours. And I'm starving."

Jamie nodded. He hadn't eaten for a while and now that Paul mentioned it he was aware of hunger pangs deep in his stomach.

"Now that you mention it," he grinned, "I could really use a hot meal." A sudden and rather desperate thought.

"Have you got any money?"

"Yep," Paul was confident.

"What is it?"

"What is...? Ah. I've got zloties, deutschmarks and some pounds. Aren't the zloties any good, again?"

"I don't know. Not for fuel, though. I'm afraid that I haven't got any money at all, and no cards either. Have you got any cards?"

"Yeah. I've got cards."

"We may need the cash later..."

Paul nodded, "We can settle up later, meanwhile it's my shout."

It's strange, Jamie thought, how even in times like this access to money is so important. Or perhaps it was particularly so in times like this. He remembered that he had read that officers in the British army in the First World War had had the option to buy their own hand guns, a better weapon than the standard hand gun, affording a greater chance of survival. Even then survival was based on how much money you had.

The Novotel was set back from the road, an unattractive black and white building. It had what Jamie thought of as an American look about it, but he'd never been to America and was only barely conscious of the feeling.

Inside, the reception area was far more spacious and attractive than he had expected. The floor was of a marble-like substance covered by the occasional rug. To their left as they entered were the bar and restaurant areas partitioned off by a light trellis. To their right was reception itself.

Several ideas presented themselves to Jamie as he paused. He could smell hot food and coffee. Suddenly, he was ravenously hungry. He had noticed the small bank of pay phones, and suddenly he was thinking of his parents. A sharp pang of unbearable pain shafted through him at the thought of the rest of his family. And he had noticed the 'Gentlemen' sign, which reminded him that it was a very long time since he'd seen a lavatory.

"Two singles, please," he heard Paul saying.

Rooms? They didn't want rooms.

"What are you doing?" he asked, perplexed.

"Rooms," Paul sounded equally perplexed, "to shower."

"Yes," he said, "Yes, of course."

"With showers," Paul continued to the girl behind the desk.

"Of course," she responded. Things didn't seem to have changed that much right here.

+

Two hours later they were dropped off by the Novotel taxi close to the railway station in the centre of Poznan. They were clean, shaven and fed.

Poznan Central Railway Station is at the end of a two hundred metre dual carriageway cul-de-sac with a small roundabout area in front of the station. It is normally crowded with cars, buses and pedestrians. The several railway lines, which lie parallel to the road, are normally full of trains.

From where they had been dropped off by the taxi they could see that there were no cars, no buses and no pedestrians. There were also no trains.

"Shit!"

Jamie nodded in agreement. The place was dead. There were obviously going to be no trains, today. Added to which, there were a dozen soldiers and a tank at the entrance to the station. Paul was shaking his head in disgust.

"What the hell are we going to do?"

"There's got to be a way."

"There isn't."

"There's got to be."

"I tell you," Paul said in a sinking voice, "there isn't."

Jamie thought that Paul might be right. If the train was out, there weren't any buses, there certainly weren't any planes; Paul had actually asked at the Novotel. Jamie had simply assumed that there would be none, and they hadn't got a car. Taxi? Could they have persuaded the Novotel taxi driver to take them to Swiecko or Slubice? He doubted it. Anyway it was too late, now. He'd gone.

And outside help was impossible. The pay phones in the Novotel had been useless. They were all dead. The hotel staff had assured them that all the 'phones in the country were down, but how would they know? How could they know? Satellite TV, maybe?

So, where to, now?

"Shit!" This time it was Jamie.

Paul grinned.

"It's not funny, is it?"

"It's not."

"How about a beer?"

"Maybe a coffee."

"Let's find somewhere."

The two men turned and walked towards the centre of the town. They were carrying no luggage. They could have been tourists except that they had no cameras.

With a horrendous clatter and roar a tank rattled past, two soldiers sitting on its superstructure. The turret hatch was open and the commander was squinting at the world through a pair of light yellow 'traffic cop' style driving glasses. The other hatches were shut. The tank looked old, well used and filthy. It was painted a very drab sandy, olive. It was mud stained, oily and dented and was blowing out copious quantities of black smoke.

"Hope the fuckers fall under it," Paul muttered.

"What?" his words had been lost in the clatter. Jamie was wondering what kind of a vehicle could dent a tank.

"Nothing," Paul grinned, "Nothing important."

"I don't feel so good about this." Maybe it hadn't been a vehicle. Maybe it had been damaged in action. It certainly looked old enough to have seen a bit of action.

"What?"

"Well, there's no one about. The streets are empty."

"Yeah," thoughtful.

"Maybe everyone else knows something that we don't."

"Like what?"

Jamie thought for a moment. He didn't know.

"Silly question, I guess," Paul continued, "Sorry."

They walked on a bit.

"I think I'd like to get under cover."

"Under cover?"

"Yeah. Find a hotel, keep our heads down, wait a bit, see what's happening. You know."

"I agree. I like the idea. Very much. This is creepy." And indeed it was creepy. The town was almost silent. No traffic and no people.

They looked around. The streets were empty. There was just the occasional pedestrian moving quickly under the cover of the buildings. There was very infrequent traffic, and most of what there was military. The buildings were dark, heavy stone. Probably offices.

"I think that we should head into the centre. We're more likely to find somewhere there."

"I agree. Which way is that?" They grinned at each other in hopelessness.

"Shit, we're useless."

"Agreed."

"A map would be handy."

"Wouldn't it just? But it might not be enough."

"Why not? We'd just head for the centre."

"Yeah, you're right. I was just remembering the first time I was in Poznan." They continued to walk up the road they were on in the same direction as before.

"I was looking for the youth hostel," he laughed, "I found it, too, but that was no thanks to the map. It was in Lenin Street. It took me half the afternoon to realise that they'd changed the name of the street. I'd been convinced that it was my map reading that was at fault."

"When was that?"

"1990. Just after the fall?"

"The fall?"

"The Berlin wall had been down for about six months."

"Ah."

"I didn't get in, though."

"What?"

"It didn't do me any good. Finding the youth hostel, I mean. I didn't get in."

"Why not?"

"I don't know."

"You don't know?"

"No," Jamie laughed, "I never did understand what the problem was. I'd only been in the country a few hours. I'd spent the night in Berlin and had arrived in Poznan in the afternoon. I had a small phrase book but I understood nothing. I thought at first that it was full, but then I thought that perhaps the warden wasn't there. The lady who spoke to me appeared to be a cleaner."

"So, what did you do? Wait?"

"No, no. I drove to Warsaw. I remember parking in the centre of Warsaw, close to the main railway station—you could park in Warsaw in those days, there weren't many cars—sometime after midnight. I ended up sleeping in the car." They had come to the end of the street.

"Does it mean anything to you? They were looking at the street name.

"Lechicka," Jamie hazarded, "No."

"Oh, well. This way?"

"Why not?"

They headed on briskly, keeping close to the buildings. This made them feel less conspicuous and somehow seemed safer. Being virtually the only people on the street did not feel good. Having nowhere to go, no home and no base, made them feel very unsafe and insecure.

With a roar and a clatter another tank sped past together with two other large armoured vehicles, spraying brown slush onto the pavement. The tank's tracks cut marks in the tarmac. It looked just as old and war-worn as the last one.

Jamie found that both he and Paul had shrunk as close to the buildings as possible, only partly because of the spray of discoloured snow. The pavement was quite wide.

"They're nasty, those things."

"Very much so," Jamie agreed.

"Is it the same one?"

"Don't think so," it had had different dents, he was almost sure of that. On the other hand the commander was wearing the same style of driving glasses. It might have been the same one, but on balance he thought not.

They reminded him very much of an express train passing a platform at high speed. The tanks were not fast, not that fast, anyway, but they gave the impression of speed. And they were so large, so heavy, so nasty.

It was really very strange to walk the streets of a major city in broad daylight and to walk them alone. The pavements had not been swept of snow and it was apparent that not many people had walked this way since the overnight fall of snow.

"What will happen next?"

"To what?"

"To Poland. What happens next?"

"Everything goes back to normal, I suppose."

"Normal?"

"Well, a sort of normal. Things will...people will go back to work, things will start to pick up where they stopped."

"Only things will be different."

"Only things will be different, yes."

"Do you reckon that Slawek was right, you know, about the Brits?"

"No," Paul shook his head, "It's not possible."

"Isn't it?"

"Well, it's not likely, is it?"

"Not likely, no...but I don't share your confidence. Do you have a Dowod Osobisty?"

"Yes, of course," Paul replied with a big grin in his appalling Polish. Up to that point they had been speaking in English.

"Good."

"Do you?"

"Yep. In fact, it's all I've got"

They had reached a major junction.

"Which way?"

"Blowed if I know."

"How about this one," Paul was indicating to the left.

"Can't do any harm."

"Can't it," Paul grinned, again, "We'll see."

It was a short and narrow road that appeared to lead to a slightly larger road that looked promising. The short, narrow road had a few small shops in it. They were all closed, which was no surprise, but the presence of the shops did suggest that perhaps they were moving towards the centre.

They hoped!

It could also be a small shopping area well away from anything much except offices and flats, although that didn't seem very likely. Judging by the age of the buildings, it looked like they might be approaching the old town.

They reached the end of the short, narrow road and walked into the slightly more major one. It looked as though they might be getting close. There were more shops, and they were bigger, too. It was distinctly looking as though they might be very close to the old town

"Ace," Jamie murmured.

"Ace, indeed."

There was the sudden and unmistakable crack of an automatic weapon. A moment's silence. They looked at each other. And a sudden roar as something very powerful responded. A few moments later it roared again, drowning out every other sound. Without realising what they were doing, they found themselves huddled together in the nearest shop doorway.

"What the hell is that?"

"Oh shit! Shit! This is not good."

They stood, half crouching, wondering whether they should be lying down or running. The gaps in the roaring sounds were filled with bursts of automatic gun fire that were obviously not very far away.

"Dear God!"

The shooting was suddenly very much closer.

"Oh, shit!"

Human noises, approaching down the road, were now audible. Shouting. Rattling. People running. And of course, automatic gun fire. The shop doorway was only about a metre deep. There was nowhere to go. Nowhere to hide.

"Oh shit, shit!"

"Do something! Don't just shout."

"Do something? Do something? Do what? Shit!" The sound of people running was just metres away. So was the gunfire.

"What the...what's happening?"

"I don't know, but it's getting closer."

"You think I hadn't noticed!"

"Time for desperate measures?"

"Shit, yes. Time for anything. What did you have in mind?" Paul reached back and smashed a small window beside the door.

"We'll get in here". But, it was too late!

"Down," Jamie screamed. And suddenly they were scrabbling around on the stone floor of the doorway, trying to fit into a very small area. Trying to disappear. Trying not to be there.

"Who are they?" Paul muttered.

"Don't know. Shut up!"

Jamie lay, hardly breathing, and watched, squeezing himself into the stone, disappearing into the stone, becoming one with the stone, his body slowly flattening until it was invisible. He wished. A series of men and women were appearing and disappearing from his field of view. They were running, pausing, hiding, shooting, running. They were running from doorway to doorway and shooting back the way they had come. They were wearing the brown uniforms that Jamie associated with the Polish army. The chatter of automatic gun fire was all around them. A figure leapt into the doorway opposite.

"Out, out," she was shouting in what Jamie took to be native Polish. They must be the Polish Army. Jamie and Paul looked at her in astonishment. Out?

She was waving an automatic weapon wildly, indicating that they should leave their doorway and run in the direction that the soldiers were running, leaping from doorway to doorway.

"Out, out!" she screamed.

"Who me?" Jamie thought to himself.

"Does she mean us?" Paul asked, his voice surprisingly close to Jamie's ear.

"Fucked if I know!" What else could she mean?

Nothing. She meant them.

"She means us," he continued.

"I don't think she means us." There was a sudden roar again and the front of a building about forty metres away folded gently in the middle and collapsed into the road.

"Dear Jesus." Three more figures ran past.

Followed by a fourth, a man, who appeared to trip on something, his arms flung forward to break his fall, a pained expression on his face. Before he hit the ground his arms had swung back, almost slowly, so that he landed on his face and chest without the protection of his extended arms. His left hand released his weapon as he slid, loose limbed, towards their doorway, appearing to bounce on the frozen, packed snow of the road.

The woman soldier in the opposite doorway screamed something they didn't understand. It seemed to be directed at the sliding soldier. There was another almighty roar. And the rumble of tank tracks.

"Oh shit, shit!"

The sliding soldier hit the kerb and began to roll, his weapon sliding ahead of him. He stopped rolling about a metre away from them, on his back on the small mound of frozen snow that lined the edge of the pavement. He didn't move. They stared at him in horror. Already a red stain was appearing on the ground at the bottom his back.

"Oh, Jesus!"

A bubbling noise seemed to come from the soldier's mouth.

"Jesus. Oh, Jesus." The woman was still shouting something. It might have been a name. And suddenly a noise. A noise as loud as hell itself. The tank was upon them, and it was not moving fast. It was taking its time. It was sweeping up the mess. It was making sure that there was nothing left behind it to cause it trouble. There was an earth shattering roar as it fired its big gun. At the same time all the glass in their shop doorway disappeared, and the woodwork began to disintegrate as thousands of rounds from the tank's smaller guns swept over them.

Jamie could feel that he was whimpering. He could hear nothing except the sound of gunfire.

In all his life he had never had so much time to be so terrified. With his naked fingers he tried to dig himself deeper into the stone of the shop doorway, oblivious to the pain of his stripped finger nails. He could feel...he could feel the bullets passing over his body. Dear God, he could feel them! The air from their movement...

There was a crumping sound in the distance as the tank's shell exploded.

Jamie half opened one eye. The tank was literally only about two metres away, which was probably why they weren't dead, yet. It looked old and well used, very much a working tank and not the sort of thing that one might see at a military display. It was not actually moving.

It was stopped!

The rubber around the gun ports was old and split and covered in flaking paint. He watched fascinated as the barrels spat and flashed their death. They seemed to be pointing slightly ahead of the tank, intent on clearing the way further ahead. The turret moved slightly and roared.

"Shit!"

He could hear nothing. The sound of shooting seemed to have faded, as though he had stuffed cotton-wool into his ears. He would have liked to have shaken his head, but any movement would have been suicide.

"Oh, Jesus!"

With a sideways lurch, a roar of worn engine, and an enormous belch of smoky exhaust the monster began to move forwards slowly. Its enormous tracks, so close, slicing through the packed snow and grinding into the tarmac, spitting out fine gravel. Oh, so slowly. Black smoke billowed from somewhere in its gut.

Its guns were still spitting fire and death. The glass and wood of the next building were disintegrating. Brickwork was crumbling into red dust and ugly, sharp chips were flying in every direction. Holes were appearing in every surface.

"Dear God!"

The tank moved slowly, so terribly slowly, but at least it was moving away. They could hear the rattle of moving mechanical parts. It sounded like a dozen large juggernauts each with a very serious problem under the bonnet.

They lay still. Not moving. Hardly daring to breathe. The noise of gunfire was still immense, but somehow they had seemed to have grown used to it. They could hear nothing else, apart from the tank's engine which must surely be a mechanic's nightmare, but the noise of the gunfire no longer seemed so acute.

There was another sudden roar as the big gun fired another shell. Yes, thought Jamie, I'm either growing used to gunfire or I'm going deaf.

Another belch of exhaust, black smoke spreading out from under the tank, and it moved away slightly faster.

"Dear God," Jamie felt that he could allow himself to breathe. The tank was a good twenty metres away. He took a couple of deep breaths. And a couple more. That ten seconds had been a lifetime. A whole lifetime in ten seconds.

"Oh, dear God," he said in relief, "Thank you God." He was still lying flat on the ground in the shop doorway. Behind him Paul was talking, too.

Neither realised that the other was talking. After another thirty seconds they pulled themselves warily into a seated position.

"Well, shit," Paul began.

Jamie said "I can't hear you."

"What?" And they both laughed.

Jamie looked back down the street. The tank was about a hundred metres away. Practically in another world, he thought. What about the soldier. In his terror he'd forgotten the man on the pavement. He lay there, unmoving. The spread of blood from the small of his back did not seem to have grown.

In the doorway opposite he could see a messy bundle that may well have been the other soldier. He hadn't realised that the Polish Army used women. They certainly hadn't when he had last noticed, but that had been ages ago—when Marzena had been a student and only the boys had had to do military service. Or, maybe, these people weren't army.

They both lay still, surrounded by debris, wondering what would happen next. All the while the tank was moving away, picking up speed slowly. Jamie found that he was concentrating on breathing.

At last, the tank turned a corner about two hundred metres away. For one awful moment as he lay rigid in the doorway, he realised that that meant that the tank's guns would be spraying back down the street while it was negotiating the ninety degree turn to its right, but he was wrong.

And suddenly, the tank was out of sight.

For another few seconds they waited.

Nothing.

"I'm going..." he began, but remembering that Paul couldn't hear him, indicated that he was going to look at the soldiers. Paul looked up and down the street and agreed. They began to get up, moving slowly—not least because of the broken glass everywhere—and looking carefully up and down the road. The war seemed to have moved on. Extraordinary.

He stood up, standing still on a carpet of glass shards and shredded wood. With a final look to the right and the left, he stepped gingerly out into the road. The soldier on the pavement looked dead, but he crouched down anyway and felt for a pulse. You never know. The man—he was little more than a boy, actually—lay facing skyward with his eyes and mouth open. Apart from the blood stain in the snow there was no apparent damage.

"Dear God," Jamie couldn't find a pulse, but he persisted for a few moments, "What a waste." The soldier was so young.

No pulse. Definitely no pulse. He looked up at Paul, shaking his head. As he stood, he picked up the soldier's weapon, looking at it curiously. He turned, and together they began to cross the road towards the soldier in the doorway.

Suddenly, and quite painlessly, Jamie's right leg buckled and failed to support him. With a grunt of surprise he tumbled to the ground, dropping the weapon and reaching down instinctively to his leg.

It seemed oddly bent...

...and bloody...

...and suddenly the pain hit him like a steam train, unbearable pain shooting up his right leg. He was lying on his side, gripping his bloody broken leg, his mouth open, screaming.

The pain was beyond comprehension. It was beyond anything that he had ever had to experience. It shot up and down his leg as though a blunt corkscrew was being used to enlarge an open wound. His mind was closed to everything except the impossibility of coping with the mind shattering pain.

He clamped his teeth shut to stop himself from screaming. Paul was lying down beside him, saying something.

He couldn't hear. He shook his head at Paul to indicate that he couldn't hear. He didn't dare unclamp his teeth. He'd start to scream again.

The pain in his leg was impossible. He lay there, halfway across the road, clutching his leg and breathing deeply.

He didn't understand! He tried to look at his leg where it hurt, but he didn't want to release his grip. There seemed to be an awful lot of blood.

Jesus! It hurt. It looked like it had exploded! Even his trousers were damaged. Torn.

He realised that Paul was still lying beside him and it began to dawn on him why. They were halfway across the road and someone was shooting.

He'd been shot! Oh shit.

"I've been shot?" he mouthed at Paul.

Paul nodded. There was a look in Paul's eyes. A different look. It took him a moment, but Jamie suddenly realised that Paul was terrified.

And in his next breath he realised why Paul was suddenly so afraid. Paul was lying between him and the shooting. He was shielding him from more shots.

Shit!

"Go," he yelled at Paul as loud as he could, "Go!" He could suddenly feel the blood pumping in his leg. It wasn't a good feeling.

"Go. Go!" His hands were sticky with the stuff.

"No move!" a voice commanded in broken Polish. Jamie looked up and realised that they were surrounded by a half dozen or so soldiers. They were wearing the uniform that he had first seen last night.

"Oh, shit."

They both lay still—Jamie on his side, gripping his screaming leg, Paul curled up beside him—as a soldier went through their pockets. They found Jamie's Polish ID and after a while Paul's.

"Polish?" The soldier demanded.

"Of course," Jamie spat through his teeth. Paul merely nodded.

"You are arrested. Subversive activities attempting to overthrow the Peoples' Republic having prohibited weapon," one of the soldiers said in one mouthful, "Now you will come with us." I'm not sure about that, Jamie found himself thinking. He didn't think that he'd be going anywhere for a while, not without help, anyway. Paul stood slowly and very carefully, and reached down to offer Jamie a hand.

Chapter Seven

WAR DAY + 89

GREAT BRITAIN
Three months later...

The policeman pressed the bell at number one hundred and fifty four. A few seconds later an attractive, grandmotherly figure opened the door cautiously, relaxing when she saw who it was.

"Hello, Charles," she greeted the village policeman.

"Hello, Mrs Ingram," the sombre tone of his voice, together with his solid face alerted her to bad news, "may I come in a minute?"

"Why, yes of course," she was nervous. They'd been expecting bad news ever since the grandchildren had got out. Tom and Trix were in Wales, with Lucy and Mark and their children Tom and Jack. It must be an absolute nightmare, Helen Ingram was thinking. Four children in place of two, added to which was the ridiculous confusion of two little boys of almost exactly the same age with the same name. That would teach Lucy—it was she and Mark who had named their baby Tom some months after Jamie and Marzena had chosen to name their son Tom.

"Would you like a cup of coffee?"

"Why, yes, thank you. I would." Police Constable Bennet answered in his slow and ponderous way. Often criticised in this fast moving world, PC Bennet generally achieved the results required by his calling without alienating the people with whom he had to work - the citizens of Much Hadham. In short, although perhaps a mite old-fashioned in outlook he was a good and well-respected copper.

She smiled, despite herself, and led him through into the kitchen. The house itself was over five hundred years old, but the fitted kitchen was light pine—bright and efficient.

"Is Mr Ingram in?" he asked. He'd removed his helmet, not only through deference to being inside a private dwelling, as he would have put it, but also because of the low ceilings.

"Yes," she paused, realising what he meant, his question confirming that he had come to deliver bad news. She called through to her husband, who ambled in. John Ingram was a tall, dark man who carried his years well. He sat at the kitchen table, greeting PC Bennet with a friendly grunt and a smile.

"It's Jamie and Marzena, I'm afraid," Bennet said. He could see from their faces that they were expecting bad news. They knew. Their son and daughter-in-law had been missing for over three months. There had been no reports at all in that time, and although no news meant that there was always room for hope, three months of silence... his thoughts trickled to a halt as he looked at the dread on their expectant faces.

"...bad news I'm afraid. I'm very sorry to have to tell you," goodness, how he hated this part of the job, "that young Jamie Ingram's car has been found abandoned close to the Polish city of Poznan in Western Poland with two," he paused for a moment, choosing his words carefully, "deceased persons in it."

He paused again. John and Helen Ingram, two people that he had known and respected for over twenty years, were staring at each other in horror, biting back the tears.

"The authorities have confirmed that the deceased persons are Jamie and Marzena Ingram, however..." he was going to continue, but Helen's tears were flowing. John reached for her and pulled her close.

He waited a moment. "However," he started again, but John's eyes silenced him.

Again, he paused. A moment later and Helen was apologising, apologies which he waved aside.

"When," John Ingram began. Mercifully, PC Bennet took advantage of the pause while John attempted to formulate his question.

"About ten weeks ago," his words hung in the air.

Ten weeks, Helen was thinking. Ten weeks of hope for us, ten weeks of prayer, ten weeks of dreaming the impossible. Her face was composed. For ten weeks, she thought, for ten weeks we had hope, a hope that was... her face collapsed, the tears streaming down her cheeks as a loud sob escaped her. She half stood, wanting to scream, to shout that this was wrong. She felt John's arms around her, holding her, supporting her. She sank into his arms, allowing him to contain her.

Visions of her son as a child floated through her mind as her tears soaked John's neatly ironed shirt, visions that grew confused...dead. Ten weeks...oh God...dear God.

+

What PC Bennet had tried to say, what he had tried to say but had not succeeded in saying was something that he had not, in fact, been authorised by his superior to say. What he had not, at first, succeeded in saying, and then later not had the heart to say—because of the images that it would invoke—was that positive identification, positive identification of a person who had been dead for over two months was something that required a little expertise. Comparison, for example, with a passport photograph would not be enough. Such positive identification would require an expertise that was almost certainly not available in Poland under present circumstances. Poland was a country with a disaster on its hands and an invading army to cope with. They would almost certainly have no time, even if they currently had the ability, to make a positive identification of two bodies out of so many—especially when it was so immediately obvious who those two bodies were.

It would have been wrong, mused PC Bennet as he walked away from the Ingram's pretty cottage, to plant hope where it would quite clearly be misplaced. The bodies had been found in their car with their passports. There could be no real doubt that it was young Jamie and his wife.

Chapter Eight

WAR DAY + 393

A Further Ten Months Later
NEW RUSSIAN CONFEDERATION WORK CAMP
POZNAN
POLAND

He looked about forty five years old. His hair was too long and he hadn't shaved for a while. His breath was bad and his mouth looked grubby and unhealthy. His skin was pale and unattractive. On his left cheek there was a nasty sore, looking damp and raw. He wore old clothes, several layers of old clothes, and did not smell good. He was tall, although stooping slightly, and very thin. Not the leanness of fitness, of exercise, but the crippling thinness of undernourishment, and overwork in an unhealthy environment.

This was Jamie. He was no longer Jamie, though. He would have hardly recognised that name as his own, now. He'd been calling himself Janus for longer than he could remember. Literally, for longer than he could remember. A good, solid Polish name to hide behind. A name to survive behind. Janus. He was Janus. Jamie was dead, Jamie was the past. Jamie was gone. Long gone. Another life, another world. That was then...

And this was... what? Hell?

Yes, this was hell.

Hell, a living hell.

He'd aged fifteen years in less than fifteen months. His eyes showed a wary mixture of fear and cunning. On his left lapel he wore a small badge. It bore the numbers 27-04267. Around his neck, deep below his clothing, he wore a chain. On that chain, on his chest close to his neck, was a disk—a dog-tag some called it— bearing the same numbers. 27-04-267. The penalty for removing either the disc or the badge was death.

He walked slowly home. The work camp, camp two seven, was his home. He lived there. It was warm, most of the time. The food was regular, although of disgusting quality and meagre proportions. He was hungry. He was always hungry. He'd been hungry all his life.

He wasn't alone. There were twenty of them walking slowly back to camp. They were silent. Nothing to say. No point in wasting energy. Energy was life. Life was all that they had. They walked in silence.

It was a five kilometre walk back to the camp, three miles if you like. It didn't matter, now. There were buses. The penalty for using a bus was death. It took an hour and a half to walk now. A year ago it would have taken well under an hour.

For thirteen hours a day they worked the machines. Sitting or standing in the oily heat, operating old and grossly inefficient machines. Today, he had been producing plastic bicycle saddles. Yesterday, it had been sunglasses. Cheap plastic sunglasses. Row upon row of ancient injection moulding machines turning out low quality products by the lorry load.

When they reached the camp the gates were open. The gates were open eighteen hours a day. You could come and go as you pleased as long as you had clearance. He had clearance to pass through the gates twice a day. Once to leave for the factory, once to return. His times were carefully and accurately monitored. No one stopped you at the open gates. No one checked your papers. They had no papers.

As they passed through the gates the sensors recorded their arrival. The discs around their necks, although slim, held positive identification tags. They were a secure form of what they had used to call 'smart-cards'. The central computer, known to everyone as 'Central', knew where each worker was at any moment. Central traced their movements day and night. There was no need for a closed gate, no need for the bright lights and barbed wire, because Central always knew where you were.

The small group of almost identical shabby, worn men passed through the open gate. Despite the discs around their necks, there was in fact barbed wire around the compound and there were bright lights during the hours of darkness.

Jamie shuffled past the guardhouse. It was dark, now. It seemed to him to be dark most of the time. As he passed the guardhouse his number showed briefly on a monitor inside, in front of a dozing soldier. Central had recorded his time of return.

He made his way wearily towards his shed, shed sixteen. It was forbidden to enter another person's shed. The penalty for entering the wrong shed was death.

In his pocket was another man's tag. Central had recorded twenty one workers in, although only twenty persons had entered the camp.

Experience had shown that physical head-counts were rare. Like so many other people the camp authorities placed rather more faith in modern technology than might have been considered wise by those who had designed it. While Central was happy that all was well the twenty first man was heading west. If he was lucky he had until tomorrow to make it.

Heading west, the thought, the silent thought, filled Jamie's mind as he lay on his bunk fingering the rough sore on his cheek. He was thirty one years old, he looked forty five and worn out. He was worn out. The sore on his cheek felt enormous and horrible, but he hadn't seen a mirror for months so he wasn't sure. He prayed as he lay in his rough wooden bunk, exactly one metre from the bunk to each side of him. He prayed that the twenty-first man would get through.

The penalty for praying was death. 'Dear God,' he prayed, 'let him get through. Let him live.' He had known the twenty first man for over a year. That was a long time. A very long time. It was almost forever. He had lost a lot of friends in that time. Made a few, lost a lot.

The twenty first man was Paul. He had less than ten hours to get away. Whatever happened, Jamie would never see him again—unless they met outside Poland. He was headed for the nearest international border, Swiecko, or possibly Slubice.

Paul was British, only there weren't any Brits in Poland. All the British had left. There were no British citizens in Poland. This was official, so it must be true. Jamie almost believed it himself at times. He was so weak from hunger that he could almost believe anything. He lay in his bunk, wearing filthy thermal underwear under the rough blankets, and prayed.

'Please God, let Paul get through. Please God let Paul get through and tell my family that I am alive.' It was official; there were no British citizens in Poland. If that were true then he was dead. Sometimes he almost believed it himself. What did his parents believe? Did they believe that he was dead? Did everyone believe that he was dead?

In his hand he held Paul's tag. It had taken an immense effort to break the chain. Although by no means heavy, it had been exceedingly difficult to cut. It appeared to be made of a light metal, but Jamie had wondered if perhaps it might have been made from a new plastic. He understood that it was possible to make plastics that were stronger than metals—apparently this was common in the space industry.

The space industry! Nothing could be further from the space industry than this.

He believed that there were just four British workers in camp 27, although nothing was certain. Each of the Brits bore the prefix 04 on their badges prior to their own individual number. Correction, there had been four. Now, there were three. Each of them spoke some

Polish and they never spoke any English. They weren't quite sure what they were doing there, whether the NRC knew that they were British or had made some other assumption or that it simply didn't care. The fact that the British Embassy in Warsaw had been reduced to rubble and that the British were no longer represented East of Germany suggested a certain lack of cordiality in relations between Britain and...and who?

Poland had ceased to exist in any real way. It no longer had its own government, not even the puppet administration of the distant past. The country had been over-run by the NRC. It had become little more than an annexed state. Poland had been swallowed by the NRC and was lost to the world - and not for the first time, as Jamie had so often heard from the genuine Poles with whom he was sharing the shed.

Jamie fell asleep, used as he was to the rough blankets and well used underclothes.

+

"Janus," the thick voice penetrated his sleep. He struggled to surface, scrambling through confused dreams and the layers of grubby cotton-wool in his mind, until finally he opened his eyes. He peered at the face.

"Janus," it was Marek. Time to rise. He pulled himself into a seated position on the edge of his bunk. A pot of coffee was brewing on the stove. He could smell the beautiful smell. Nothing smelt better than brewing coffee.

He almost smiled to himself.

Almost. He looked around him. Fear.

On every face. Fear. He wondered at his own face. No mirrors meant not knowing. He rubbed his chin. Time for a shave. He didn't want to die like this.

He paused. The fear...today one of them would die. That was the price. Somebody would die today.

It was not so much the fear as sorrow that ate slowly up from his stomach. He didn't want to die. Neither, though, did he want to continue to live like this. He wanted...but that was useless.

There was something particularly awful, though, in the thought that if he died today no one at home would know. He dropped from his bunk and made for the huddle around the coffee pot on the stove.

"Mornin'," he grunted in Polish. He didn't know with any great certainty who was actually Polish and who wasn't. The less that you knew the safer you were. They all used Polish, no one wanting to admit to anything else. Jamie's Polish was so appalling that he found it quite impossible to know whether another man's Polish was his own language or not.

"Mornin'," they all grunted back.

In his hand he was still grasping Paul's tag. Central seemed happy. If it hadn't been they'd have known soon enough. Some reckoned that it was important to keep the tag warm, but no one actually knew.

"We are in Shit Street," a voice whispered. Jamie peered at the crinkled old face, and got a grin for his trouble. A grin full of stained and damaged teeth, a grin with more than its fair share of irregular gaps.

"Too right, Stary," he agreed. The problem was straightforward. While Central remained happy there were rarely any headcounts in the camp. Even en-route they should be all right. Central monitored them all the way to work and back, but once at the factory it would immediately be obvious that their number was one down. If the guards assumed that the runner had made his break last night and that he had been covered by one or more other workers in the meantime, the punishment would be death. Or deaths. At least one death.

If Paul was discovered, he too would die. It would not be difficult, if Paul was caught, for the guards to estimate for how long he had been covered by the other workers. The more protection that they gauged had been given to Paul, the more would die in retribution.

The only hope, the only way to escape a death would be if Paul was never caught and the guards simply failed to realise that anyone had covered for him at all.

A slim chance. A very slim chance. In fact, it was, really, beyond possibility. And as for who would die, that had become established practice. The runner was always shot—without fail. And the guards would carry out a brief investigation to discover who had helped the runner. Almost invariably, the 'investigation' showed up nothing so they would choose a victim—or victims— apparently at random.

And execute them. Murder them.

Jamie shivered. He grasped the mug of coffee ever harder, staring deep into the black coffee. Looking for what? For a moment he remembered how in the distant past he had attempted to cut down on coffee for health reasons. Health!

There was a rattling at the hatch at the end of the shed as the bread arrived. Still hot from the ovens, it was beautiful to eat, but it was none-the-less less than exciting when it was all that they ever received in the mornings.

Jamie clasped his mug in one grubby hand and a wedge of bread in the other. His hands were old and worn, where a year ago they had been soft and pampered. For a moment his mind leapt to Marzena's legs and how once, despite his hands having been so pampered, he had managed to ladder her tights merely by running his hand along her leg.

He winced, discarding the memory instantly. That way led to disaster. He examined his left hand: the nails were cracked, broken and dirty the skin rough and ingrained with a fine grey filth. He grimaced.

"What's up?" Little Jacek was peering up at him.

"Nothing," he replaced the grimace with a grin.

"Nothing," Little Jacek was grinning at him, "nothing? How can 'nothing' be up?" his demeanour seemed to indicate their surroundings. The large wooden shed, the disgusting bunks, the fifty dirty men...forty nine, actually, Jamie corrected himself.

"Nothing special," he corrected himself, "okay?" He spoke softly. Little Jacek was okay.

+

For the twenty men walking from shed sixteen to the factory, the walk was long and hard. And at the end they knew what awaited them.

Death.

Someone would die.

The twenty men were very quiet.

Maybe more than one would die.

POZNAN
POLAND

The screwdriver slipped silently into the lock. A quick twist, an energetic wrench and the whole barrel turned. He removed the screwdriver, opened the car door and slipped in. For a few moments he sat, silent. It was dark. He was a long way from a working street lamp, but he could see that there was nobody on the street.

However, he reminded himself, any number of people could have seen what he had just done. The car was parked under an enormous block of flats. He was, in fact, exceedingly lucky to have found a car that was not in one of the dedicated parking areas that were constantly guarded by a night-watchman.

Whilst these thoughts were crossing his mind he was systematically dismantling the steering lock. Had the owner of the vehicle seen him, he would have said that he was destroying it.

Moments later the dashboard came alive. Before he started the engine he wanted to check that the car had fuel in its tank. It was useless without it and he couldn't possibly buy any. Not only had he got no money, but even if he had had any he would have been unable to purchase any. Fuel for private use was very carefully controlled.

Added to which, anyone who saw his work camp uniform would immediately know that he was a runner. Giving assistance to a runner was a serious offence—for which the penalty was death. Ignoring a runner and failing to notify the authorities was deemed to be assisting a runner. Even seeing a runner was considered to be very bad news indeed.

The needle climbed, slowly. It had some fuel.

A door slammed. He looked up. About twenty five metres away three men were leaving the block of flats. They were ageless and shapeless in their bulky coats, scarves and hats.

The needle had drifted gently to almost half. Was it still moving? Would it make any difference if the three shapes were heading for the car?

No. He put his foot flat on the throttle, checked the gearstick, and held the two wires together. The old Ford gave a tired groan. Once, twice she turned over and suddenly she was firing...and running.

He eased his foot off the throttle, grinning despite himself. Not one of the three men had missed a beat in their stride. It obviously wasn't their car.

His grin widened.

+

Seven floors up, in flat 286, Bogdan rolled off Anita's beautifully smooth young body. One of the perks, he called it, of the new regime. Not that he spoke aloud of such things. Some things were best left unsaid. He lay, for a moment, looking at the dimly lit ceiling. White painted concrete with the inevitable poorly fitting light unit. He grinned to himself.

"Lovely," he murmured, "that was lovely." One had to be careful what one said. Who knew who was listening. It was certain that someone was listening, one simply didn't know who. His grin lingered.

Anita, he thought, was a lovely girl. He reached for a cigarette. She lay silent, thinking only of her family. Her parents and two brothers who had been taken to the work camps for she knew not what. Her father, who had died an old man at fifty, her mother who had been given soft duties...soft duties, because of her health, and on condition that Anita provide special services. The tears pricked behind her eyes. What other decision could a daughter have made?

"Is there any vodka?" Bogdan asked, lying on his back and enjoying his cigarette. He hadn't offered her one. They were good cigarettes, an expensive luxury.

With a murmured affirmative, Anita climbed off the bed. He turned to watch her shapely, lithe young body. Her large breasts still young and firm, her small, tight buttocks...he grinned despite himself.

She returned with the vodka and two glasses. Vodka was one of the perks of her job. It was freely and inexpensively available in the shops and it made the job altogether easier.

She was indeed a beautiful girl. She was tall and slim with a shapely body. She still looked fit. Her long blonde hair had a healthy sheen to it. She looked good, really good, and she carried herself with the grace and outward confidence of an educated Polish girl. This was a quality that the new regime particularly admired, but mainly in their whores. Bogdan reached out and fondled her bottom as she poured the two glasses of clear liquid. 'I'm going to kill the fuckers,' she thought to herself, grinning inside herself at the suitability of the obscenity, an obscenity that she wouldn't have let cross her lips a few months ago.

She'd worked it out. Whatever happened to her she knew now that she couldn't survive, wouldn't survive. She had seen that from almost the start. Blackmailed into providing special services to local collaborators and a number of the local NRC, she was despised by everyone. Her own kind and the invaders. The other residents of her block took every opportunity— every safe opportunity—to let her know how much they despised her, but what would they have done?

Only her own family would understand, and even her brothers would find it very hard...perhaps impossible.

Oh God. She nearly spilt the vodka.

Anyway, she was going to kill them. All of them. And it would cost her nothing, because she had nothing, she had nothing left to lose.

Freedom, she thought, is just another word for nothing left to lose, a line from an ancient Grateful Dead tape that a visitor had brought to the flat.

She shuddered, Bogdan put out a reassuring hand; 'I hope you die covered in shit, you fucker,' the thought roared through her mind. God, she hated these men more than she could ever express.

She just hoped that she'd take as many of these bastards with her as possible. She grinned to herself.

"Good, eh?" the creep, Bogdan, asked her. She grinned even more.

"Good? Yes, Bogdan, that was very good."

+

An hour later, when Bogdan left the flat, he found to his horror that his car had been stolen. He stood for a moment, speechless. He shouldn't have been in such a rush when he had arrived. He should have put the car in the pound. Stupid, stupid...he stared at the empty space in disbelief. Who on earth would have stolen his car...the penalties were so high?

"Oh shit," he stamped in frustration and disbelief. He had begun to believe in his own power. He had begun to believe that he was powerful, important, a big wheel, but at this disastrous moment he realised that he was simply in trouble.

When a car was stolen there was always trouble, big trouble. It was always somconc's fault. If you had a driver, it was his fault. If you had parked it in a pound, it was the night-watchman's fault. But, if you had no driver and you had parked in the street...

"Oh, shit," he swore again.

+

Bogdan, being something of an idiot as well as being a very small minded and narrow sighted young man, made a desperately unintelligent decision. He made a decision that even he would be unable to justify when finally the shit hit the fan—which it surely would.

He decided to go home by taxi and to pretend that his car had not been stolen. He was, in effect, hiding his head in the sand, putting off for tomorrow what ought to have been dealt with immediately in what his boss would have called a damage control operation.

He was driven, in part, by the fact that he was a married man, and that whilst his new bosses actively encouraged the use of Anita's 'courtesy' services, it was not something that he expected his wife to understand.

"Oh, shit!" he practically shouted, managing to restrain his voice only at the last moment as it climbed out of his throat, "Oh, shit!"

He turned and stomped angrily towards the taxi ramp...and the end of his life as he knew it.

+

The stolen Ford was a nice car, Paul was thinking. It was cold outside, not desperately cold, but cold, and now that the Ford had been running for a while and he had mastered the heating controls it was beautifully warm. The car was by no means new, but it was smooth and fast. After a while he had discovered the radio cassette and he had tuned in to a radio station that he assumed was beamed across from Germany. He spoke very little German, but he was able to recognise enough to understand patches.

170

He was heading west. It was easy enough, he simply had to follow the road signs. His big problem lay with the careful policing of the curfew regulations. None of the camp workers had real up to date information on how the curfew was enforced. Was it shoot first, ask questions later? Would there be road blocks, or just patrolling militia and police? Would the entry and exit points to major towns, Poznan for example, be controlled? Did the same curfew regulations apply outside urban areas? And what, exactly, were the current curfew regulations? It had been impossible, in the camp, to get any clear answers. Of course, they'd overheard other workers—voluntary or civilian workers in the factory, rather than prisoner workers like themselves—discuss things from time to time, but the penalties for speaking to a prisoner worker, a tagged worker, was high and the passage of information was subscquently very restricted.

The only thing that was absolutely certain was that by removing his disk he would inevitably be shot if he was apprehended, and that by escaping from his authorised area he would also incur the penalty of death if he was apprehended. It was also unfortunately true that anyone who saw him in the car—dressed as he was—would know him for what he was. His only hope was darkness...and luck, lots and lots of luck.

+

As soon as Bogdan had left, Anita had put on a light dressing gown and had run a bath in the tiny bathroom. While it was running, she had made herself a coffee which she drank quickly in the kitchen, and had enjoyed a cigarette from a pack, stolen from a 'visitor', standing in the kitchen, the light turned off, staring sightlessly out into the night.

Her mind was full of hate, an absolute turmoil of hate. No confusion, no doubts, just pure hate and loathing. Hate and loathing. Mixed and twisted in her mind. She'd get them. Unlikely as it might seem, she'd get them. She would take several of them with her. And their families. As many as she could.

She glanced at her watch, stubbed out her cigarette, walked from the tiny kitchen into the tiny bathroom in four strides as she shrugged off her dressing gown, and climbed into the bath, lifting her long blonde hair and tying it into a knot in one fluid, practised movement.

Ahh, she sank back into the hot water with an almost audible groan of pleasure. Allowing her knees to bend, she lay on her back in the glorious, cleansing, soaking water.

She had about thirty minutes until the next one.

+

Bogdan arrived home at about the time that he was expected. He sat down to a meal lovingly prepared by his wife. He kissed Malgorzata a perfunctory hello and dug in. She was a good cook and he very much enjoyed her meals. He

172

also enjoyed the other benefits of a loving wife. Their first child would be born in just over seven months. This was something that they were both very excited about.

What Malgorzata didn't know, of course, was that her husband was a regular visitor to two courtesy girls laid on, so to speak, by the NRC. Neither did she know that Bogdan had allowed his car to be stolen and had not reported it. The penalty for aiding and abetting an escaping worker, whether deliberately or by negligence, was death. The penalty for merely failing to notify the authorities that an unauthorised person had possession of a vehicle registered to you was the work camp.

All things considered, it seemed unlikely that the future would be quite as rosy as either of them imagined.

+

Anita dried herself off carefully, walking into the bedroom as she did so. Opening the wardrobe, she selected white knickers and bra, full length black skirt and a cream cotton blouse, and placed them carefully on the bed. She had no clean tights left, but that wasn't important. The next one was a new one. She had no idea what he would like, so she was going for an elegant look, without shoes, socks or tights. A sort of sexy, elegant, peasant look, she thought. It normally had the right effect.

She let her hair down, brushed it carefully, and then expertly pinned it up, glancing at herself sideways each way in the mirror, to ensure that it was perfect. It was. Swiftly, she put on knickers, bra and skirt, giving herself a tiny squirt of Chanel, a gift from a visitor, and then put on and buttoned the blouse. Another quick check in the mirror...good!

She leaned across the bed and straightened the bed clothes. And stood. She was ready.

A couple of minutes later the door buzzer sounded.

As she walked to the door she almost smiled. She was going to take as many of the bastards as she could with her. As she opened the door she was smiling.

+

Getting out of Poznan was easy. There were no roadblocks, nothing. No visible control of any kind. Things had obviously quietened down and a lot of reliance was presumably now being placed on electronic control. Despite himself, Paul smiled.

Paul was correct in thinking that there was no visible control, but his assumption that there was electronic control was also correct. As he drove carefully towards the edge of Poznan he passed an electronic sensor that noted the car tag number. Every vehicle was tagged. If the vehicle had been attempting an unauthorised journey or if it had been reported stolen, Central would have alerted the police and it would have taken only a few minutes to put a roadblock in front of it or a police car behind it.

But the Ford had not been reported stolen and it did have the authority to cross Poznan so Paul's movement excited no interest. As he left the city he put his foot down and cruised at 90 kph, the speed limit outside urban areas. He was being very careful, he wasn't about to get picked up for speeding.

+

It took the young Colonel rather less time to remove Anita's blouse than it had taken her to put it on. They were in the living room, on the sofa. He had removed his tunic, but was otherwise fully dressed. She was blouse-less and her skirt had been pushed high up her legs. His hand rested on her bare leg just millimetres from her knickers. He was in a state of high excitement.

Anita didn't even know his name. This was his first time with her. She didn't know how it worked, and neither did she care. She just did what she was told. She knew when she was to be at home, and she had learned how to please. It was important to her that she pleased. The more that she pleased, the more men would come to her. The more men that came to her, the more she could destroy ...the more she could take with her.

The bastards!

She smiled, lifting herself slowly from the sofa, "Vodka?"

He was looking very over-excited. She'd like to give him a chance to cool down.

"Yes, please," he was very polite. Some of them were.

He pulled at his tie, taking it off and laying it carefully on the floor, and unbuttoned his top shirt buttons. It made him look much younger.

She poured two generous vodkas, smiling sweetly at him as she turned back to face him.

Wow, he thought. She is gorgeous. He had heard about her a while ago, had heard that she was lovely and very good in bed, but there was a bit of a queue. As word had spread and her popularity had increased her waiting list had grown. And as her waiting list had grown word had spread even faster. She was a rising star.

Unknown to her, she had been upgraded. She was beginning to be denied to minor officials and was being offered to more senior. She was being 'taken care' of. As the more senior men discovered her, she was being sent fewer visitors, thus allowing the men more time with her, and allowing her more time to herself....There was no point in slaying the golden goose, after all.

She held out her hand, and led him into the bedroom.

+

A few miles west of Poznan the Ford turned right down a minor road, its lights picking out familiar landmarks. The road was a narrow lane. On each side, it was lined by a shallow ditch, sparse leafless trees and snow covered fields. The road itself was coated a treacherous white from ice, snow and salt. Paul drove with great care. This was no time to put the car into a ditch.

Twice, he turned at unmarked junctions. Twenty minutes after leaving the main road, on the edge of a small village, the Ford's lights picked out a stone-built farmhouse no different from a million others. He pulled carefully into the farmyard and drove straight into the barn, killing the lights as the car stopped.

He paused, allowing his eyes to get used to the lack of light. In the blackness of the barn, the wooden wall of the barn slowly faded vaguely back into sight in front of him. To his right, a pile of baled straw or hay, he'd never known the difference. To his left, the stone wall of the farmhouse itself. If he had not been there before, and known what he was looking at, he would not have been able to make out what was around him.

There was no sign of movement or of light.

He waited a moment longer. Nothing.

He pushed open the car door carefully and stepped into the darkness, cursing silently as the interior light came on. Stupid mistake. He'd been away too long. He pushed the door closed, swiftly but silently, and padded gently across to the door in the wall of the farm house, every nerve wide awake. Everything was completely still, totally silent.

The old handle turned silently on the unlocked door, and he slid himself into the farm house kitchen without a sound, pushing the door to, behind him.

It was almost totally black in there.

It was immediately apparent to him that the room was unheated.

Feeling his way around carefully, he found the fridge. As he opened the fridge door, he was hit by the powerful stench of rotten food. No internal light came on.

"Shit," he muttered, more to himself than out loud. He shut the door, and felt for the cooker. With his face close to the ring, he turned on the gas. Nothing.

"And shit."

Still in almost total blackness, he made his way silently through to the living and dining area.

The room smelt damp and was also clearly unheated. Walking across the room he trod on some broken crockery. Feeling in the old dresser drawers he found nothing. Empty. Abandoned. The place was abandoned.

"Shit!" Things were looking very bleak.

Leaving the living/dining area, he found the stairs, noting immediately that their concrete was no longer covered, and crept carefully up them, feeling with his hands ahead of him for obstructions. It was beginning to look as though this was a wasted trip.

Upstairs, in the three bedrooms, there was slightly more light from the moon. He could make out three furnished, but clearly abandoned, bedrooms. Damp, unmade beds in freezing cold rooms. Largely empty wardrobes, some broken glass on the floor of one of them. In the bathroom, no water in the taps. Probably frozen.

"Shit."

In the smallest bedroom, Paul carefully pushed aside a small writing bureau, felt for a loosened section of flooring in the concrete floor, and pulled out a small metal box. Fumbling, his hands now feeling the cold, he snapped open the box and spilled out the contents into his hand. Three trackers, each the size of a pen, each wrapped in cloth.

Putting two on the floor beside where he was crouching, he activated one. *Batt Low* appeared in tiny LEDs, followed by *Enter User Code*. Using the tiny multifunction keys embedded on the side of the tracker, he punched in 0444.

Batt Low flashed.

Confirm User Code.

0444.

Batt Low flashed, more urgently.

"Shit."

Send? followed immediately by *Replace Batt* flashing twice, and the tiny LEDs faded out.

"Shit, shit!"

He picked up the second tracker, slipped out the batteries and cradled them in his hands, hoping to warm them up.

Crouching on the floor, wondering what had happened to this place, he found his mind wandering to the past. The fun that he had had, not realising how serious it would all become. Being recruited by Mac so soon after leaving university. The training, and the two boring years in London, followed by a fantastic eighteen months just outside Venice, when he had gained operational status. Then, more training in the States. And then his days 'attached' to the British Council, touring Eastern Europe, and most recently Poland, promoting the English language and British culture. And Anne. Had she got out? He'd thought so much about Anne.

He slipped the batteries back into the tracker and activated it. *Batt Low* appeared in tiny LEDs, followed by *Enter User Code.*

"Shit."

He punched in 0444.

Batt Low flashed.

Confirm User Code.

0444.

Batt Low flashed, again.

"Shit."

Send?

He confirmed.

Sending.

"Thank you, God," he muttered. He meant it. He started to count.

Batt Low. Sending. He only needed five seconds continuous.

Batt Low. Sending. Four seconds.

Batt Low. Sending. Five seconds!

Batt Low, very urgent now.

Sending. Six seconds.

"Thank you, God."

Batt Low. Replace Batt. Replace Batt. The LEDs faded and died.

Carefully, he removed the batteries from the two trackers that he had used, to ensure that their memories were 100% wiped, wrapped them all up in their cloths, replaced them in their tin, put the tin back into its hidey hole and slid the writing bureau back into place.

There was nothing more for him, here.

It was time to go.

GREAT BRITAIN

Three minutes later the VDU in front of the duty operator at Eastern Ops One flashed up the message 0444 positioning signal, followed by a series of co-ordinates.

The operator selected 'Decode', and the VDU responded with:

Lieutenant Anthony Higgins. Nojewo.

Current status: Missing.

And then, *Signal now lost* flashed across the top of the VDU. The operator selected 'Signal Quality': Single six second burst with one second fade. And then, 'Verify Signal': 98% true. That was as good as certain.

The operator picked up his phone.

+

Twenty seconds later the phone rang in the living room in a small cottage in Markyate, Bedfordshire.

"Restell."

"We have an unexpected signal, ma'am. We'd like you to come in." Restell had recognised the caller's voice. Despite the line being secure, no information of any value was ever put into words on the phone.

"I'll be there in fifteen minutes," Restell was standing as she spoke. It was unusual to be disturbed whilst off duty. Must be a good one.

+

Thirteen minutes later, Captain Restell's dark green MGF slowed at the brightly lit barrier to the government compound, as the four metre outer cage door slid open. When the outer door was fully open, she drove into the cage, and the door slid shut behind her. A moment later the inner cage door slid open slowly, she drove swiftly to her parking place, got out and made for one of the three buildings in the compound. Inside the building, she cleared security, took a lift to floor sub 3, and entered Eastern Ops One.

"What have we got?"

"It's Lieutenant Higgins, ma'am."

She was standing behind the operative, her eyes on the wall-sized screen above his work station. To her right, three more operatives were at work at their VDUs.

She nodded, "Yes?"

"A six second tracker burst, ma'am. Nothing more."

"Hmm," she grunted.

"Position?"

"Nojewo, ma'am."

"Just west of Poznan?"

"Yes, ma'am."

"We lost him on War Day plus one, right?"

"Yes, ma'am."

"In Poznan?"

"Yes, ma'am."

"What do you think?"

"It could be him, ma'am. The right number coming from the right area. I think it's too much of a coincidence to be anything else."

"Why terminate after six seconds?"

"Battery fail, probably, ma'am. The signal faded before failing. Those trackers have been abandoned on site for over a year, and temperatures have been sub-zero."

"Hmm," she agreed.

"Lieutenant Tony Higgins," she thought out aloud, "Alive and well. Poor sod."

"We can't help him, can we?" a rhetorical question.

"We can't even track him. We can't do anything, ma'am. Not a thing."

"Except watch and wait," she paused for a moment, "Have you told our American cousins?"

"Yes, ma'am."

"What ground cover have they got in that area?"

"Nothing, ma'am."

A moment's thought. What the hell was Tony Higgins doing out there, loose, over a year after they'd lost him?

+

Bogdan wiped his mouth with a smile and opened his third bccr. This would be his last beer before bed. He smiled at his wife who sat across from him. She loved to look at him; he was so good to her. She knew that this would be his last beer. She sipped her tea. Bed soon, and they would cuddle up together - so warm, so lovely. She smiled back at him.

He took a mouthful of the beer. Polish beer. He'd always preferred the Polish beer to the more western beers that had been available for the few years after the turn in the very early

1990's. Now, of course, there was only Polish beer. He took another mouthful of the yellow liquid, Okocim beer.

This would not only be his last beer tonight, this would be his last beer. He licked his lips.

+

What the hell was he going to do, now? Paul sat in the car, still parked out of sight in the barn. He had precious little choice. He could make a break for it, he could stay put, or he could go for another safe house. The only option that offered any real chance of survival was to go for the next safe house - but it was a thin chance and a long way.

"Shit!"

He sat, staring at the darkness in front of him. He could get close to the border and cross on foot. He knew his geography; it had been part of the training. Towards the north, near to Szczecin, the river Oder was inland of the border. He could cross the river and then cross the border. The border itself, not being protected by the river, should not pose too much of a problem. But perhaps there were now enhanced security measures on the bridges crossing the river inland of the border.

"Shit!"

Alternatively, there were spots where the river could be waded. But he didn't fancy that. Even if he could be sure of the correct spot, which he couldn't, he didn't fancy his chances in the freezing water.

"Shit!"

The nearest safe house, then. But for what?

If it was abandoned, too, it would be wasted time and dangerous. And heading back east would be dangerous too, regardless.

Stay put? Pointless.

"Shit!"

Make a break for it, then?

He was going round in circles.

"Shit, shit!"

He couldn't think. He was tired. He was wrecked. The camp had taken it out of him. He felt far older than his years. He just hadn't got what it took, anymore. I mean, look at me, he was thinking: I'm sitting here swearing instead of doing whatever I should be doing...because I can't decide what I should be doing. I've lost it! I've bloody lost it!

Another moment's thought.

Perhaps a night's sleep? No, that would be a mistake. No one would be looking for him, yet. Tonight was his best chance, whatever he decided to do.

"Shit!!"

He made up his mind, reached up and pushed the internal light switch to the permanent off position, opened the door, climbed out and silently re-entered the farm house.

Time for desperate measures. Heath Robinson, anyway.

Once inside, he went straight back to the writing desk in the small bedroom, pushed it aside, pulled out the trackers, and took the one that he had not yet used and the batteries that he had taken out of the two that he had used

Carefully, he replaced the other two trackers and pushed back the writing desk. He dragged the writing desk chair out onto the landing, climbed up, opened the hatch into the loft and tried to pull himself up. It was impossible.

"Shit!"

His arms simply weren't strong enough. He went back down into the kitchen, found a stool, placed it above the chair, climbed up the chair and the stool, wobbled a bit, and pulled himself into the loft. It was absolutely black in there. No moonlight penetrated the roof at all.

Feeling across the boarded floor with his finger tips took ages. The floor of the loft was made of rough fibreboard in two and a half metre by one metre boards. He was looking for the one that was not screwed down. He knew that it was at 2 o'clock from the entry to the loft as he had entered. By the time that he had found it the ends of his fingers were numb and bleeding.

With an almost silent grunt of pain, he prised up the corner of the loose board with a table knife from the kitchen and his fingers, and pushed it slightly to one side. The section of the void below the floor that interested him was filled with electronic gadgetry. Using his fingertips in the darkness, he selected what he thought he needed, and took it down to one of the bedrooms to examine it in the moonlight. It looked like what he was looking for.

In the barn, he raised the bonnet of the Ford, connected the piece of pulse circuitry to the car battery, took the six tiny tracker batteries and taped them together, connecting them to the output from the circuitry, and taped the whole bundle to the side of the car battery. If he was lucky, that would do the trick.

He returned to the loft, replaced the loose board, closed the trap door, replaced the stool and chair, and returned to the car.

It really was time to go, now.

He was going to make a break for it.

He started the car, reversed out of the barn, swung the car back onto the road, and headed back the way he had come.

+

Paul pulled the car into a secluded lay-by, killed the lights, and then the engine.

Silence. He waited a moment. Nothing. Silence. He had been heading north, using the lanes. It was tortuous work. He had just crossed route 22 and was now heading north west, planning to converge with route 10 (or E28) just east of Szczecin, where it should be possible to cross the river Oder before reaching the border.

He eased open the bonnet, removing two of the batteries from the makeshift charger, resealing the other four. Back in the car, he fitted the two batteries into the tracker, and activated it.

Enter User Code.

0444.

Send?

He confirmed.

Sending.

He watched it for twenty seconds. No *Battery Low* signal appeared.

Fantastic. He smiled.

He selected the battery life indicator. Twenty minutes.

Wow! Fantastic! He was still smiling. He popped the tracker into his pocket, and started the car.

+

"He's sending, again, ma'am," the screen was flashing 0444 positioning signal followed by his co-ordinates. The operator selected 'Decode' as Captain Restell came up behind him.

Lieutenant Anthony Higgins. Lipie Gory.

Current Status: Missing.

"Where the hell's that?" she asked.

"It's a village just north of route 22, just east of Gorzow Wielkopolski. He's heading north west," he glanced at her. She hadn't recognised the town name, so he added, "He's to the east of E65, headed in the general direction of Stargard Szczecinski.," or Szczecin, he thought.

"Hmm," she grunted, "put him on the screen."

He turned to his keyboard.

"And track his route back to his first signal, at Nojewo."

"Yes, ma'am."

The image on the wall-sized screen changed to the north western quartile of Poland. The operative punched in his selection and a straight red line appeared joining the two co-ordinates.

"Hmm," she grunted, again. He was clearly headed for the north western corner of Poland. And clearly he had wheels. What the hell was he doing out there? And what had he been doing for the last year?

"How's the signal?"

"Constant and strong, ma'am."

"Any ideas?"

"Ma'am?"

"Have you got any ideas? What's he doing out there? Why has he popped up, now?"

"He's going to Szczecin, ma'am. The border has always been harder to secure up there."

"Yes. But why now?"

He shook his head.

+

Twenty minutes later, Paul pulled over, and fitted the last two refreshed batteries into the tracker, and reactivated it. The battery indicator gave him two hours.

He popped the tracker back into his pocket.

+

Signal Now Lost flashed across the top of the operative's VDU, and the tip of the growing red line on the big screen stopped pulsing.

"We've lost him, ma'am."

"Right."

She was behind him.

One hundred and twenty seconds later the message reappeared 0444 positioning signal, and the tip of the red line began to pulse and to move forward at a snail's pace.

The operative smiled.

"What was that?"

"There was a little bit of fade first, ma'am. I'd say that he's changed the power supply."

"More flat batteries?"

"Almost certainly, ma'am, with that fade."

"Poor sod."

+

The Ford tripped an electronic device on the outskirts of Choszczno, a minor town, just south of route 10, about fifty miles from the German border. This was not a tightly controlled area, but access was restricted to those who lived or worked there or who otherwise needed to be there.

In the centre of the city, on the fourth floor of what had originally been the communist headquarters, which had then become a school and which was now a Control Centre, the young duty officer noted that a vehicle with standard access had crossed into a restricted access area. He timed the crossing at 02.57.

It was not an offence to cross the line from a standard to a restricted access area, in fact it was not even public knowledge, although it was widely understood, that there were such lines. It was simply standard practice that when a person without prior authorisation crossed the line he was apprehended and was asked to explain where he was going. And why.

At 03.06 the young duty officer passed the signal on to the local duty Policja.

At the small, local police headquarters, the old man who took the call had been on the force for almost thirty years. He went back to not only before the NRC had arrived, as did most of them, but also back to the big changes—some called it the turn, others called it the first turn—between 1989 and 1992, but also to way before the hard times of the early 1980's: martial law, heavy policing and real police power. He'd seen it all.

He paused, his cup of hot sweet tea halfway to his mouth, as the telex stuttered out its message. By leaning forwards he could read it without leaving his seat, but he raised himself slightly and tore it off.

A voice at the door. He looked up, "Upstairs," the young policja said with a smile, "Cap wants a word."

Gorzegorz grimaced, glancing ruefully at his tea. The younger man's smile turned to a grin as he turned to go. They all liked Gorzegorz, he was all right.

Gorzegorz put his tea and the telex on the desk, stood, tucked in his shirt, straightened his jacket and made his way to the Captain's office wondering what it was now.

+

The Colonel didn't leave the flat until the early hours of the morning. After he had left, Anita flushed another unused condom down the lavatory, ran herself another hot bath, scooped up her clothes, briefly tidied the flat, and allowed herself a long, hot soak. Glorious! She washed herself carefully, cleansing herself as best she could with soap and water.

Another one down. Thank heaven for the constant supply of hot water piped into the block.

She had a late start the next day, so she could afford to relax for just a moment. With the door shut in the tiny bathroom and the walls damp from the steam she felt certain that she was safe from the prying eyes of a surveillance camera—if there was one, which she considered unlikely. But it was still nice to hide, to be certain that no one was watching. The bathroom was the only room in which she felt totally secure. She was convinced that her flat was bugged, but this was something about which she knew very little, but she had learned a lot about human behaviour and she believed that the men who came to her assumed that the flat was bugged. They never said so; it was just the way that they behaved. But in the damp of the bathroom, although they might be listening, they couldn't see, and there was nothing to hear.

Another one down. She'd got another one. She had lost count of the number of men who had visited her in the past few months, and she was too bright to have put anything down on paper, but she had just added the Colonel to her score. They were so stupid, these men. When it came to the crunch, when it came to that moment, they simply forgot everything that they had ever learnt and just went for it.

Fucking animals! She smiled.

+

After changing the tracker batteries again, Paul had found a pack of cigarettes in the car and was struggling with the car's cigar lighter. It kept popping out before it had got hot enough to light a cigarette—it was maddening. Finding cigarettes and then not being able to light them. After several unsuccessful attempts to hold the lighter in by hand, he gave up and began to feel around with his right hand for matches instead. If he couldn't light a cigarette with the car cigar lighter, then it was fair to assume that the owner hadn't been able to, either.

He glanced at the fuel gauge—in fact, it would be more accurate to say that he was constantly glancing at it. Fuel was life. He had tons. He was travelling at just under 90 kilometres an hour. When he hit built-up areas he dropped his speed and tried to disappear from sight. Although a lot of it was not working, a fair bit of the street lighting was still functioning in built-up areas.

At last! His hand fumbled against a matchbox. He gave it a quick shake. Yes, there were matches in it. But were they dead or alive? He was in luck. A few seconds later and he was drawing the smoke down into his lungs.

Ace!

He could feel it like he had never felt it before. He grinned, a wide grin, not only for himself, but for the whole world.

By now he had travelled some miles west of Choszczno, the town in which he had tripped the electronic warning. Any militia or policja that came looking for him would find him almost immediately.

However, Gorzegorz, the seasoned policja man was still with his boss. The young man who had taken Gorzegorz's place had simply disregarded the telex. It was some two hours later that the older man returned, casually relieving the younger man of his position and the comfortable chair. He, in turn, had assumed that the telex had been dealt with by the younger man, had muttered something about people not putting things away, and had filed it.

It was an inefficient system. However, its main failing was that few of the policja had their hearts in the job now that they were doing the NRC's dirty work. All this made little difference, because when the Ford hit the ten kilometre line it would be stopped. No car with standard access authorisation could pass beyond the ten 'k' line without prior authorisation.

Paul was smoking his seventh cigarette - and rather regretting it. He'd really smoked too many in the last couple of hours, but not only were they something of a treat, he was growing rather nervous. Since he had found the safe house empty, with no chance of a guide to get him across the border, it was almost inevitable that he would die.

To say that he was growing rather nervous would have described his feelings in his own words. However, a more honest appraisal would have concluded that he was terrified.

It was almost impossible that he would live for more than a few more hours.

+

At soon after 5.15 am Central located the Ford crossing the ten 'k' line. Mere minutes later Paul didn't even see the roadblock until he was within yards of it. It had been very cleverly done. The road was gently winding, although quite broad, and the roadblock was immediately past a rather sharper bend than most in a rather pretty glade surrounded by beautiful trees.

Instantly, he jumped on the brakes. The car squealed to a halt, veering slightly as its tired tyres gripped the road unevenly. In one movement he threw it into reverse, twisted his body to face backwards, let up the clutch and pushed the throttle flat to the floor.

For a moment the Ford moved away from the roadblock, and then it hit the olive militia vehicle that had just blocked the road.

He sat there for a moment—ten yards in front of him the road was completely blocked with vehicles. A Ruskie built four wheel drive vehicle was behind him placed sideways across the road. There was no road to the sides.

He was going to die. He knew that. He'd known that really, since he'd realised that the safe house was abandoned.

Pity, he half thought to himself, there's so much to live for. Or, there would be outside this God-forsaken country. And he was so close, he must be. He nearly smiled at the thought of the old phrase, so close and yet so far, but he was altogether too frightened to raise a smile.

He felt sick, and suddenly he wanted the lavatory. Rather badly.

He began to open the door. The militia were still a few metres away, strolling—perhaps rather warily—towards him. They knew that they had him, but they couldn't know whether he'd try to take any of them with him. His thought of a smile had flickered across his face as a grimace.

Shall I go quietly, he thought, or what? It was too late really...

Still...he thought, flinging open the door, heaving himself out of the car, and making for the near side bank. Three paces up the muddy incline he was reduced to scrabbling with his hands to make progress.

Someone grabbed his right leg and pulled. Suddenly he felt a most terrific pain in his head and realised rather dully that he'd been hit with something nasty.

He found himself lying at the feet of several large men. At least they looked large from his worm's eye view. He felt as though he'd been hit around the side of his head with a baseball bat. He peered at them through the pain.

"I'm British," he said in Polish. He wasn't quite sure why he said it, but somehow he wanted to make it clear. Recognising belatedly that the uniforms the troops were wearing were Russian, he repeated this statement in perfect Russian.

"So what?" a voice asked in very broken English. Two soldiers took each of his arms and lifted him, not without a certain gentleness now that they had him. He found himself in a kneeling position, his bottom on his heels. His head was spinning with pain. Blood dripped from the side of his chin. He looked dully at the empty space in front of him—the men had moved to the side—and began to speak;

"Dear God..." the thought had formed in his mind that he shouldn't have listened to Mac. It had been a terrible mistake to join the service. But, it had been fun...

A picture of his parents, his two brothers and his sister flashed across his mind.

"Dear God..." were the only words that passed his lips.

The soldier behind him shot him twice.

And then once more, as he lay in the mud.

+

"Ma'am," the operative's voice was urgent. Captain Restell was beside him in a moment, her eyes glued to the wall screen.

"Sod it!"

"I think we've lost him, ma'am."

She nodded in resigned agreement.

"Sod, sod, sod," she was muttering just below her breath, "sod it!" her eyes remaining glued to the screen.

The thin red line that marked Lieutenant Higgins' route had been moving erratically north west for hours, until he had been within just a few miles of the border. Now, without any apparent pause the line was heading east, fast, probably on the E28.

"Sod it!"

+

Chapter Nine

WAR DAY + 394

POZNAN
POLAND

Anita let herself out of the flat and down the flight of concrete steps into ulica Fabryczna. She was dressed sensibly against the harsh cold, wearing a black woolly hat and scarf, black thick wool calf length overcoat buttoned to the high collar around her throat, and black leather boots that reached slightly above her knees, buccaneer style, so popular in Poland in the winters. She looked every millimetre the lady.

She walked to ulica 28 Czerwca 1956 and waited for the number 2 or 9 bus.

The number 2 arrived, and she travelled the few minutes to the edge of the old town, and then walked the last bit into the central square.

It was impossible to be sure that she wasn't being followed, but she didn't think that she was worth the effort of that kind of surveillance. She imagined that those who watched or listened at the flat were more interested in what her 'visitors' might or might not say, to ensure that security was not compromised.

She chose a cafe almost at random—they were all very pleasant, and recently her allowance had increased slightly and she could afford to indulge herself occasionally—and ordered scrambled egg and ham with a coffee.

Something pleasant and hot. After eating she went to a phone booth and telephoned Grzesiek.

Grzesiek, poor old Grzesiek was the answer. She'd been seeing Grzesiek for three weeks, now. He'd been at the same school as her before the invasion had interrupted their education. He was older than her, of course, several years older. He must be almost twenty.

He'd been a lovely boy at school. She had always rather fancied him. He'd been one of the boys her brothers had known quite well, but things had gone badly for Grzesiek in the last couple of years. He was a drug user, now.

"Hi, it's me."

"Hi," instant recognition at his end. No need for names.

"Can I pop round?" Not really a question.

"Of course," genuine pleasure in his voice.

"I'll be there in a few minutes." Grzesiek lived in an old building just a few minutes from the centre of the old town. She hung up, and seven minutes later was leaning on the buzzer of the ancient five story block.

"Hello?"

"Hi, it's me." A low buzz as he released the catch, and she pushed the heavy door open. The stairway was poorly lit, dirty and built of solid stone. A typical old town block. She unbuttoned her coat and removed her hat as she climbed the worn stone stairs to the third floor.

Grzesiek's father opened the front door, "Hello, Mr Morawski," she beamed at him, as she removed her scarf and slipped out of her coat. It was baking hot in the flat.

"Hello, Anita," he indicated that she should help herself to a pair of leather house shoes as she slipped off her boots.

"Hi," Grzesiek poked his face around a half opened door, his eyes taking in her black tights, red mini skirt, and plain white blouse as she paused in front of the mirror for an instant to shake down her hair. He smiled a big welcome.

The flat was small, but generous by old town Polish standards. The hall had no outside windows, but each of the four rooms that led off it had large windows. The largest room was the living room, also used by Grzesiek's parents as their bedroom, the smallest room was Grzesiek's living and bedroom, the middle-sized room was his grand parents' room, and the fourth room was the kitchen. There were two more doors, leading to the bathroom and to the lavatory, neither of which had windows. The whole flat totalled seventy five square metres.

Anita, being a familiar visitor to their flat, went into the kitchen with Grzesiek, while his father returned to the living room. Anita sat on the kitchen work top with her feet on a stool and her back to the window, and watched Grzesiek make the tea.

With the kettle on and the door shut, she pulled him towards her, her hands in his hair as she kissed him. With his arms around her, his body firmly between her legs, he could feel the warmth of her whole body against his.

"Wow," he said, coming up for breath. This had been happening for a while now, and he loved it.

"Wow, indeed," she replied, releasing him and kissing the end of his nose, "Let's make that tea." She slipped down off the work top, running her hands down her skirt to straighten it down, and pushing him towards the kettle.

Back in his bedroom they drank their tea and ate a little cake, sitting at a little table in the window. The room was very small, with the table at the window end, a large wardrobe down one wall, and Grzesiek's bed settee against the wall opposite the window. The stereo was on softly.

She smiled at him, wiping a crumb of cake from her lip.

Wow, he thought, she is so lovely. And all mine. He smiled back, stood and walked to the bed.

"Come here," he said pleasantly. She stood, went to the stereo, turned it up slightly, and began to dance gently, but rather provocatively.

"You come here," she had such a sexy smile.

For a moment he watched, but was unable to resist standing and joining her. Together they swayed gently to the music. As she held him to her, she could feel him begin to grow. She slid her hand into the top of his jeans, sliding it down his painfully thin stomach.

Half an hour later, with her skirt around her waist, she got up from the bed, found the rest of her clothes and put them on. It was time to go. She had to be back.

Grzesiek was half asleep and very happy. There was a smile on his face. The smile of a contented cat.

+

Acquired Immune Deficiency Syndrome: she savoured those words as she waited for the bus home.

Anita didn't know very much about AIDs. It wasn't something about which she had received much education at school. They'd been taught, of course, about how to avoid AIDs, but no one had thought to tell them how to tell if they were infected. If they had caught AIDs.

Grzesiek had AIDs. He had got through his drug taking activities. Dirty needles, probably.

She was having regular unprotected sex with Grzesiek. She wanted a weapon with which to destroy the men who used her, and she hoped that she had got that weapon.

She didn't believe that she would be able to tell if and when she had AIDs...she just hoped that she'd take as many of these bastards with her as possible. 'Take them out,' she murmured to herself, 'Take the bastards out,' she felt a bit like a secret agent, working behind the lines. Meanwhile, Grzesiek thought that it must be Christmas. She grinned to herself. She'd get them yet. And their families. And their children. All of the fuckers. Wipe them out.

+

The truck pulled up outside the factory with a grumble, black exhaust curling away into the air. The olive saloon pulled up close behind it.

"Bring them out," a voice yelled. It was the commander. He didn't need to specify who he meant. The foreman, a likeable enough fellow

202

who had never caused any problems for the prisoners and even, at times, had seemed to sympathise with their plight, blew the whistle.

Trouble. The word passed through every man's mind. Death.

Each of the tagged men knew what this was about. An unnecessary glance at the wall clock confirmed what they already knew; that this wasn't a break time. An unscheduled stop meant trouble. This unscheduled stop today meant death. The two columns filed out; workers and workers, the only difference being that one group was prisoners and that the other was not. That one group was tagged and that the other was not. They stood huddled in two small groups. Tagged and civilian. A few metres away the truck grumbled on, black exhaust trickling into the crisp cold air.

"Okay," the commander yelled. Yelling was quite unnecessary. "Tea break," he yelled at the group of civilian workers, the non-tagged workers. After a moment of confusion the message sank in. The foreman began to say something, but thought better of it. It wasn't the commander's job to tell his men to take an unscheduled tea-break. At least, he didn't think that it was.

However, it was wiser not to argue with one of Ruskie's men. Pimp, he thought to himself as he trailed behind his men. The canteen wouldn't be open, anyway.

"Okay," the commander started yelling, again. He was a short and rather unattractive young man. Possibly teutonic, definitely Polish and undeniably considered a complete and utter bastard by each of the men standing in front of him—most of whom were also Polish, the rest of whom were pretending to be Polish. He smiled, a seemingly genuine smile reflecting real pleasure.

It was an unattractive smile in nature. Added to which, several of the man's teeth were bad.

"We've brought him back for you," he continued. He waved at the truck. A soldier in the back of the truck kicked down the flap at the back of the truck. A moment later a shapeless bundle thumped to the ground. It appeared to be wrapped in an old blanket.

"Jesus," Stary muttered. Tears had sprung into his eyes. Two soldiers pulled at the end of the blanket. It was lumpy and difficult, but after a few moments Paul was lying in the dust. A ragged shape.

Jamie closed his eyes, "Dear God."

Paul's upper torso and face were dark brown with the stain of dried blood. Any wounds in his chest weren't visible, covered as they were by his prison tunic, but the damage to his face and head was clearly visible.

"Oh, God," someone muttered in a voice full of the despair that they all felt.

"Take two," the commander yelled, this time at his soldiers. Four of the armed men moved towards the group of undernourished prisoners. For a moment the group was frozen...

...for a moment they were frozen.

"No," a voice from their midst.

"Take that man," the commander spoke. For a split second Jamie could imagine leaping at the commander and wringing the life out of the man, his hands around his throat. He could almost feel the man's fleshy neck under his nails. For a split second.

The armed men broke into the tightly knotted crowd and hauled out Bartek and Piotr, apparently choosing them at random. Neither of them said a word as they were hauled away, their stunned faces showing their understanding and horror.

They were flung to the ground on their faces, a soldier stood on each man's back and their wrists were tied roughly together. Each man was lifted sharply to his knees and left kneeling in the dirt.

"My wife," Bartek pleaded in a broken voice. He was a young man. He had once had a wife and a family. They'd lived in a happy home and had worried about things like buying a second car or redecorating the living room. Now, before he'd reached thirty, he was about to be shot as he knelt in the dust.

"No," yelled Stary.

It had come out as a squeal, a croaky squeal, his voice collapsing in terror. He pushed forward, turning crimson with embarrassment at what he was doing.

"Stary," Jamie muttered urgently, pulling at his clothing. Stary ignored him and pulled free.

The commander had turned to watch the old man with an air of amusement. With a wave of his hand he stilled the soldiers.

"Take me," Stary said. His voice was all croaky. He was very frightened and not at all sure of what he was doing. But, he had no wife. No one would miss him.

The commander looked him up and down, the same rather cynical look of humour on his face.

"Next time," was all he said to Stary. He turned and waved at his men.

The soldiers moved away from Bartek and Piotr. Piotr was murmuring, possibly praying. Bartek was silent, staring into the middle distance, seeing nothing.

Two shots.

The two bodies slumped to the ground. Two soldiers moved forward.

Four more shots.

"Okay," the commander yelled, "back to work."

+

One hour earlier Bogdan had heard his front door buzzer with horror. His heart was in his mouth as he opened the door. His fears were justified.

Standing politely outside were four policja. They looked at him and read the look on his face. They didn't need to ask any questions. His face said 'guilt', where perhaps he might have tried 'what's happening?'

Malgorzata appeared behind him, emerging from the living room door in the small flat, wondering who would be calling at this hour. The sight of the policja at the door neither dismayed her nor really surprised her. She knew that Bogdan was moving ever up in his job and that he was mixing with all sorts of people. What alerted her to the fact that this was a disaster was the look on her husband's face. That the shit was hitting the fan right now, to use his favourite phrase, she did not doubt. Her jaw opened in horror, she began to speak...

"No," Bogdan stopped her.

"What...?" she began.

"No," he repeated, "later." He couldn't bring himself to even start to try to explain.

She stood, not knowing what to say. Not understanding what was happening, but at the same time perceiving that this was a disaster, without being sure of its exact proportions.

"When...?" she wanted to know when he'd be back.

"SShhh," he put his finger to his lips, gave her a quick and exceedingly weak smile, touched her cheek with his lips, and walked out of the flat. At all costs he had wanted to avoid any questions while Malgorzata was within earshot.

It was cold outside and he'd left in too much of a hurry to pick up his coat. He and the policja trotted down the stairs and into the cold. The car was parked a few metres away.

He walked in his shirt and slacks across the concrete path, between the empty flower-beds, among the careless, bustling, laughing schoolchildren wrapped up against the cold. Above him, the sky was bright and blue. Around him, the tower blocks peeled and faded.

One of the policja held open a rear door of the car for him. As he slid into the seat he turned to look at the block - his block - where he had lived so happily with Malgorzata.

+

The walk back to the camp was long and hard. The eighteen men walked slowly with their heads bowed. Each man with his own thoughts. Heavy thoughts, desperate thoughts. In twenty four hours they had lost three of their number. In some of their minds thought had turned to submission. To total compliance to the new order. To survival in a foul world.

These eighteen men were not special. They had not been hand-picked, nor had they been trained for this role. These men were normal. These men had led normal lives in a normal world. They had had wives, girlfriends, parents and family—and only the good Lord knew if they'd see them again. These men had had all the trappings of life in a capitalist world. They had had cars, homes, washing machines, jobs and lawnmowers. They had had deadlines to meet, partners to satisfy, neighbours to impress. They had been happily married, or not as the case might have been—some had had girlfriends, some had had wives. Some had been successful, some had not. Some had been happy, others had not. But today, today...

...today they all had one thing in common. They were normal men, ordinary men thrust into a living hell. Thrust into a life that would have been impossible to contemplate only a few short months ago. Thrust from the world into a hell - a place where each man was alone, dirty, overworked, undernourished, and captive.

If some of their minds had turned to submission, to total compliance, most of their minds had turned to a more positive course of action. Many of these men had been successful in the short years of free enterprise in Poland. They were not used to submission. They had been beaten, both literally and emotionally, and their minds were turning to a violence that they themselves would have found unacceptable in their previous lives. These men who had been used to freedom were now prisoners, men who had been accustomed to free choice were now subjected to a rigid and vicious regime, men who had been accustomed to a lightness of heart now dreaded every new day. These men had once eaten well, now they ate bread and scraps. They had had warm, spacious homes, now they had six square metres in a draughty wooden shed that was heated by a couple of smoky pot-bellied stoves.

Captive. Prisoners. Deprived of their freedom.

They were used to the warmth of friends and family. They were normally peaceable men. But now, now their minds were turning to a new course of action. An action based on violence. Each man had been horribly sickened by what had happened today. It's one thing to read of a death in a newspapcr, cvcn to see the victims on television, but to see a friend at your feet. To see his mutilated body rolled out at your feet—this could turn a man from a pacifist to a fighter, perhaps a killer. To show him the body of a friend and to show no remorse...it was impossible to gauge the effect on young men still capable of purposeful action. And although these men were tired and undernourished they were still capable of a lot.

And then...the thought was almost beyond comprehension...to shoot down in cold blood, to shoot them dead in moments, to kill, to destroy two more men...in the dust...to see their life-blood mingle with the dirt on the ground.

To see this was too much. It was more than any reasonable man could be expected to cope with without major change.

The desired effect, the desired major change, of course, was submission. But...

None of them had any real ideas, no real germ of hope had yet been sown in their dulled and frightened minds—but something was growing. They were frightened yes, but their fear was making them, in most cases, angry - not submissive.

They walked. The eighteen men. Each alone with his own thoughts.

Eighteen very angry men. Eighteen very frightened men. Walking slowly home...

Their heads low, their feet heavy...

Hearts of lead...

Eighteen men...

Eighteen men...with ideas...growing.

Ideas burning away in their minds. They were desperate men in a desperate position. Men like you and me. Men thrust into a living hell from a life like yours or mine. Men who needed a way out. Eighteen desperate men.

+

And the beauty of it was, thought Anita, as she flushed another unused condom down the lavatory, that however often it had been drummed into the bastards who came to 'visit' her, however often they had been told, when it came to the crunch, when it came to that moment, when it was time to put on a condom, most of them wouldn't choose to do so. The lure of warm pussy was just too much for these old men. They just couldn't say no.

She loved it. She'd kill them all. Even the bastards who did wear a condom at first normally gave way to temptation after a few visits. She couldn't see their logic, but she loved that, too. She smiled as she turned on the bath.

One by one she was going to wipe them out. And their families. She was still smiling as she stepped into the bath.

WAR DAY + 394

THE WORK CAMP
POZNAN
POLAND

Jamie lay on his back fighting back the tears. Above him he could see faint light through the slats in the roof of the shed. The stars. Or, more likely, the moon. Of course, it was the moon. Or, maybe it was the arc lamps. It was the same moon that had given him so much pleasure just a few months ago. The taste in his mouth, he realised, was blood. He was biting his lip in his attempts to stop his tears.

Today had been too much. Today was the hair that had broken the camel's back. Today, he had seen three men - three men that he had known for months - he had seen them cut down, destroyed. He had seen their lives taken away from them. And for what?

For what? The tears were coming.

He couldn't stop them. Oh! How he despised himself, how he hated his weakness. He bit harder, screaming silently at himself. This was no place for tears. This place was for...

...for what? Why had they died?

He didn't even like Piotr or Bartek. Not really, not particularly. He hadn't really had a chance. There was no time for anything in the camp except sleep, work and walking. But that wasn't the point. They were dead. And so, too, was Paul. He had really hoped that Paul would make it, whatever the cost.

He lay still, his eyes on the ceiling. His body dirty and uncomfortable. He was fully clothed. He hadn't taken these clothes off for over a month. He hadn't been issued with a change of underwear for nearly six weeks, and he'd been wearing his outer clothes since he'd arrived over six months ago. Some men would try to wash their clothes, but most found it impossible, and those who tried normally gave up after a while. There was a single cold tap for each shed. One tap for fifty people. It was only at the factory that he was able to wash his hands and face.

He was foul. And he hated to think of the life that must be going on in his underclothes. He felt really dirty, really nasty.

He squirmed. He couldn't make it. He knew that much. He wasn't tough enough. He wasn't a survivor. Some people had the inner strength, some simply didn't. He didn't. He was suffering from no delusions. He was a loser. He was too soft. He was finished. It was all over.

And what was the point of making it, anyway. Outside, he had nothing.

This evening, on the walk back from the factory, he had given up. He had been beaten by the new system. He had acknowledged defeat. He was finished, and he knew it.

So, he would die.

Now, for a certainty he knew that he would never leave the camp alive. For the first time he acknowledged to himself that his life was finished.

It was not an easy thing to do.

But today, today had been...

But he'd done it. He was dead, as good as dead. Still, he fought back the tears. He was finished. His life would end in this camp. And his life in the camp was no life.

Therefore, he was dead. It was over. There was no point. Whatever happened now made little or no difference. His life was over.

Whatever he did his life was over. He would never get out of the camp. He would spend his whole life in the camp. But...

...he completed the full circle for the second time...

...a life in this camp was no life.

He lay still. He stared straight up at the cracks where the moon glimmered through into the shed. Nothing he did would make any difference. Carefully, he fumbled with the rough knot on his neck-chain.

Jamie was finished. He knew that. He was going for the wire. Better to die on the wire tonight than to have no life in this hellhole.

He had nothing to lose.

He had nothing.

And still he held back the tears. Still he struggled to keep the visions of his family out of his mind—all the hopes and aspirations that were now in ashes. The future that could have been.

He pushed himself into a sitting position, and dangled his legs over the side of his bunk. His was on the upper layer. He dropped down, lightly and silently, and padded over towards the latrine buckets. He wouldn't need his boots where he was going, and someone here could make good use of them.

He stopped for a pee in a bucket, at the same time fiddling with the window shutter. It took just a moment to loosen the catch. He finished his pee.

In one movement he pushed open the window, put his hands on the sill, and rolled out in a forward somersault. Still a young man, despite his appearance, he landed on his feet and ran directly for the wire.

It was twenty metres to the nearest point.

"Runner," a voice yelled, hard and desperate. There was a scrabbling noise as several inmates of his shed ran to the opened window in horror and shock. His action was immediately recognised for what it was. A bid for suicide. It was understood and accepted that escape over the wire was impossible.

Someone was hissing at him to turn back. But he'd had enough. He wondered what would get him. He hoped that it would be a mine. He hoped very much that it would be a mine.

He'd seen a man shot on the wire. It hadn't been very nice. They'd left him there a while before taking him down.

And the dogs...he almost faltered, but still his legs carried him forward.

He was at the wire.

He began to climb.

Several voices were yelling at him—at least their hisses sounded like yells in his ears.

He pulled himself up, climbing arm over arm, his toes gripping the wire through his socks. Every moment could be his last.

Every thought his final...

Don't, he shouted silently to himself, don't.

He had three fences to cover. Between the inner and the central fence there were mines. Between the central and the outer fence there were dogs. Every hundred metres there was a watch-tower. There was no nonsense with searchlights swinging back and forth - the whole area was permanently lit with blinding arc lamps.

Each fence was about four metres high. Alternate strands were barbed wire. It was believed that each plain wire could be electrified at the touch of a switch. The fences were sound, good quality structures. The posts were reinforced concrete, the wires spaced far too close to each other to allow a person - or a dog - to pass through.

At the top of each fence there was a 'T' section, each arm of the 'T' at an angle of about 135 degrees to the upright. The arms of the 'T' section were of barbed wire.

You'd need a miracle to get through.

He was a dead man. Jamie was history the moment he'd flung himself through the window.

Up fence one, hand over hand, he reached the barbed wire 'T'. He swung himself out and over, grasping with toes and hands, and hauled himself into its arms.

For a moment he seemed to pause, balanced precariously four metres up, brightly lit by the arc lights. A solitary moving object less than fifty metres from the nearest watch-tower.

Every man in the shed was praying. Jamie was a dead man. It had been a bad day already. Several had turned away from the window. For some it was too much to stand—another death.

For a moment he wavered. He was full of fear. He wanted a bullet, now. He glanced at the smooth and soft-soiled minefield between this and the next fence.

Okay. This is it.

With a prayer, he leaned across, gripped the wire, and swung himself out over the other side of the 'T'. So far, he had managed to avoid drawing blood on the barbed wire.

With a mighty leap, he was in the soft soil of the minefield. Another moment's pause.

Now, it must be now!

Run a few paces. Each step his last.

He wasn't breathing.

He was running on his toes.

He was praying, he suddenly realised that he was praying. Praying for death. Praying for peace. Praying to join Marzena and the kids.

There were tears on his cheeks.

One, two, three paces.

His feet sinking slightly into the soft soil.

Each one his last...

And suddenly, with astonishment he realised that he had reached the central fence.

He was through the minefield.

Without a thought, without a pause, and without a glance to either left or right, he gripped the central fence.

Up...up the central fence. Fingers clawing at wire. Stockinged feet almost gripping wire, monkey-like, up he went, strand by strand.

Sudden pain!

A slip. One foot sliding from under him. Desperately he gripped the wire, grabbing wildly...

...dear Jesus, the pain...

...barbed wire stripping flesh from fingers, palms and upper arms...

Impossible not to cry out...impossible...but, hanging for just a moment, his full weight on both hands, each hand wrapped around a barb, he swallowed his scream...

...silence. Not a sound from his mouth. He would die with dignity. He would die a living man.

Scrabbling. His feet scrabbling for a grip, finding wire with his toes, taking the weight off his screaming, bleeding hands.

Hanging on the fence, floodlit, loosing each hand gently from the barbed wire. Biting his tongue to remain silent.

Visible, oh so visible from the watchtowers to his left and to his right.

He could feel the bullets.

He could feel them coming.

The small of his back flexed, flinching, waiting for the flash of pain that would take his life away.

Silence - no bullets. Anyway, he wouldn't hear the ones that got him. Would he?

Hand over hand, now more carefully than before, he hauled himself up the central fence— a small fly on an enormous and well lit spider's web. Visible for several hundred metres in every direction. The only moving object in sight.

He reached out, gripping the arm of the 'T', swinging himself out and into the arms of the 'T', pushing himself gingerly with his feet..

...and over the top.

Every nerve ending praying for the bullet. Anything rather than a dog.

Please, please, a bullet. See me now, his mind was praying. See me now. Shoot, shoot, shoot!

Don't shoot, don't! Another part of his mind was praying.

Freedom was just one fence away.

Oh Jesus!

But, freedom was impossible.

His feet hit the ground, a harder ground than the soft soil of the minefield. This was the worst stage—the dogs.

As he ran silently to the third fence his ears strained to pick up the sound of dogs.

Nothing.

Wiping the blood from his maimed hands on his jacket, he risked a glance to either side as he reached the final fence.

No dogs.

He gripped the fence...

Oh! The pain, as his slippery-sticky hands gripped the wire.

Still...

Up he pulled, hauling himself gently and carefully to the 'T' of wire at the top. The final hurdle.

Up, up, up he went. Hands, fingers and toes feeling carefully, gripping firmly, the impossible pain searing through his hands...and yet not a sound passed his lips.

Gripping the outer section of the 'T', swinging himself around, gripping with his hands, searching and clinging with his toes, he hauled..

...a sudden slip..

...and he was hanging...

...swinging free, dangling, suspended on the outer edge of the inner arm of the 'T'.

The bright lights...

His body dangling...

Marksmen less than fifty metres away...

Surely to God it was all over, now...

His feet less than two metres from the ground...the ground of the dog pound...

For a moment he swung, dangling, helpless...

It must be over...dear God, it must...

He seemed to swing there for moments. He seemed to accept that it was all over. For an age, it seemed, he waited for the bullet, for the dog...

But no. The searing, tearing pain in his hands brought him back to reality...he was alive.

With his feet he sought the fence. Gingerly feeling for a wire that wasn't barbed, finding a grip.

Working his feet back up the fence, relieving the pain in his hands, in moments he was in a position to swing over the top.

Again, he paused. His body tired, his arms and legs aching. The sweat streaming down his face and beneath his clothes.

And over, he swung, over the bundle of barbed wire at the top. And as he went he felt it tear at his chest...

...the pain searing, desperate and unbearable...

... but he wasn't going to let anything stop him on the last fence.

Suddenly, and quite unexpectedly, he could smell life.

A freshness in the air.

Life!

He leapt to the ground, knees bending gracefully with the weight of his body as his feet found the ground.

Without a pause, without turning back...

...without believing...

...he ran...

...and ran...

The ground was well lit for about a hundred metres. He ran across it, barefoot and praying.

Nothing.

Just himself and silence.

He wondered if he were dead.

But he wasn't.

He wondered if this were possible...

...and he knew that it wasn't...

He was alive—and out.

He was free.

For a second, safe in the darkness...

...he allowed himself to pause and to look back.

It was impossible!

He'd achieved the impossible!

He took a deep breath. And another, and pushing his hand down inside his clothes he pulled at the cord around his neck, loosened the knot and pulled the tag free. For a moment he held it in his hand, savouring the moment, and then he dropped it at his feet.

Another deep breath.

Now what?

POZNAN
POLAND

It didn't take long. It took just a few hours to seal his fate, to determine his future—or lack of it. He had been taken, shivering, into the warm policja building, and left in a room. It was a bare room. The walls were a sort of off-white, completely free of decoration or graffiti. The floor was of worn lino-style tiles in a sort of colourless grey. The ceiling was the same as the walls. It wasn't actually a cell. The window was barred on the outside, true, but then so were most of the windows in the building. The room contained three wooden and rather upright chairs and a plain wooden desk. Nothing else.

Happily, it was warm. The large, painted, coiled, cast-iron radiator under the window pumped out heat. He sat, uncomfortably, and stared into space.

'Oh, how the mighty have fallen,' he thought. 'What an idiot I am,' he suffered no delusions. His predicament was of his own doing.

When the policja in the police car had told him that a runner had stolen his car and what had happened his heart had sunk into his boots and beyond. Things were as bad as they could be. What a fool he'd been. Oh, what a fool. His lack of action, his failure to report the theft, had allowed a runner to get to within a few kilometres of the border. He was aware of the penalty for assisting a runner. The rules were quite clear. Assisting a runner was a capital offence. He was aware of the penalty for allowing an unregistered person to drive a vehicle. The rules were quite clear. The penalty was the work camp. He was aware that failing to report the stolen car would be accepted by any court as assisting a runner. He was finished. Yesterday, he'd been a man with a future. Today, he was a man with a past—but not for long. But it was worse than that. He could accept that—he could accept the penalties that he would incur. He had made a very stupid decision, he could see that now, and he deeply regretted it. How very, very stupid and short-sighted he'd been, and now he had to pay the price. He could accept that.

But, what he found so very difficult was that the process of the law would also punish his wife. Malgorzata would be removed from their home, of that there could be no doubt. The state would not provide for one who was assumed to know of such a criminal an act as the rendering of assistance to a runner. Within twenty four hours of his conviction, she would be physically removed—if she had not already moved out. Most people moved out well in advance in order to avoid the unpleasantness of a forced eviction.

Her job, too, would be taken from her. The wife of a man convicted of subversive action was not considered suitable for work. Jobs were for those who deserved them. Subversives didn't even deserve consideration. He sighed, a deep draught of despair. He'd really spoilt everything, hadn't he? He sat in the upright wooden chair, his head in his hands, his elbows on the table, and stared at the surface of the table.

'Oh, shit!'

Two floors up, in a far more comfortable room, three plump, middle-aged, and smartly uniformed men were deciding Bogdan's fate. One of them sat behind an attractive and uncluttered desk in a well sprung swivel chair upholstered in a rather splendid material. The other two sat in slightly more upright, but none-the-less very comfortable office chairs upholstered in the same material.

The three men were colleagues of many years. They knew and understood one another, and were comfortable in each other's company. Each man was powerful in his own right. Together, their power was ominously awesome. In practice, they held the power of life and death, although in theory their power was rather more limited. On an almost daily basis they decided the fate of subversives.

Bogdan was a dead man; each of the three men knew this. So, too, did Bogdan. Bogdan had no right to expect anything other than death. Termination was inevitable. But yet...

...the most powerful of the three men, the man behind the desk who was at present dipping his chocolate biscuit gingerly into his cup of sweet tea, was listening with interest to an idea that one of his colleagues was putting to him. It was an interesting idea. A most interesting and novel idea. He rather thought that he liked it. A spy - or an eye - in one of the camps. A wonderful idea.

Chapter Ten

WAR DAY + 394

POZNAN
POLAND

Now what, indeed? There had been only one thing that he could do—and that was to put as much ground between himself and the camp as quickly as possible. At first, Jamie had begun to run at a gentle trot directly away from the camp itself. Once he'd got used to the comparative darkness of the night beyond the arc lights, he had found that he could really see quite well by the light of the moon.

His only real problem lay in the fact that he was running in bare feet. One bare foot, anyway. Somewhere, whilst going over the wire, he had lost one of his socks. The remaining sock was of little value. What he needed was a pair of shoes.

When he'd been jogging away from the camp for about twenty minutes he crouched against a tree to pause and to consider. All in all, things looked good. Every minute of life was an extra minute. Right then he should have been being removed from the wire. Or pieces of him should have been being scraped off the sheds, or been being prised out of slavering dogs' jaws.

He shivered. And smiled at himself.

Such was life.

That would have been a fine moment for a cigarette. He had paused, smiling, looking at the sky.

Beautiful sky!

His smile remained on his face as he considered the stars. He knew just enough about them to have charmed potential lovers in the long distant past, and—which was of far greater importance at that particular moment—to know which direction was west. If he was right, and he was far from confident, that meant that the huge yellow glow that was the city of Poznan was to his north. Which was a relief. Going through Poznan would have been suicide, and if he had had to circumnavigate the whole city it would have taken an age.

After a final wistful look at the moon, his moon, he had begun to trot west in his bare feet.

+

Jamie was warm and comfortable. He stirred slightly, the tone of his gentle snore hardly changing. Warm and comfortable. He smiled to himself as he slept, much as large tom cat might smile in self-satisfied pleasure as he curled up in front of a warm fire.

He was on the outer edge of the city of Poznan. His night of gentle jogging had carried him less distance from the camp than he thought. He had jogged for several hours, but Poznan is a very large city and he had been jogging around the perimeter of the city giving it a wide berth. Added to which, rather than heading due west during the night he had constantly erred towards the north, towards the city of Poznan. It had been easier to keep the bright yellow of the city lights to his right than to follow the stars. The net result of which was that he was now on the outer city limits to the west of the city.

And he was comfortable. And asleep. And at peace with the world. Had he been awake he might almost have smiled.

Towards dawn he had begun to consider the question of what to do with himself during the coming day. Dressed as he was in prison garb, not to mention his lack of footwear, he could not consider anything other than lying low. But where?

All sorts of ideas presented themselves, but they all had flaws. The first and most obvious idea was to hide in a barn. But, in order to do that successfully he had to find a barn first. The farms around the city were all tiny, more like smallholdings, and they had no need of large barns in which to store feed or produce. Most of them seemed to have either small buildings close to the farmer's home or to have a lean-to on the side of the farmhouse. Neither of which was suitable.

He had finally settled for one of the small concrete rubbish sheds in an estate on the edge of the city. It had seemed a silly idea, at first, but investigation had showed that it was quite large and dark inside. It was also unspeakably disgusting.

The shed, which was similar to thousands like it all over Poland, was a concrete structure with a roof made of a corrugated material. It had two rather large metal doors, the top half of which were perforated. Inside the shed there were eight rubbish carts—large, wheeled metal containers with swing lids—into which the residents of the estate would place their daily rubbish.

As dawn approached, Jamie had strolled into the shed and selected an empty cart. It wasn't actually totally empty, but it was as empty as a rubbish cart can be when its contents are emptied just once a week and when that process of emptying involves simply tipping the contents into a crusher. The carts had probably never been washed.

With an eye on the doors—it seemed unlikely that many people would choose to empty their rubbish bins before dawn, but Jamie knew that there was no accounting for taste—he had scrabbled around the fuller bins looking for insulation. He had been astonishingly lucky. He had found a lot of newspapers, some of which, it was true had obviously been thrown into the bins containing some fairly unpleasant objects. He had used these to line his chosen bin, using some choice pieces of cardboard under the paper. His most astonishing luck, though, was to find both an old overcoat and a pair of incredibly worn snow boots.

He couldn't believe his luck. With the coat to cover his prison uniform and shoes to cover his feet he could pass for an everyday tramp—if they still had them in Poland.

Shivering in the cold, he had stripped off his uniform and replaced it inside out, and covered it with his coat. His new coat. With some excitement he had pulled on his new boots. He wished that he had had a mirror. He was sure that he looked ace, just ace.

And he did...as tramps go he looked just perfect. He was lean, with a hungry unshaved face. He wore a coat of nondescript colour covered in unspeakable stains, although closer examination would have shown that it had once been a fine coat, a very long time ago. He had fixed the coat closed with string at his waist and wrists. Between the lower hem of the coat and the top of his horribly worn and stained grey—at least they had been grey once—snow boots were several inches of trousers whose colour was also an indistinct grey. It would have taken a very alert person to recognise those few inches as inside out prison gear.

Having dressed himself for the occasion, he had climbed into his prepared cart, struggled for a few moments with a bundle of newspapers, made himself comfortable under them, and had almost instantly fallen asleep.

+

Some hours later, a figure dressed in an ancient coat, worn shoes and several layers of filthy clothing wandered into the rubbish shed. On his back he carried the remains of a small, brown canvas rucksack. Both the waist of his coat and the sleeves were fastened with string. Quite clearly, he hadn't shaved or washed for a very long time. This figure ambled into the shed wondering at life. Every new rubbish cart was a new adventure, every cart held the promise of new wealth. He was looking for bottles.

A lot of people, despite the current hard times, discarded glass bottles on which they had paid a small deposit. Ten empty bottles, for example, would buy a full bottle of beer. Forty empties would buy a half litre bottle of vodka. A loaf of bread, together with a healthy chunk of cheese or a mackerel would cost about sixteen empty bottles. His was a gentle, serene life.

He shuffled in, his perpetual good humour visible only through the glint in his electric blue eyes. The laughter lines around his mouth were disguised by his undisciplined beard and moustache. Hardly anyone got close enough to notice his eyes.

No one loves a tramp, no one cares for a tramp - no one even really notices a tramp after his existence has registered.

In short, our amiable figure was able to come and go unnoticed. The authorities, the new authorities had made a few half-hearted attempts to register these vagrant characters with Central, but all that had ever happened was that they had kept doing as they pleased and had ignored the restrictions placed upon them, which, in turn, had meant that they had ended up in the policja cells. But the policja didn't want them and there was no point in holding (and feeding!) them when they weren't doing any harm.

The net result was that the attempt to control their movements with Central had been abandoned. No one liked to say that it had failed, but it had certainly not worked.

Our amiable friend began to poke through the carts with his stick. Every now and then he would grunt, a quiet grunt, either in pleasure at finding a bottle or some other valuable, or simply because from time to time he fancied a grunt.

Slowly his ears, which were perhaps more attuned to small noises than most, became aware of the quiet suggestion that he was not alone. He paused for a moment, allowing his work to take second place to his curiosity. He had no need of hard work—he had enough money in the deep recesses of his clothing to keep him in food and drink for almost seven days. If he wasn't good at much else, it would have been impossible to fault his personal budgeting—except perhaps to suggest that he could have applied his financial prowess to something more rewarding than surviving from his fellow citizens' rubbish.

For a moment he listened intently, then abandoned his cart. It had been a long time since he'd had a pet. Some months earlier he had had a small dog as a companion, whose company he had greatly enjoyed. Unhappily, one night his companion had gone his own way and had never returned. The noise that he thought that he could almost hear was that of a contented cat purring.

He moved slowly and carefully towards the cart from which he imagined the noise was coming. You had to be careful not to startle a cat. Its first instinct was always to run. He wasn't certain as to the suitability of a cat as a pet to a man in his situation, and he hadn't fully worked out why he was doing what he was doing—except to the extent that he knew that he was allowing curiosity to take over his other instincts—when the noise stopped.

He paused, silent, unaware that he was standing on his toes. A ridiculous, pantomime figure, he would have laughed aloud if he could have seen himself.

For a moment...he balanced, his ears awake to every nuance of sound. It was a time of day when there was very little constant background noise, but this simply seemed to accentuate those noises that were there. The sound of a car starting some one hundred metres away, for example, seemed far louder, far more sudden than it would have if there were the background noise of people, buses and passing cars that was normally there during the bulk of the day. He grinned at himself...the bulk of the working day.

Very carefully, almost silently, he tip-toed towards the cart that the noise had been coming from. He noted with surprise that the lid was closed. It was not an old cart, so it was unlikely that there were any rusty holes in its bottom, and it hadn't been damaged in any way that would seem to allow the passage of a cat whilst the lid remained closed.

Strange.

He moved carefully, his feet automatically avoiding the noisy pieces of discarded rubbish on the concrete floor, which was littered with the odds and ends that fall out of plastic rubbish buckets the moment before—or the moment after—they have been upturned over rubbish carts.

He loved a mystery. Maybe someone had...no, they wouldn't bother. For a moment he had considered that someone might have purposely discarded a domestic pet, but the thought was nonsense. It didn't make any sense.

He reached out, his hands gently gripping the two greasy handles on the lid.

He held his breath...

...and lifted the lid...

...gently, oh so gently...

...he lifted...

...still holding his breath...

...he held the lid halfway open. Nothing.

Well, nothing special, anyway.

It was one of the carts further towards the back. People preferred not to come into the rubbish sheds if they could avoid it, so the carts close to the entrance were invariably filled to well above overflowing before people would venture further into the shed to discard their rubbish. The carts at the rear were commonly quite empty.

He grimaced in disappointment, carefully lowering the lid. He would return to it in due course. He had a long established routine and he saw no reason to abandon it now. If he did things as normal there was less chance of missing a cart—and possibly something of great interest. People threw away the most extraordinary things—sometimes.

He smiled pleasantly to himself as he returned to his half-sorted cart, counting in his head how many bottles he had in his rucksack.

Halfway through the next cart he found a suitcase. He pulled it out with ill-concealed pleasure. He didn't, it was true, actually need a suitcase. He didn't, it was also true, even want a suitcase, but nonetheless it was quite a find. He grunted with pleasure as he viewed it.

True, it was old, but what did one expect? True, one of the fasteners was missing and the other one had no spring, but that was of little importance. He carefully placed it on the floor, after first kicking a space clear, opened it and gently laid his half-filled rucksack inside it.

Lovely.

He grinned to himself.

He closed the lid, fastened the one remaining catch, lifted it by the handle and continued his labours with the air of a satisfied entrepreneur who, having concluded one deal, is immediately on the lookout for another.

Some minutes later, he was startled into a second's immobility. He was not a man who startled easily, living as he did, and nor did he like to admit to anyone—least of all to himself—that he could be startled by anything. However, startled he was.

He was just lifting the lid of one of the more distant carts, towards the back of the shed, where the light was fairly dim. To his astonishment and horror...

...there was a body in it...

...a man's body had been thrown into the cart...

...it was an old, dirty body. He noticed with distaste that it was dressed in rags. It was partly covered in rubbish, although the upper half of the torso protruded...

...who could possibly have callously discarded rubbish on top of a body? He could understand that some people on some occasions found it necessary to commit murder, especially these days, but how could normal everyday citizens simply ignore a man's body and dump rubbish on it?

He stood, astonished...

...more shocked than he cared to admit by the callousness of the human race...

...and let the lid slam down with a crash of metal on metal.

Jamie, who had been fast asleep after nearly twenty four hours without sleep—not to mention a run of several hours—awoke with a sudden jerk.

He was in total darkness.

He had no idea where he was.

With no conscious thought, he jerked himself into a sitting position as he woke.

His head slammed against the metal of the lid...

...and with an astonished moan of dismay he raised his hands to his head.

Suddenly, aware of the pain in his hands, arms and chest where the barbed wire had torn at him, he groaned again.

IIis fingers scrabbled at the unfamiliar inside surface of the lid.

On the outside, our amiable friend was—for the moment—consumed by a nameless terror. The confused thought rose in his mind that he had somehow disturbed the living dead, although at the very moment of thinking this he knew it to be nonsense.

He took two great, plunging, clumsy steps away from the cart before slipping on a piece of slimy cardboard, momentarily losing his balance, grabbing at a cart to steady himself, and pausing...to think...as he regained his equilibrium.

There was a moaning and a scratching coming from the cart.

He stood, breathing heavily, for just a moment more. For just a moment before reason took over and he understood that he had simply disturbed someone sleeping...sleeping, it was true, in a somewhat unorthodox place...his mind conjured up a mental picture...a truly dangerous place! What would happen to such a poor soul if the cart had been emptied into the crusher? If the bin men had arrived whilst he was asleep?

This man was obviously a newcomer to the game. He obviously needed guidance from a true veteran, a true gentleman of the road.

And...he paused with a smile...wasn't it time that he, the true veteran, had an assistant or even...an apprentice?

With renewed confidence, with the bounce back in his feet, he moved back to the cart - with just a glance around him to ensure that no one had witnessed his recent discomfort - and gently lifted the lid.

POZNAN
POLAND

Jamie sat in the opened cart, bleary eyed and blinking in the bright light. It wasn't actually very bright, but it seemed very much so to him.

He was a little unsure of his ground, right then. Was this kindly gent who had opened his lid for him going, perhaps, to dispute the territory?   Were tramps—and, Jamie asked himself, was that word acceptable in such circles?—were tramps territorial?   He struggled with his thoughts; he knew, for example, that lobsters amongst many other animals were strongly territorial, but that was of little use now.

He shook his head. And instantly regretted it as a blinding pain shot through it from the base of his neck to the back of his eyes. He raised his hands to his head, and allowed it to sink gently into them. That had the added bonus of not only soothing the pain, but of blacking out both reality and the blinding light.

As his head settled he became more aware of a shocking pain in his arms. Without removing his hands from his eyes he carefully considered and remembered. He'd caught his hands and lower arms on the wire!

And his chest, too!   But he could feel little pain in his chest. Perhaps the damage to his chest was insignificant. Or his chest was numb?

After a few moments of further consideration in which he made no further advances, he peered carefully through a small gap in his fingers. He was met by a most piercing blue gaze.

The man who was looking back at him was ageless. That is, Jamie would have been unable to say with any confidence that he had any idea of his age. He would, however, have been able to say that he was neither old nor young. His face was stained, that part of his face that was visible and not hidden by beard, was stained a slightly darker than natural colour than flesh, much like a mechanic might allow his hands to become gently discoloured by oil over the years.

The most marked features about the man, apart from the fact that he was obviously a homeless tramp, were his eyes. Their gaze was strong and steady and an astonishingly bright blue.

The man's beard had been dark, but was now very much more grey than it would once have been, although his hair still retained most of its colour. From his seated position, Jamie estimated him to be a little over six foot, but accurately judging a standing man's height whilst one is seated in a rubbish cart is not easy.

There was no look of aggression; Jamie was relieved to see, in the man's face or stance. Realising just how incredibly stupid he must look he dropped his hands slowly from his eyes.

"Hello," he tried, hoping that it wasn't obvious that Polish wasn't his first language, a fact that he would like to keep to himself.

The eyes lit up, the mouth split into a grin and the man stuck his hand out.

"Janus."

"Orszulik, Tomek Orszulik."

Jamie gripped the proffered hand and shook it, grinning.

"Hungry, Janus?" the man asked. The man didn't need to ask twice, and nor did he have to wait for an answer. Jamie's eyes had lit up at the question. He began to haul himself out of the cart.

"Ohhhugh," he groaned, flinching at the pain in his arms - and his chest! Yeeow! For a moment, they felt as though he was on the wire again. Unbearable! His face contorted with the tearing pain. And his legs! What was wrong with them? They felt terrible.

It must have been the running. It wasn't that long since he'd gone for a jog every day, not that long. Or perhaps it was. His legs were full of ache.

He was a wreck. He hauled himself very gently out of the high-sided cart and lowered himself gingerly to the ground, successfully stifling all his grunts and groans, but looking very fragile as he moved.

The older man led him outside, carefully carrying his suitcase. They walked together for a few metres by the side of the road, a pair of tramps. Perfectly matched. Each of them walking slowly and carefully, each of them with their eyes on the ground. Each of them dressed in unarguably ancient clothes, each of them tall and lean. Each of them unshaven and grubby, each of them blinking in the light.

They walked slowly past a taxi rank. The lone taxi driver ignored them—they were a part of the scenery. Anyway, he was watching the tasty blonde in the truly tiny mini skirt and ridiculously short fashion coat who was pushing the pram up the pavement. She had a lovely pair of legs that looked absolutely stunning in those knee-length leather boots. He groaned to himself.

She was there every morning. And so was he—he was a government man. He drove a taxi, but his real job was simply to watch, and that's what he was doing.

He followed her with his eyes, and as she passed he kept his head facing forward. In a moment he'd be able to see her in the mirror.

The two tramps shuffled past, headed for the rear of the heating shed. The taxi driver would have been able to tell you where they were probably going even though he hadn't consciously noticed them. He knew that they normally ate around the heating sheds because it was warmer there.

Around the back of the heating shed, away from prying eyes, they paused and considered. It was quiet. Jamie kept his mouth shut. He just watched. He wanted to learn.

The older man carefully chose a spot and sat with his back to the heating shed wall. With a flick of his eyes he indicated to Jamie that he was invited to sit, and so he did, carefully crouching and then dropping onto his bottom.

Oh! How his legs ached!

The pain in his head seemed to have gone, but his arms and chest were agony. It felt as though wounds that had begun to heal had been torn open, and he had an idea that the cloth of his thermal vest had stuck to the wounds on his arms.

Right now he didn't dare to look. Not many innocent tramps would have lacerated lower arms and a shredded chest. He supposed.

As he crouched the material of his vest strained against his arms, bringing tears to his eyes, but still he didn't cry out.

His new friend looked on with casual interest, saying nothing. He pulled his case towards him and flicked open the single catch. He had to push it with his thumb because the spring was broken.

He smiled to himself. And pushed open the case to reveal his rucksack. His smile spread to his face. He pulled a small loaf and a healthy chunk of yellow cheese from one of the rucksack's pockets. Breaking the loaf in half, he handed one half to Jamie. He paused for a moment with the cheese. Normally a piece this size would have lasted him several meals, but...

...well, his new companion looked as though he needed some decent food...

...he broke the cheese into two equal halves and offered one to Jamie, who accepted it with a grateful grunt.

The older man very much appreciated the grunt, the appreciation. It looked as though they might get on.

Chapter Eleven

WAR DAY + 395

THE WORK CAMP
POZNAN
POLAND

Mariusz had watched Jamie getting over the wire. He'd been astonished when he'd seen him reach the other side, when he'd seen him reach open ground and run on into the darkness. Even then he'd expected to hear the sound of gunfire. They'd all expected it. No one got out over the wire. It simply wasn't possible.

It was also astonishing that Jamie had attempted it. He hadn't put him down in his mind as being either a runner or a suicide. It took something, some inner strength, to make a man decide to take his own life - especially on the wire. He hadn't thought that Jamie had had that strength. In short, Jamie had seemed rather soft.

He and Jamie had been quite close. They were on the same work detail. Had been. He'd shown Jamie how to cut through his tag chain with the heat lance, but he hadn't expected it to come to anything. So, now he was out there in the big wide open.

Or, maybe he was dead. Who knew? But the fact that there had been no retribution killings in the camp suggested that he had neither been found nor killed. Although, in fact, the one added up to the other. To be found running was to be killed.

If they had found him, almost certainly there would have been retribution at the camp. It followed that they had probably not found him.

It wasn't even clear to the inmates of the camp when Central had become aware of the missing prisoner. Naturally, virtually every prisoner simply assumed that Jamie, seeking suicide on the wire, would have been wearing his tag—there being no reason to remove it, and even less apparent possibility of so doing.

However, once he'd gone there had been no response. There had been no sudden invasion of the shed by guards. No alarm had been raised.

Mariusz, knowing that Jamie had been able to leave his tag behind, assumed after a few minutes that he had in fact done so. The others had been perplexed, and it had been a sleepless night for most of them. Mariusz lay back, gazing at the ceiling. It had been twenty four hours, one whole day, since Jamie had made his break.

Central knew that he'd gone, of course, because he hadn't arrived at work as expected - or, more accurately, Central would have noted that he didn't leave the camp to go to work. For the present, it was difficult to see how Central could know anything except that some time between coming in in the evening and the time that he was due to leave in the morning, Jamie had made a break.

Or...

...and this, in Mariusz's opinion was far more likely...or, Central would assume that Jamie could not have escaped over the wire and that he must therefore have not come in the night before—that someone else had brought his tag in in order to give him more time to make good his escape.

In which case...

...Mariusz trembled with both excitement and trepidation...

...this meant two things. Firstly, there would, in all probability be retribution among the work party rather than in the shed. This meant a far greater risk of death to Mariusz, because the work party was so small in number compared to the number of prisoners in the shed, and secondly, if Central didn't realise that someone had got out over the fence, Central would not have increased vigilance on the perimeter.

Which meant, in short, that it might still be possible to get out, and...

...that staying was all the more dangerous.

Mariusz lay on his back, staring at nothing, thinking these thoughts. The conclusion was inevitable.

And he knew it.

It looked like a good opportunity.

And he knew it.

At least, it looked like as good an opportunity as he would ever have.

And he knew it.

And still he lay on his bunk.

It's not an easy decision to make, the decision to put the whole of the rest of your life on a single card. To put everything that you are, everything that you might be, and everything that you ever were, on the turn of a single card.

It's not an easy thing at all.

And he wasn't sure that he could do it. He wasn't sure that he had it in him.

He lay on his bunk, staring at the ceiling, thinking...wondering...and, finally, sleeping.

Sometime later he was woken by sudden movement.

Someone had said something rather loudly.

It took a moment to sink into his sleep-clogged mind.

Runner! It was a runner!

His immediate reaction, as he ran to the window with the others, was that he'd missed his opportunity, that it should have been him out there...

...at the window, he could clearly see the slight figure brightly lit by the arc lamps. Already he had reached the first fence.

"Who is it?   Who is it?" people were whispering.

No one seemed to know.

The figure was reaching for the top layer of the inner arm of the 'T' at the top of the first fence.

Silence.

The figure swung around, pulling itself over and into the arms of the 'T'.

For a moment all seemed well.

The figure was crouched in the arms of the 'T'.

He paused...the watchers held their breath...

He moved, reaching out for the end of the inner arm of the 'T'.

Somehow, it seemed too far to reach...

...his outstretched arm, his body balanced above the barbed wire...

...then he seemed to slip...

...his outstretched arm thrust through the wire, his body fell flat on the barbs...

He called out in pain—they heard his cry in the shed—the barbs tearing at his lower and upper arm, pinning his chest and perforating his abdomen.

All was lost. That much could be seen from the shed. He was finished. He hadn't a chance.

The distant figure tried to pull himself up, but the barbs caught at his legs, tore at his feet. He was lying, almost horizontal, in the arms of the 'T', on barbed wire.

He was pinned down. His whole body was pinned to the wire. Each and every movement pinned his body deeper onto the barbs, causing unbearable shafts of pain...

...for a moment he was still.

He lay, on a bed of barbed wire, four metres above the ground bathed in bright light.

A movement. He tried to free his arms, but slipped even further onto the barbs with...

...a sudden scream as the pain took over. A piercing scream. A sound that could be heard in each of the two watchtowers. A sound that curdled every man's blood...

...a shot.

A single shot. A warning?

Suddenly everyone was crouching below the opened window.

A guard was despatched from the gatehouse while the guards in the two watchtowers simply watched. That, after all, was their job.

Then the figure started to scream, again.

WAR DAY + 397
POZNAN
POLAND

"Bottles," the old man was saying. Well, he wasn't so old, but Jamie thought of him as old. He seemed old. He didn't actually look old—in fact, up close he looked quite fit— but somehow he seemed to exude the air of such timeless experience that he must be old.

He turned a smiling face at Jamie, ensuring that his audience was paying attention. It was. His smile widened. It was a beautiful day.

"Spring," he murmured, "I love spring." It was, too, it would soon be spring. Spring in Poland was a truly beautiful time.

"Bottles," Jamie reminded him gently.

"Ah, yes," for a moment he seemed to consider, staring into the middle distance, lost.

"Ah, yes," he repeated, "you can get virtually everything you need from the carts," Jamie had noticed that the old man seemed to like to avoid referring directly to rubbish, "but, of course, sometimes you might need a little cash," he paused once again for thought.

Why, wondered Jamie, would this old man want cash?

For the past two days they had wandered gently though the outer suburbs of Poznan. The old man had shown him, to his astonishment, that you could feed like a king from the carts. Jamie hadn't eaten so well for a long time. In fact, you could find virtually anything in the carts—the only real problem being that you could never predict what you would find and when you would find it.

Maybe, for alcohol? But the old man hadn't mentioned alcohol once. Maybe for heat? It wasn't so important at this time of year, but perhaps when the temperature was really low you had to buy heat? Perhaps? But there were places where you could find heat, free heat.

They moved gently, meandering along the side of the road.

Jamie's shoes, his new shoes, were ideal. True, a couple of years ago he would have considered them well past their best, to say the least, but today he was well pleased with them.

He smiled to himself. The old man hadn't asked him a single direct question about himself. Not one. But after they'd been together for a few hours the old man had suggested that a new pair of trousers for Jamie wouldn't go amiss. He had said nothing else. Just that a new pair of trousers wouldn't go amiss.

Jamie had looked down in guilty shock at the few inches of inside out prison uniform that was visible below his coat. To be quite honest, having considered that he'd solved that problem he had rather forgotten about it.

"Yes," he'd replied after a moment's consideration, "it would be nice to have a complete change." And, true enough, the old man had led him to what seemed to be an abandoned building site and had taken him up to a first floor room—a room without any outer walls—and had pointed him to a cardboard box on the floor.

"This is my wardrobe," he had grinned, "help yourself." The old man had descended the concrete steps without turning back. Meanwhile Jamie had chosen the most nondescript clothing that he could find in the box. When he had followed, taking care on the banister-less concrete steps, he had found that the old man was tending a small fire. He was heating a small can of water and sorting out a couple of tea bags.

Jamie had grinned uncontrollably. "You're impossible," he had laughed. The old man had looked up with pleasure.

"Would you like sugar and or lemon with your tea?"

Jamie had laughed, but the old man had meant it. From somewhere in his coat he had produced a small bag of white powder and a whole lemon, together with a tiny, but deadly-sharp knife and a small silver teaspoon.

"Is that silver?" Jamie was still laughing. The old man was really quite incredible.

It was. The old man had nodded solemnly, his eyes twinkling. He had begun to explain that he'd found it some years back in a cart, when he had paused, his nose to the air like a dog. His electric eyes had searched the surrounding building site. His ears had seemed to quiver...

"Here," he had said, reaching out his hands. There had been an air of deadly seriousness about his voice. A crispness that had not been there a moment before...

...four militia men had appeared at the top of the next building, another unfinished concrete shell, about seven floors high...

...maybe fifty metres away...

...a shout...

...who was shouting at whom?...

...one of the militia...

...at whom...

...and in his hands...Jamie had his prison uniform...

...waving. They were waving. Two of the armed militia were waving...

...at whom?...

A nameless terror had seized Jamie. He had frozen. He couldn't move. He could feel the bile rise in the back of his throat. The camp...

...he couldn't go back. He could picture the impossible in his mind. He knew that he couldn't do it.

He had forgotten, in his wild and headless panic that he wouldn't be sent back to the camp...

...the old man had had his arms outstretched...

...his hands had been reaching...

...Jamie had stood, his eyes wide, his breathing shallow. He had seen nothing, nothing except the four militia. He had felt nothing, nothing except the all pervading, disabling fear...terror...panic...

...he could see the end. He could smell his own end...death...dead...

...the camp...

The old man had leaned gently forward without a word. He had carefully removed the two rolled-up garments from Jamie's hands, and had bent to tend the fire, at the same time turning his back on the militia.

With one hand he had fussed with the container of water. With the other he had slowly fed the clothing to the fire.

"Sit," he had commanded, as though to a dog. Jamie had crouched, allowing his bottom to rest on a piece of concrete.

"Relax," Jamie's eyes had caught his, "Breath easy. Slow, slow, slow," he had murmured as though to a small child. His electric blue eyes had burned fiercely.

"Slow, slow," he had continued, "they don't want you. They haven't even seen us. We're nothing." He had continued until Jamie had finally realised that the militia literally hadn't noticed them. They, the two tramps, had simply been a part of the scenery. They had sat there, tending their fire and drinking their tea while around them the militia had seemed to be engaged in some kind of an exercise.

"Money," Jamie murmured, making it sound almost a question. He was still wondering, vaguely, why the old man would want money. However, just as the old man seemed happy not to ask direct questions, Jamie felt uncomfortable about directing any at him.

"Yes," the old man picked up, "everyone needs money," he paused, some long-distant thought seemed to have attracted his mind for the moment. The familiar smile, a little more distant than usual, crossed his face.

They walked on a few paces. Jamie was learning to scan the pavement, the road and the grass for...anything! You never knew what you might find. Only a few minutes ago the old man had been over the moon to find an almost new boot lace. It had been perfect apart from one of its ends being a little frayed.

Yesterday, Jamie had found enough good food to feel that he was contributing his proper share to the day's meals. He had been disproportionately pleased with himself. Acquiring a new skill, however simple it might seem to the outsider, always gave him pleasure.

In the distance was a rubbish shed. It was quite a small one, a modern one with a thin roof supported about a foot above the walls by metal piping. The old man nodded at it, the question clear on his face. He wanted Jamie's opinion.

"I'd say," Jamie began slowly, recalling everything that the old man had told him, "its maybe a four carter. Probably quite clean." He looked around at the surrounding area - newish, but poor, "Not much for us, I'd guess."

The old man was nodding. "But..." he prompted.

"But," Jamie grinned, "it's always worth a look." He looked sideways at the old man.

The old man was grinning. It was always worth a look.

+

Lying in the bath, she tried again to count them. But, she found that it wasn't possible. There had been too many men. She lay back and stretched in the hot water. In the background, a Leonard Cohen CD drifted in from the stereo. Both the stereo and the CD were gifts from 'visitors'.

She felt good. Despite everything, she felt good. She was doing something. She was achieving something. She knew that if her own people had known what she was doing they would be proud of her. She was helping to destroy the enemy, to undermine the enemy where it really mattered. She felt really good about what she was doing.

The music was good, too. She almost knew these lyrics by heart, and sang along with them as she lay in the bath.

"Give me back the ..."

She loved it. Somehow, Leonard Cohen seemed to sum it all up. Things are going to slide, to slide in all directions. These words often passed through her mind as her visitors used her. Things were sliding, all right. It was late. She'd had her last one for the day. This was a final hot bath before sleep. She lay in the frothy water luxuriating in the warmth, absorbing the 'relaxing' bath oil that another visitor had given her. It had been part of a set of four, one of which was 'sensuous', which was almost certainly the one that had caught his eye. Time for sleep! She was beginning to drift off in the bath. She shook herself awake, and pulled herself out of the bath, reaching for the towel. Tomorrow, she was going to see Grzesiek.

+

She didn't enjoy the sex with Grzesiek. She had never actually enjoyed sex. She enjoyed what she was doing with Grzesiek and why she was doing it, but she derived no pleasure or enjoyment from the sex itself.

Anita had never had the opportunity to enjoy sex. She had been a virgin when the Russians had arrived, which was not unusual for a sixteen year old in Poland then, and apart from turning to Grzesiek, had never chosen a sexual partner for herself. They had, instead, been thrust upon her. She had been used and abused in the most literal sense.

But she was stronger than most, and much stronger than she looked. When she had realised that the only way her mother would stay out of a work camp was if she, Anita, provided 'services', she decided to knuckle down and do what was necessary. She had always been a fast learner. And learning to act for her visitors was no exception. What they wanted, she could provide, but at a high price to herself.

The brittle shell of her composure sometimes came close to cracking. It was all she could do to keep up her act, but what gave her her strength was the fact that she was helping to destroy the enemy. That the enemy would, one day, be destroyed she did not doubt. She knew her history. Poland had been trodden under before, it had even disappeared completely from the map for a while, but it had always bounced back up. And she was a part of that bounce. She was using her body as a deadly weapon. She was doing her bit. History would repeat itself.

She did like Grzesiek, but she doubted that she would ever choose to have sex with anyone unless there was a reason for it. A compelling reason. Liking someone was nowhere enough.

And as for love, that was a word that she hadn't even considered since the day that her family had been taken and she had been raped in the interview room by the two young militia. Russian animals! Sex for Anita was not 'making love', it was a tool for making war. And on that front she was a good warrior. Tantalisingly good.

Sitting on the bus, returning from Grzesiek, she smiled gently to herself as she recalled the ancient Polish joke: If you stand a Pole between a Russian and a German and you give the Pole a gun, who will he shoot first? The German, of course. Why? Business before pleasure. Despite its age, it seemed a particularly fitting joke now.

She pulled herself out of her seat, aware of the momentary glance of admiration from the good looking young man who had caught just a glimpse of her long leg below her calf length coat as she moved to stand up. I'm not for you, she thought, you look like a nice Polish boy. I'm just a toy for the enemy to play with—at their peril.

Chapter Twelve

WAR DAY + 422

POZNAN
POLAND

Four weeks had passed since Jamie had left the work camp. Four weeks of blessed life, four weeks of the gift of life that he had expected to lose that night on the wire.

Four extra weeks. Four weeks that he might never have had. He stretched luxuriously. It was a beautiful morning, and the night had been fabulously mild. Mild nights meant that they didn't need to be so choosy about where they slept. Mind you, they always kept their heads down at night. They'd find somewhere unobtrusive to settle down and then stay put until dawn.

The old man had constantly reassured Jamie that both the Policja and the Militia would leave them alone, would in fact ignore them, but it had made no difference. Jamie wouldn't go near them.

Still, the old man had asked no direct questions, but he'd seen the uniform and there was only one place a uniform like that could have come from. And Jamie had said a lot more in general conversation than he had realised—he had grown very relaxed with the old man—and the old man had put two and two together several times and had generally come up with four.

What particularly puzzled the old man was not why Jamie's first language was obviously not Polish, a fact that neither of them had ever actually mentioned, but which was painfully obvious, nor was it why, or even how, Jamie had escaped from a camp and nor was it why he had been in the camp in the first place, but the big puzzler was why Jamie used a Polish name when, if his first language wasn't Polish, he presumably wasn't Polish.

The old man had often pondered this imponderable. He liked puzzles. The better the puzzle, the more he liked it. And he would have put money on his hunch that his companion's real name was not Janus. Real money. He grinned to himself.

He didn't ask Jamie direct questions both out of respect for the man's, for every mans' privacy, and out of the joy of watching the facts unroll gently over the days, weeks and months...at any moment another piece of the puzzle might fall into place. Or, perhaps, it would never be complete. Perhaps the puzzle would never be complete. It wasn't important. It was all part the game. He smiled.

Across the room, on the first floor of the rather grand abandoned building, he saw that Jamie was struggling into a sitting position. Looking at the light pouring through the window, it must be a suitable time to start the day.

He struggled up. He always found it a struggle, actually getting out of the warm comfort of bed. They'd been staying in this house for a few days now, he wasn't sure how long exactly, because it was so ridiculously comfortable. They even had running water.

It felt a bit like cheating. They really should be out on the road! Last night they'd heated the water over a home-made boiler and had had hot baths. Fantastic! Ridiculous! His grin widened.

Across the room, Jamie was sitting, still wrapped in blankets, grinning sleepily back.

"Good morning," the old man sounded on top of the world. He felt on top of the world.

"Good morning," Jamie replied. The old man's grin was contagious. The weather looked fabulous through the window.

As they prepared breakfast the old man said that he thought that they ought to be moving on.

"I don't feel comfortable in a house," he had concluded. Jamie had looked at him, questions all over his face. He had just shaved in hot water—it had been glorious! He rubbed his chin.

He said nothing. He'd learnt a lot from the old man, an unimaginably large amount, and he particularly admired him for not asking direct questions. 'Just roll with it', he'd told himself once or twice, or was it a million times? 'Just roll with it'. It had worked. The old man knew what he was doing.

After a few moments the old man continued in answer to Jamie's unasked questions.

"If we keep moving no one will notice us..." he paused. He knew that he wanted to move on simply for the sake of moving, but he also knew that his words were true and that they would give Jamie a reason to move, too, " but if we stay here we become a part of the community. We'll begin to belong here, and then one day someone will notice us and maybe ask us for papers, or they'll expect taxes or they'll want to know what we're doing here."

Jamie's face showed that he'd answered the unasked question.

"Our strength is in our moving. So long as we keep moving, and so long as we look like this," he stroked his grey beard with the air of a General praising a new tank, "people won't see us."

It was true. Jamie wouldn't have lasted more than half a day on his own. With the old man he'd managed four weeks. Twenty eight days! Life!

"You're right, of course," already Jamie wondered if he should have shaved. He rubbed his chin reflectively. It felt good, though.

They began to gather together a few things to take with them. The things that they wouldn't take they would hide and perhaps return to them when they needed them. All over the edge of Poznan they seemed to have hidden little caches of valuables. Second line valuables, things that they didn't actually need today, but which might come in handy at any time.

A short while later they emerged from the house, looking for all the world like a pair of tramps. The sort of people that no one notices, except perhaps with a hint of sympathy or distaste. A closer look, had you had the inclination, would have told you that they were clean, happy and well fed. But it's best, and most common, that you don't look at all.

The older man trod carefully and gently on the grass beside the pavement. He was particularly fond of his shoes and wanted them to last the summer if possible. They were quality leather trainers. True, they weren't new, indeed they'd seen perhaps a little more than their share of life already, but quality trainers like these were hard to come by.

The younger man walked beside him, happy to walk on the pavement itself.

As they went they chatted quietly in the brilliant sunshine of the early morning.

+

They were discussing geography and navigation. Well, one or the other. He wasn't sure. What they were actually doing was that the old man was asking him where he thought that they were and discussing with him how to tell where they were.

It wasn't difficult. There was none of that nonsense with the stars—the old man called it nonsense because it was too complex, Jamie kept his mouth shut. He wasn't sure if the old man meant that it was too complex or that it was too complex for Jamie. The old man used two things, and they were both simple and they both worked well enough for their own needs. There was the sun. Since most of their walking was done during daylight, especially now that their day was growing longer and that Jamie was so patently paranoid about being on the road at night, the sun was the ideal tool. A glance at the sun let you know which way you were headed.

So long as you knew where you were when you started you knew where you were headed. Like the old man said, it was simple.

And the second thing that he used was street maps. Every village, town and city had a large map, normally painted on a large wooden board at the bus station, the railway station, if it was in a different place, and in the larger towns and cities these maps would be dotted around the place. They generally showed the built up area in some detail as well as showing where the town lay in relation to other populated areas. So far, though, they'd spent all their time on the outskirts of Poznan, so Jamie hadn't seen so many of these.

In answer to the old man's question, Jamie responded, "I reckon that we're headed North...Northish. Perhaps North West," he peered at the sun. It was early yet. Difficult to be sure, "Yep, I'd say North West. Poznan's on our right, most of it, anyway, so we're walking up the bottom left hand side of Poznan." He paused.

The old man was nodding, a smile on his face. The smile on his face. He was always smiling. Jamie found that he was smiling in return. Contagious.

"So, we're at about eight o'clock," he meant that if you viewed Poznan as the face of a clock, they were at the position of the eight.

The old man nodded. "Closer to nine, I'd say," he said, "it's early. A little later I think we'll find that we're actually heading North and that the city is all to our right. Yep," he agreed with himself, "about nine." They walked on.

Jamie brought the conversation back to the stars and mentioned that he'd once had a poem published. The connection wasn't immediately obvious to the old man, but he was happy to listen without interrupting. Poems, eh? He'd thought that there was more to this young lad than met the eye.

+

She wondered how long it took. She knew that you could catch AIDs from a single sexual contact with an infected person, but actually how likely was that? And presumably, one increased the likelihood by repeating the contact. She hoped so. She hoped most fervently that she had caught the virus right at the start and had been passing it on ever since.

It was impossible to tell. And, of course, if she was to display any symptom of the virus she would no longer be able to pass it on. Whatever she did, she had to appear healthy. Any indication that she was not one hundred percent healthy and she would be out of business. Out of the war.

But right now, she was young, beautiful, desirable, and willing. And the visitors kept on coming. And one by one they fell to her charms, ignoring common sense and years of indoctrination, the animal in them choosing unprotected sex. The animals!

A bit like nine pin bowling. She smiled. Strike! Her smile grew broader. She rolled out of bed, padded into the living room, and flicked on the stereo. Leonard Cohen, again. She loved the death in his voice. She stood in the window, lighting her first cigarette of the day, breathing in the throat-biting smoke with intense pleasure. One of her few real pleasures.

"I've seen the future, baby: it is murder," she sang along with the CD, exhaling smoke. It is murder. Too right.

She watched the life outside the flat. The large expanse of worn grass, criss-crossed by concrete foot paths. A few kids, a few adults. A dog messing in the children's sandpit. A squeaking swing. A dozen other five story blocks within two hundred metres, each painted a different colour, but otherwise identical.

So what was new today? Sweet FA!.

Except that she had been given a bleep. Now, she was booked by bleep. She glanced at it. Blank. It was new idea. Whoever was keeping her diary had become voiceless. She would receive a name and a time, a first name only, and she had to be ready. The bleep could also accept whole messages, so she supposed that if anyone had any special preferences they could send them on in advance, too...if they didn't mind their preferences being on record, which didn't seem awfully likely.

It did mean, though, that she could leave the flat without the fear of missing a telephone call.

Neat! That meant that she wouldn't miss an opportunity to infect someone. Anything that increased her contact with the enemy was a good thing.

+

She opened the front door. The man who came in was a stranger. The bleep had told her that his name was Igor. He was much older than she had expected He was wearing the uniform of the Russian military intelligence, possibly the most despised and feared Russian form of militia in Poland. His face was round and ruddy, his stomach large and soft, pushing against his perfectly pressed tunic.

Oh dear, she thought. This might be hard work. She shook his hand formally, but he held her hand and kissed her cheek. He smelt faintly of expensive after shave. He removed his shoes, and looked around vaguely for a pair of house shoes.

"Would you like a drink?" she asked very formally.

"Yes, please. What have you got?" She had got used to this drawing room formality, and it seemed to be appreciated.

"Vodka or juices," she smiled sweetly. He slipped his feet into a pair of leather house shoes, and looked at her—and felt his loins twitch. He had only just heard about Anita, but having heard what he had heard he had decided that he had to visit to see her for himself, and he had instantly liked what he saw. An obviously educated girl from a good family, and pretty to boot. Very pretty, in fact, and dressed very nicely in a short plain black skirt and a white cotton, embroidered shirt. Very nice. And his for the taking. His loins were definitely waking up. She followed him into the living room.

"A vodka, please, I think."

"What would you like? I have several."

He smiled, appreciating her very much.

"Wyborowa?"

"Not Smirnof?" Was she teasing him?

"No, Wyborowa, please. If you have it."

"Of course," she turned to the drinks cupboard, "I just thought that you might prefer something from back home."

He didn't respond, but let himself down heavily onto the sofa, watching her pretty legs as she poured the drinks. It was a long time since he'd had sex, and she was truly appealing, but it wasn't really what he wanted. He was no longer young. She had turned towards him, still standing at the other end of the room at the drinks cupboard, her hips thrust very slightly towards him.

He could almost imagine running his hand up the inside of one her thighs. Almost. But, the fact that she was available—provided by the state and so definitely available, took some of the attraction away.

"Sit down," he suggested. She moved towards him.

"No, no. On the chair. Where I can see you."

She smiled. "Security?"

"What?"

"It was a joke. I wondered if being able to see me was a question of security," she indicated his uniform with a movement of her head, brushing her long blond hair back from her face with her hand.

He smiled. This was probably the first time a Polish citizen had made a joke for his benefit. He was totally aware of the effect that his uniform had on the Poles. He was generally feared and loathed. He put the vodka glass to his lips and emptied it.

"Ah...good."

"Thank you." She took a sip from her glass.

There was a moment's pause. She got up, and walked to the stereo. He watched her legs.

"Would you like to go to the theatre?"

"The theatre?" Had she heard right? She refilled his glass and left the bottle of vodka with him.

"Would you like to?"

"I don't think I can."

"I'm sure you can. Would you like to?"

She knew that her next visitor was due in ninety minutes. Weekend evenings were a busy time. She couldn't possibly go out.

"No, I'd love to. I really would. But I can't. Really." She had returned to her chair.

"I can arrange it," he said with complete confidence.

I'm sure you can, she thought, I'm sure you can. What was he? "Are you a very important man?" The direct question was often the best way.

He smiled, "Not very," he lied.

"A Colonel?" She knew that he was more than that.

He nodded.

"But the stars?" He was wearing three stars on his collar.

"Ah, yes," he smiled again, this time more gently. Anita realised that he was very tired.

"You're a General, perhaps?"

"Perhaps, yes." He emptied his glass again, and refilled it.

She looked at him, a pretty smile on her pretty face. Without thinking, he shook his head very gently.

"Would you like, perhaps," she asked, "to listen to a relaxation tape?" .

He looked at her quizzically.

"It's very quiet, very gentle. We could just lie down, on our backs, perfectly still. It's...," what was it? "...very relaxing." This sometimes worked. She would get them onto the bed, play the tape, and before long...

"That sounds nice."

"You go and lie down," she opened the living room door, stepped into the hall, and opened the bedroom door, "I'll just put the tape on." The flat was so small that when the doors were open, she could speak from any room to anyone in any other room and be heard with ease. It was just 50 square metres. Big enough for two, sometimes three, generations of Poles.

He lifted himself to his feet, and walked into the bedroom, letting himself down heavily onto the bed. When she had put on the tape and returned to the bedroom, he was lying flat out on one side of the large bed, his eyes closed. She kicked off her house shoes, slipped off her skirt and shirt, and lay down beside him, gently

Two minutes later she realised from his gentle snoring that he was asleep.

WAR DAY + 442

THE WORK CAMP
POZNAN
POLAND

They shot the priest at midday. They had made him dig his own grave in the morning. The whole camp had been kept in. There had been no factory work and the main gates had been closed all day, opening only to let in the night workers. No one left. Extra guards patrolled both inside and outside the wire.

The prisoners had been called to the parade ground at 11.15. Hundreds, thousands, who knew how many, dirty, smelly, half-starved and dog tired, they stood, apparently almost senseless, and yet knowing what was coming. They had been turned about face so that they could see the priest standing beside a mound of earth just outside the wire. There was nothing to show that he was a priest, nothing except his resignation. He seemed prepared for death.

He was not tall, he was not good looking. He looked old and very tired. His face and hands were smeared in sweat and the soil that he had been digging. His clothes were the same as theirs, standard camp uniform. His hair was too long, grey and dirty. His beard was several days old. Despite the way he looked, they knew that he was probably in his middle thirties. He looked the way they felt.

268

He was a Roman Catholic priest. A few of the prisoners recognised him from before the second turn. He'd been a popular man during a period in which the Catholic Church itself had been suffering a downturn in popularity because of its stance on contraception and abortion and its desire to bring these into the field of politics and legislation.

All morning this man had sweated over his grave. All morning his mind had been in turmoil. It was not for himself that his mind suffered. His own fate was set. Unlike the early martyrs he had not been offered an alternative to death. He had not been offered life in exchange for denouncing his faith. He would die whatever, and to that he was reconciled.

What concerned him was the fate of the man who had informed the camp authorities that he was a priest. What concerned him was what the other prisoners would do to this man.

At midday he had stood beside his mound of earth. His morning's work. His last morning's work. His muscles ached; he wasn't used to the exercise. Digging was very different from the factory work to which he had recently grown accustomed.

One of the soldiers offered him a cigarette. For a moment he considered refusing, but decided that that would have been an empty gesture.

He'd love a cigarette! He drew hard on the filter tip cigarette, his first for some time. A very long time, he thought. His fingers were damp from the soil and the cigarette quickly became shapeless in their grip.

It reminded him of the cigarettes that he had shared as a schoolboy. They, too, had become shapeless under their schoolboy fingers, as a result of the unusual demand that a shared cigarette is subjected to.

As he approached the end of his cigarette, they asked him to move around to the front of the hole that he'd dug. He moved around slowly and carefully, the raw soil sticking to his shoes. In his right hand he cupped the cigarette.

It was difficult to imagine that this was happening. A part of him wanted to cry, to cry not because he wanted sympathy but because this all seemed so terribly...what?...poignant? This was an awful moment.

Not for him. For him this was a form of fulfilment. Not a form that he would have chosen and not a form that he had foreseen when he had entered the priesthood, but none the less a form of fulfilment. No, this was an awful moment for Poland, for the world.

To stand a man before his comrades and to execute him for what he believed, to cut him down in public because he believed that the same had been done to another man two thousand years ago was a dreadful step backwards.

A soldier stepped forward, turned him and placed something leather around his wrists, holding his hands behind his back. The hole didn't look very deep, although it had taken so desperately long to dig. The soldier turned him back towards the parade ground—where he could see hundreds of faces looking up to him—and took a hood out of his tunic.

"No," he shook his head. He didn't want to die in darkness.

The soldier glanced at his warrant officer, who shrugged. He smiled, perhaps kindly, and said something quietly in poor Polish, before turning away. He didn't catch what the soldier had said.

He stood. His arms were fastened behind his back. In front of him, four soldiers. Beyond them, and slightly to his left, the parade ground.

He didn't hear the shots. He didn't feel the bullets take his life.

At midday, almost to the second, his lifeless body slumped into the grave.

+

That night there was hell to pay in shed nine.

Bogdan, who had hoped that life would be made easier for Malgorzata in exchange for the information about the priest, would never know if she was going to benefit. That night, he was torn apart by his fellow prisoners.

The next morning Bogdan's body was found by the guards, a bloody mess in the corner of his shed.

That afternoon six men were chosen at random from the shed and were shot in the parade ground. The seven bodies were taken away in lorries.

+

The entryphone buzzed. It was one of her regulars.

"It's Leszek."

271

"Come on up," he could hear the welcome in her voice. He climbed the steps quickly, shut the front door firmly behind him, dropped his thick woollen overcoat onto the shoe rack, and pulled her into his arms.

This was the kind of visitor that Anita liked. Fast and to the point.

In moments, her blouse was open, his hands unclipping her bra, his lips on her breasts, while she was unbuckling his belt, unbuttoning his trousers, sliding down the zip, and slipping her hand into his underpants.

"Wow! You're big, today," she whispered into his ear.

Half an hour later he had left, a big smile on his face.

Quick work, she thought, as she pushed the front door closed. A job well done. She smiled to herself, as she lobbed another unused condom into the loo.

WAR DAY + 450

POZNAN
POLAND

The old man mentioned the car on a Tuesday. At least, Jamie thought that it had been a Tuesday. He had started to try to remember what day it was each day. Just as a sort of mental exercise. It hadn't been important for so long, and it was of no importance now, but somehow it felt like a good thing to do.

Like jogging, or aerobics, before the second turn. Something that one felt that one ought to do. Actually, he'd rather enjoyed jogging. Not the actual act of jogging, but the feeling of general health and goodwill that it had seemed to bestow. Aerobics was fun, too, but he'd had so much trouble getting the routines right, and just when he'd managed it the teacher—normally a sickeningly fit young woman—would change the routine and he would have to start learning again what seemed to come naturally to the others. He did not seem to understand the rhythm. He had no feel for the movement. He'd always felt such a fool being at least half a step out of sequence for a large part of each session. He had, he supposed, been out of step both physically and metaphysically.

He remembered what a friend of his had told him—Jane, was it? A long time ago—that she had been told. She'd been going to a counsellor after her marriage had collapsed. She and her husband, her ex-husband, had attended counselling for several weeks. Apparently it had helped, although Jamie had never really understood how. Anyway, what Jane had told him was that one day when she had just said that she felt that she ought to do something, the counsellor had stopped her and asked her, "What's this ought? What do you mean ought?" It had taken Jane a moment to figure out what the woman was asking, but when she did the message was clear. After that, whenever Jane (or her ex husband) had used the word 'ought' the counsellor had stopped them and had asked them to work out who wanted the thing that ought to be done. After a while they had both learned to avoid using the word 'ought' altogether. Apparently, it had helped them to put into words, and then to understand, who it was that was making the demands.

The old man had mentioned the car in passing. At the time it had seemed of little significance to Jamie. He should've known better than that. The old man hardly ever mentioned anything that remained insignificant for long. Apparently this car had been in a private garage in an abandoned house since before the second turn. The significance of this also escaped Jamie who knew nothing about the tagging of vehicles.

One day, probably a Friday, the old man took him to see the car. They'd spent the night in an abandoned house, not unlike a hundred others, when he mentioned that the car was in the garage in the basement. After breakfast they'd gone down to have a look.

Jamie had been astonished at the vehicle's condition. It looked as though it had been properly looked after rather than having been abandoned for over a year.

At the time, Jamie's most valuable possession was a Sony personal compact disc player. He'd found it, naturally enough, in one of the carts. It looked as though it might work perfectly. Astonishingly enough he'd also found a compact disc. Just one. Well, he'd been lucky to find that. Naturally, the disc had been Vivaldi's *Four Seasons*.

But he had a problem. Batteries. He had none, and nor did the old man have any. Occasionally they found batteries in the carts, but so far they had always - not surprisingly - been used. Completely used. Flat. Dud. Finished. Useless.

He hadn't got enough money from bottles to buy any. Batteries were desperately expensive. They seemed to be one of the many things that the new regime had either put onto a back burner for the moment or that they were simply incapable of producing. But, none the less, he carried the compact disc player with him everywhere. He kept it in one of his coat pockets. The old man didn't say anything, but Jamie suspected that the old man thought that it was a waste of time.

Sometimes, he'd take it out in the evening and look at it. It was useless.

He supposed that the old man felt the way about the car that he felt about the compact disc player. It was a wonderful find, but absolutely useless.

+

"I have this dream," Grzesiek was leaning back on his sofa bed, drawing luxuriously on one of Anita's rather splendid cigarettes. She grunted, encouraging him to continue.

"To get out, to get away from all this."

"How? Where to?"

"Just across to Germany."

"What would you do there?"

"Go to college," he smiled. The dream was very much alive in his head.

"How would you do that?"

"What?"

"How would you go to college? How would you live - support yourself? Do you speak German?"

"I'd work. Pizza boy, or something. There's plenty of work over there."

"How do you know?"

"I listen to the radio, their radio. German radio."

"I thought there was a lot of unemployment in Germany."

"Maybe. That's what the Russians want us to believe. Who knows? But even if it's true, there's always work if you'll do the work that no one else wants to do...like delivering pizzas late on a Saturday night, or..."

"Yes," she interrupted, "but what would you study?"

"What would I like to study, or what would I study?"

"What would you like to study?"

"Don't laugh?"

"Of course not," she was smiling her beautiful smile.

He paused. "What I'd actually like to study is medicine, but I haven't got the grades," he paused, again, to see if she would laugh. She didn't. Her beautiful smile was still flickering around her mouth and eyes, but she was regarding him seriously. "What I would probably study is law."

"Law?"

"Yes. I'd like to do something that would let me help people. I know it's a dream, but to be able to help people would mean so much."

"Is your German good enough?"

"My German is very good. I got very good grades in German, and I study it every day. It's all I do."

"I had no idea," she was impressed. "My German is very poor."

"Yes, but you studied English," she had, too. She hadn't realised that he would remember. They had been to the same schools since she had been seven, but he was way older than her. She had noticed him, as one might notice an older pupil, but hadn't considered that he might have noticed her. She grinned a big grin.

"How do you know that?"

"You told me," he laughed, "Anyway, you gorgeous lump," he pulled her towards him, "We've got to get out, first."

"We!?" she was startled.

"You don't think I'm going to go without you, do you?"

She sat up straight. He was serious!

"Can we get out? What do you mean?"

"Like I said, it's a dream. But it must be possible."

"How?"

"Get a scholarship to a university in Berlin?"

"That really is dreaming!"

"Take a package holiday to Prague, and just not come back?"

"We'd never get an exit visa, let alone a passport."

"I have a passport."

"Jesus," she was shocked. Anita instantly covered her mouth with her hand. She had been a devout Catholic before the churches had been closed. For an instant she prayed for forgiveness for using His name in vain.

He was grinning.

"You've got one," she asked. He nodded.

"How? Have you got your Dowod Osobisty, too?" she was astonished.

"I just didn't hand it in. Yes, I have."

"And nothing happened?"

"Nothing happened."

"Wow!"

She looked at him in a new light. It was a very serious offence to hold both a passport and a Dowod Osobisty at the same time. One or the other, normally the passport, was always to be stored with the policja. There had to be good a reason to have possession of a passport.

"Anyway," she realised, "that makes it even more difficult for you to get a visa. In fact, you can't get a visa, because that would mean telling them that you've got your passport. And then they certainly wouldn't give you one."

He nodded. "But I do have a passport, which means that I would be recognised outside Poland as a legit person."

"Is a passport that important?"

"I don't know, but it would help me establish who I am, if I got out." She nodded her agreement. He continued, "And it must have some significance, otherwise why would the Russians want to control our passports so tightly?"

"I guess so. I don't know."

"I reckon that having a passport makes you a real person outside Poland."

She lit another cigarette, shaking one out for Grzesiek. "So, how do we get out?" she didn't believe that it was possible.

"Steal a car and drive through the border?"

"Not a chance."

"Cross on foot?"

"Where. What about the Oder?"

"Up North, where the border is west of the Oder."

"What, and walk across, just like that?"

"I don't know. It must be possible."

"I think not."

"Something's got to be possible!"

"I'm not so sure," and she wasn't. If there was a way, people would be doing it, now.

"There's no life for us here, Anita."

She looked at him. His young old face. Her heart reached out for him. He was so full of hope. She shook her head gently, her eyes on his. We are condemned, she thought. There is no escape. Only in your dreams, dear Grzesiek. She leaned towards him, and for the first time in her life she kissed an adult male, other than her father, because she wanted to.

+

In the back of the big limousine, Anita stretched out luxuriously. The car was longer than any car she had been in before and it seemed to move both effortlessly and noiselessly, as the lights of Poznan flashed past.

"How did you enjoy that?" He was referring to the ballet.

"It was beautiful, Igor. Absolutely fantastic," she was positively glowing. The two glasses of sparkling wine had gone straight to her head. She wrapped herself around him, stroking his thigh, letting the new evening dress ride provocatively high. She wanted to intoxicate him with her body. The car was filled with the gentle air of her expensive perfume. The music was slow and sleepy.

He was quiet. They were going to his town flat. She hadn't been there, before, but she hoped that this would do the trick. He'd been to her flat four times, now, but not once had they had sex. He had simply chosen to talk, or to sleep as the relaxation tape played. She wanted this man. He was obviously important. She wanted to screw him, to infect him, to destroy him. He was almost certainly the most important member of the invading force that she had yet had as a visitor.

A few moments later and they were there, the limo pulling over, the driver leaping out and opening the rear door, his eyes and face expressionless as the couple climbed out. The flat was beautiful, truly beautiful. It was also enormous.

"Sit down," he commanded, gently. She chose a large, voluptuous sofa, and sat, tucking her legs under her, demurely pulling her tiny black dress back towards her knees.

"Vodka?"

"Yes, please."

He poured her a generous drink and sat in an armchair opposite her with a glass and the bottle.

Half an hour later, still in the armchair and still fully clothed, the bottle almost empty, he was asleep.

"Shit!" Experience had shown that waking him was a waste of time. She picked up the phone and ordered a taxi.

Chapter Thirteen

WAR DAY + 492
POZNAN
POLAND

"You want to get out, don't you?" It was the first time that the old man had asked him directly. The first time that he'd asked him anything in the way of a direct question. But it was a fact. A fact that they both knew. He didn't need to expand. They both knew that Jamie wanted to get out, and they both knew that what Jamie wanted to get out of was what used to be called Poland.

They'd been drinking. This was the first time that Jamie had had any alcohol for over a year. More than that! For a long time, anyway. It was also the first time that he'd seen the old man drink.

Earlier that day the old man had paused thoughtfully outside a bottle shop. He'd dug his hands deep into a couple of interior pockets and had started to count notes. Jamie had dug deep, too, and they'd bought themselves more alcohol than they could decently expect to drink in one evening.

The old man had favoured vodka, and he hadn't messed around. He'd gone for quality. Jamie couldn't tell the difference personally, but he had known what was quality and what was not, in the past, and he'd noted the shop assistant's response. Himself, he'd gone for beer. He liked a strong beer. The weak beers were a waste of time and vodka, he found, was altogether too efficient.

They'd returned to their shelter, an old heating plant, and had sat outside in the sunshine. They didn't touch the alcohol until dark. As darkness fell, the old man had lit a small fire around the back and together they had created a light meal; fresh vegetables boiled lightly, rice and a little grated cheese. Jamie would have liked to have prepared a white sauce for the vegetables, but they had no fresh milk.

They had crawled into the heating plant with their meal. A street lamp almost directly outside shone in through the high windows. It gave everything a yellow glow. No one could see in because the row of windows was up near the ceiling.

The old man opened a bottle of vodka, twisting the top with the audible sound of the seal breaking.

Which reminded Jamie with a start of dismay that he hadn't got a bottle opener for his beer. Which was incredibly stupid. The old man must have read the look on his face, because he reached into his waistcoat and pulled out an opener.

Wow!

"Thanks," Jamie was embarrassed by his continued reliance on the old man. He didn't know how long it had been now, but it had been weeks. Several weeks.

He opened a bottle of beer, and lifted it to his mouth.

"Lovely!"

The old man grinned at him. He grinned back. He always did. He couldn't help it. They ate their food in silence. They ate slowly and carefully. It was good food and it deserved all their attention.

Some time later, the old man said to Jamie, "You want to get out, don't you?"

He looked at the old man in surprise. He paused. He'd learnt a lot from the old man, maybe he'd learnt everything that he knew from him. It certainly felt like it. He'd learnt not to rush things. "No point," the old man had told him. Simple as that. "No point."

He paused, and tried to think this through. But there was nothing to think through. He trusted the old man, that was all that counted. If he trusted him, he could answer him. If he didn't trust him, what was he doing here now? He trusted him.

"Yes," he said slowly and carefully.

They looked at each other. The old man's electric blue eyes penetrating deep into his own.

"I can show you," he said, "a way."

"You can?" he hadn't meant it to sound like a question. Asking a question suggested doubt, and if the old man said something he didn't doubt it.

"Yes," he took a slow swig from his bottle. Jamie was surprised that he hadn't produced a vodka glass. That would have been more in the old man's style.

"If you want to go, I can show you the way."

"I want to go." Did he? Yes, he did. This life was all very well, but it couldn't last. One day he'd get caught, and that'd be it. And if something happened to the old man? Well, he'd learnt a lot from him, that was true, but he doubted very much that he'd learnt enough to survive on his own. And if there was a way out, a way to civilisation, a way home he'd take it. Yes, he'd take it.

"Where're you from?" the old man was still looking at him. His electric blue eyes probing his face. He'd told Jamie once just how much he could learn from a person by looking at them. It wasn't so much a person's words, he had said, as the way they said them and the way that they looked while they said them.

Jamie looked away and took a mouthful of beer. When he looked up the old man was still looking at him, his face gentle, his eyes bright. The old man smiled.

"Which camp are you from?" Was that what he'd meant when he'd asked where he was from? Jamie had thought that he'd meant which country was he from.

"I'm from Konin," the old man said slowly and carefully, naming a town some kilometres to the east of Poznan, "big work camp on the east side of the town. Walked out one day. I'd had enough. Couldn't take any more."

Jamie stared at him. It hadn't occurred to him that the old man had got out of a camp. He just sat and stared. They each took a mouthful from their respective bottles.

"I got out of the camp around the south side of Poznan. The day before...the night before you found me in the cart," they both grinned.

"How'd you do it?"

"Over the wire," Jamie tried to sound neutral.

"Over the wire!" the old man was amazed, "you must have been desperate."

"I was. Reckoned I had nothing to lose...and now you've shown me what I could have lost," he lifted the bottle, looking at the label. But he didn't mean the alcohol, oh no. He meant life.

The old man's grin was still stuck on his face.

"Oh my," he said, "Over the wire, over the wire," he said it slowly and carefully, his voice expressing wonder and perhaps admiration. It was difficult to be sure; the beer was going to Jamie's head.

"I've got a daughter," he said suddenly, and seemed to sober up.

"Yes?" Jamie was surprised. Somehow he hadn't seen the old man as the family type.

"She's seventeen," he seemed to think for a moment, "she's a lovely girl."

In Jamie's opinion, every father considered his daughters to be lovely, but he kept his mouth shut, and just nodded.

"When they took me," he was shaking his head, "they took my wife and my sons, too."

For a moment he said no more. Jamie could see the struggle on the old man's face. What he was about to say was going to cause him some pain to get out. To put into words.

"They put her in a flat," Jamie assumed that the old man meant his daughter. Jamie kept his mouth shut. Again, the old man said nothing for a moment. He could see the tears in the old man's eyes.

286

"Men visit her. They send men to her," the old man lifted the bottle to hide his face from Jamie. For a moment Jamie wasn't sure what the old man had meant.

"She was a school girl! She hadn't left school, just a child..." his voice faded. It was too much for him, but Jamie had got the message.

"...and they use her like a whore!"

They sat, then, for a while saying nothing. Each man alone with his thoughts. Some minutes later, the old man asked,

"Will you take her with you?" His meaning wasn't entirely clear to Jamie. His head was befuddled with beer and the old man seemed to be taking conversational short cuts and leaving him behind. He looked up. The old man's eyes were electric blue and tearless again.

"Out?"

"Yes."

"Yes, but how?"

"I can show you the way if you'll take her out."

"Won't you come?" something in the old man's voice had suggested that he wouldn't be there.

"No," the old man said rather sadly, "I've got a wife and sons in this country."

"You show me how," Jamie promised, "and I'll take her out."

+

General Igor Siemiornowicz sat in his spacious office reviewing the surveillance report. The computer traces were consistent and displeasing. The girl was visiting the Morawski's flat regularly. He flicked the screen back and forth between the days. A couple of times each week, sometimes more often, Central showed her at ulica Grobla. Maybe more, if she was leaving the bleep behind. Silently, he swore again, and picked up the phone.

"I'd like you to pick up the Morawski boy. Turn the place over. As soon as you can fit it in," he paused, "but make sure the Orszulik girl's not there before you go in." He turned back to the screen, the frown still on his face.

+

There was no knock on the door. One moment all was tranquil in the flat, the next moment the front door had appeared to implode with the sound of splintering wood, and the hall was full of uniforms.

"Freeze," a voice had bellowed.

And within moments, they had spread through the whole flat. Grzesiek Morawski was held face down on the floor of his room, a military boot firmly in the small of his back. In their room, Mr and Mrs Morawski looked up stunned as the militia stormed into the room.

"What...?" Mr Morawski started.

"Shut it!" One of the militia was holding up a piece of paper which Mr Morawski assumed was authorisation for the raid. He shut his mouth. Very quickly, they were patted down. No surprises. No weapons.

"Stay there," indicating the sofa, "and stay silent. We'll be gone in five minutes. If you're no trouble, you'll not see us again. If you make so much as a peep, we'll bust your teeth." A wave of the butt of his weapon indicated how the damage would be done.

It took them two minutes to turn Grzesiek's room upside down. Every single item, from clothing to books, from cigarettes to school notes, and even the drawers themselves, was thrown onto the floor. Grzesiek lay on the floor, held down by the militia's booted foot, shouted down into silence each time he began to protest. Nothing of any interest was found.

Two of them reached down and lifted him by his armpits, and dragged him stumbling out of the flat. In another moment the flat was empty of militia. The whole thing had taken less than three minutes from start to finish. Mr and Mrs Morawski rushed into Grzesiek's room.

"Oh my God, dear God, dear God," Mrs Morawski was in tears. Her Grzesiek was gone.

She would never see him, again.

+

"They've what?" She couldn't believe it.

"They just knocked down the front door," Anita could see that, "threw everything onto the floor and took him away," Mrs Morawski was in tears.

"I don't believe it." She couldn't. She just stood there, halfway into the hall, her mind blank. No thought process would happen. She stared sightlessly at Grzesiek's parents. She shook her head, screwing up her eyes to hold back her own tears.

"When?"

"This morning."

"Ten o'clock."

"Did they say anything?"

"No."

"Did they have any papers?"

"No...Yes. But we didn't see them."

"Who were they? Do you know who they were?"

"No. Just Russian militiamen."

"They were so fast."

"And so violent. And there were so many of them."

Anita looked around the hall, helplessly, "May I?", she asked, indicating Grzesiek's room.

"Of course."

She went in, still in boots and coat. The floor of the tiny room was covered with the contents of the drawers and cupboards. Even the bedding had been pulled out from under the bed-settee and thrown onto the floor.

Her mind still blank from the shock, she sat slowly on the bed and began to cry.

+

TWO DAYS LATER

Anita lay on the bed, triumphant. It had taken a long time, but at last she had achieved it. She grinned broadly, not trying to hide it.

"Was that good?" she asked. She knew that it had been good for him. He had leapt into her, and had made a great deal of noise about enjoying it.

"That was good," already Igor was going to sleep. She curled herself around her enemy. Another one down. This one a big fish, too.

Her wide grin faded slowly. She'd beat the fuckers, yet. As many as possible. She lay there, not allowing her eyes to close, staring sightlessly at nothing. If she closed her eyes unbearable images of the hope on Grzesiek's face kept returning.

She prayed that she had the weapon that she needed.

Chapter Fourteen

WAR DAY + 546

WESTBOUND ON ROUTE E8
LEAVING POZNAN
POLAND

It was a beautiful car to drive. They seemed to speed almost silently through the darkness. Beside him, the girl was silent. She'd said hardly anything. A few hours ago she had simply turned up, obviously by prior arrangement, although he hadn't been aware of what form the arranging had taken. These were strange times.

She was a lovely looking girl, although she must surely be older than the old man had said. Well, she looked older than seventeen, anyway. If she was his daughter though, the old man ought to know how old she was. Oughtn't he? She had long blond hair, a tall slim frame and an attractively trim shape hidden inside a calf length woollen overcoat. He was suddenly and acutely aware that he had hardly seen a woman for a very long time. Let alone sat beside one in a Mercedes. After a while in the warmth of the car he had become aware of a slight scent. She was either wearing something with a slight but beautiful fragrance, or there were traces of it on her clothing. She smelt lovely. With an unpleasant jerk, it took him back a while.

The old man had explained about how cars were tagged and about the electronic sensors that monitored their movement. The Mercedes was a particularly valuable find because it wasn't tagged, which meant that it could go anywhere unnoticed...but if they were stopped by the policja or the militia they were dead. Quite apart from anything else, the penalty for driving or for riding in an untagged car was death, (which had come as no surprise to Jamie).

The old man had been full of ideas and they'd spent several weeks getting the car ready. They'd fitted a series of lights to the roof so that in the dark it might pass for a military or law enforcement vehicle. The old man had had an idea that perhaps these vehicles weren't tagged. He also felt that as there were at least two completely different law enforcement agencies active in each area that it was possible that neither department would know where all the untagged cars in any one area were at any one time. Added to which he was certain that around the border area there would be a lot of untagged vehicles belonging to various government departments.

They had even tried to fix a large piece of steel behind the two front seats, but the task had been beyond them. And they had tried for days. In the end they had propped the thick piece of steel behind the front seats with cardboard boxes. Not exactly ideal, but if the boxes held it in place the idea was that the steel would protect them from people shooting from behind - if they crouched down on the floor. The piece of steel that they'd got was only about two foot high. Still, they had grinned, beggars can't be choosers. And they now had the best part of an armoured Mercedes.

So, the thick piece of metal protected the smalls of their backs. The old man had made Jamie promise to make the girl crouch down on the floor whenever there was any trouble. If they saw it coming! If she would do what he asked, Jamie added to himself.

Fuel looked like it might be a problem. The old man had reckoned that petrol went off after a fairly short period. Jamie had thought that that was very likely to be nonsense, but all he had said was that they should try it.

Starting it had been tough, too, but they'd managed. They'd got the thing ticking over in the garage, terrified that someone would come and see what was going on. It had seemed to make an awful lot of noise.

No one did. But the garage had very quickly filled up with noxious fumes. They hadn't dared to open the double doors, so they'd smashed the windows that opened out onto the garden behind the house.

They were almost ready by then. They would spend only a couple of days at a time in the house, and then they'd move on. The old man was paranoid about becoming a part of the community. Jamie, too, was a lot more nervous about everything, now that he knew that the old man had escaped from a camp. Somehow he'd lost a little of his magic.

So the work was slow, but in the end it was done.

One evening the old man had said that perhaps tomorrow was the day. He had definitely been asking a question. He wasn't pushing.

Jamie had given it a moment's thought.

Why not?

He had nodded.

+

It was about a hundred miles, which was a hundred and sixty kilometres from Poznan to the border as the crow flies. And that was the way they were going.

Make or break.

A straight line.

The way the crow flies.

The other reason why the old man was so insistent that Anita crouch on the floor at the first sign of any trouble was that she was in the driver's seat. The car was a UK model. The steering wheel was on the wrong side. So, anyone trying to knock out the driver would go for the front off-side seat. Where Anita was sitting.

She could have sat in the back, behind Jamie, but then she wouldn't have been protected by the steel sheet. She could even have hidden in the boot, but the thought of what could go wrong if she was in there was horrifying.

No. The front off-side seat was still the best option. A right hand drive model! Amazing!

One hundred miles. That meant that he could think of the journey in terms of percentage done and percentage to go. So far, they'd covered a mere ten miles, ten percent. Ninety percent to go.

"Smoke?" she asked. He shook his head.

"Mind if I do?" He was watching the road, but even in the dark he could see the swing of her long blond hair. Or could he just imagine it?

"Please do," he shook his head. He didn't mind. He was expecting the flare of a match, but she used the cigar lighter. The soft glow almost lit her face. She inhaled the smoke with almost audible pleasure. Before exhaling she leaned forward slightly and wound down her window a little to let out the smoke. Each time she exhaled she was careful to blow the smoke through the window. He liked that.

"Where're you from?" she asked.

What did she mean, exactly? In the darkness ahead a pair of headlights! He didn't answer. Neither of them expected an answer. Their four eyes were simply glued to the oncoming pair of lights. Could be anything, they were thinking. Could be a civilian going about his or her lawful, legal business, could be Policja, could be Militia, could be...the end of their lives.

The oncoming lights didn't slow, just carried on going wherever they were going. They both breathed out in relief.

"Wow!" she said. There wasn't much traffic around and they were still ages from the border. He glanced at the dashboard. Over eighty percent to go. She looked at him.

He could feel it. Or maybe he could see the swing of her hair, but he knew that she was waiting for an answer to her question.

"Work camp," he found that he wanted to choke on the words. He tried again.

"I was in the camp on the south of Poznan."

"Kotowa?"

"What?" he hadn't understood what she had said.

"Kotowa," she said it more slowly, pausing for just an instant whilst she realised that he still didn't understand, before continuing, "the camp in Kotowa?"

For a confused moment he was silent.

"Kotowa?" he repeated, "I don't know. It was the camp on the edge of Poznan."

"The camp," she almost laughed. He looked sharply at her. "Do you know how many camps there are in Poznan?"

"No," she could hear a waver in his voice. She realised that perhaps she was being unfair. His veneer of normality was obviously still very fragile.

"Nor do I. But there are loads," she pressed the cigar lighter and fumbled for a ciggie.

"Oh!" He sounded both surprised and shocked. And indeed he was. He had had no idea.

"My brothers are in Kotowa. The camp in Kotowa. I used to see them sometimes."

"You could see them?" it must have been a very different kind of camp.

"No, no. I mean that I used to watch them go from the camp to the plant."

"Were you," he wasn't sure what he was asking, "I mean, were you allowed to?"

"Allowed to? I don't know. There weren't any rules about being in the street, and the prisoners used the same streets." She drew hard on her new cigarette.

Despite himself the aroma of woman, scent and cigarette smoke, was almost intoxicating.

+

They passed the 80 kilometre line. With no electronic tag in the Mercedes no one knew that they were there. And then they were gone.

All around them militia and policja snoozed behind their silent consoles. Five miles on they passed a blue and white policja Polonez parked in a lay-by, sideways on to the road.

He'd just glanced at the dash—they'd got 45 miles to go—when she grabbed at his arm, saying something fast that he didn't understand. He understood her tone, though.

At the same moment he saw the blue and white. He stifled an obscenity. Quite why he stifled it, he wasn't sure. He thought that it was something to do with not wanting to die with an obscenity on his lips.

"What are we going to do?" It was far too late to do anything but to go on. Any deviation now would certainly encourage interest. If they continued there was always the chance that they would be allowed to pass.

He didn't slow.

"Pray," he answered. She wasn't sure if he was joking or not. Nor was he.

They stared stiffly ahead as they passed the Polonez. Both of them were praying. There are times when praying is easy. They prayed in silence.

They passed the policja car. There was no sign of movement. Maybe, the guy—or guys—were asleep? Maybe, they would wait a few moments, then flick on their headlights and tail the Mercedes. Maybe, they were running a check with Central. It would take a few moments. Maybe, they were just playing with them.

Maybe.

They didn't seem to breathe. They said nothing. Jamie found that it was suddenly very difficult to watch the road ahead. Every nerve wanted to watch the rear view mirror. He forced himself to look forwards. Allowing the Mercedes to wander all over the road wasn't going to help them any. He grinned at the Americanism.

"What're they doing?" she hissed, as though perhaps hissing would help.

"Nothing," despite his grin, he was hissing, too.

This was ridiculous. It was hardly believable. This was the world. This was their lives. This was all that they had, and it was hanging on a thread. How did this nightmare happen? How could it happen that they were fleeing for their lives? What had they done? Were they criminals? Foul fiends? Were they evil?

No!

What were they? Two individuals fleeing, hoping to keep their lives. Nothing else. They had nothing. Except life.

And they were surrounded by people who wanted to deprive them of that. Of life. It was a bit too much like an American movie. Only it didn't feel like an adventure. It felt more like blinding panic.

Another glance in the mirror.

Nothing there.

Maybe...but maybe not. Who knew?

Another few moments in silence.

Another glance in the mirror.

Nothing.

He breathed again.

+

"Sandwich?"

"What?"

"Would you like a sandwich?"

"No," he was struggling with his thoughts. Did he want a sandwich? "No, thanks."

Twenty percent to go. Twenty miles.

"Twenty miles," he said.

"What? What's that?" She didn't know what he was talking about.

"Just over thirty kilometres."

"Oh," he could hear the tension in her voice.

"Go on, have one." What was she talking about?

"They're very good." The sandwiches. She was still going on about the sandwiches. "I made them myself."

We may be dead in minutes. Dear God. And she's talking about sandwiches. His stomach was churning—butterflies they'd called it as kids. This was more like a threshing machine in the pit of his stomach. He thought that he might want to vomit.

"I couldn't, I'm sorry." She turned to look at him.

"Vodka?"

Vodka? What was this woman? A walking larder? Or what? Vodka?

"No, thanks," he'd never liked to drink and drive.

"Go on, it'll make you feel great. It'll take away the pain." Which particular pain was that?

"You know they give soldiers a shot of alcohol before a battle." Yes, he had an idea that he'd read about that. Sometimes, it was the only way to be sure that they'd go over the top. He nodded slowly. And was it such a bad idea? It might give him that extra edge...it would certainly make him feel that he'd got it. She unscrewed the bottle top.

"I feel sick," he said, surprising himself.

"I know," she handed him the open bottle.

He clasped it in his hand. Was it shaking? And lifted the bottle to his lips. Two large swallows. Surprisingly, it was rather pleasant. He'd imagined that it would be rough, make him cough or something. He paused, the bottle against his leg.

"Like it?" she sounded as though she was smiling.

He nodded, "Yes."

He lifted the bottle again, taking another mouthful, and handed it back to her. Their fingers touched.

"Perhaps," he started. He felt a sudden glow of optimism. They might make it. They might just make it. They might be all right.

"Perhaps, a sandwich."

She laughed. She actually laughed.

+

"Janus?" she hadn't used his name before. He nodded. His mouth was full of bread. She sounded nervous, hesitant. Quite unlike the Anita he had grown to know in the last hours.

He wasn't sure that the sandwich had been a good idea. It seemed to have had some kind of cold meat in it. More fat than meat, actually. It wasn't going down so well over the vodka. He swallowed.

"Yes?"

"Do you have anyone over there?" she made it sound like over there was a long, long way away. "You know..." she finished rather lamely.

He knew. The old man had told him quite a lot about his family while they'd been working on the car. About his wife, his sons and about the beautiful nymph that the NRC had taken and abused.

The girl had nothing. No one. She was alone. On the other side of the border she would be even more alone.

"No," he shook his head, a vivid picture of his lost family flashing through his mind. A moment's silence. They hadn't got much time. They'd be there very soon. Quite where there was, he wasn't sure.

"Could we," she paused, "I mean..." he wondered if he knew what she was going to say, but he couldn't say it for her. She pushed in the cigar lighter.

"Can we tell them that we're..." she seemed lost for words, "...that we're together."

No problem. He wasn't sure exactly what she meant, but that would be no problem. He nodded.

"Yes."

He had an empty home in north London. At least, he supposed that he had. If it was still his. He supposed that it was. And what about his mortgage? If that house wasn't there for him, there'd be something, he was sure. What happened when a 'dead' man reappeared? If his estate had been distributed? For a brief moment of madness, Jamie's mind flashed to the thought that his parents, or sister, might have collected on his life assurance. What would happen if he got out? As soon as these thoughts had entered his mind, they were gone. They were totally irrelevant. They formed no part of his current world. This was here, that was then. Back to the present. He certainly owed it to the old man to help her out. He owed the old man everything.

"Do you have any money?" What could she have? What would she do? She could have only what she was standing in. He had only a few zloties.

"About a million."

"Zloties?"

"Yes."

Worthless, they were worthless outside Poland. Bound to be. And not worth very much in Poland either, for that matter. He grunted.

"I've got a place...I had a place. I can give you a home while you sort yourself out..." If, he was thinking, if. "...it would be a pleasure."

A moments silence. A home, she was thinking. A home. I like that word.

"Thank you," she said softly.

Another moment's pause. She lit the cigarette.

"Here," he held out his hand. She looked at him in surprise.

"But you don't."

Where we're going, it won't make any difference. He almost said it. He knew that they were going to die. It just wasn't possible that a tramp and a schoolgirl whore could beat the system. Not a system like this. They were dead. Dead. His foot lifted off the throttle.

"Anita," he began.

"Don't say it!" it was as though she had read his mind.

He turned to her. She was looking at him, daggers! Silently, she handed him the cigarette. He lifted it to his mouth and took a deep drag. Smooth! The smoke curled down his throat. He held it in his lungs. Beautiful. He breathed out gently. She was looking at him in astonishment. He caught her look, glanced at her, and grinned.

"Used to smoke at school. That was a while ago," he added for her benefit. Just in case she imagined that he'd recently left. He realised that the alcohol must have gone to his head.

"That's better," she said, rather like a mother to a child.

Ahead of them they could see a soft glow in the sky. It had been there for a while before becoming noticeable.

"Must be the border," she said.

He began to pray.

+

"The idea," the old man had said, "is to go through just after something else. That way there's a better chance the barriers will be open." It had sounded simple at the time. Simple. And 'there's a better chance the barriers will be open'. 'Chance'! Now that they were there they wanted rather more than a mere chance. A chance!

Oh shit! They couldn't even see the border crossing, the way everything was laid out. It was in a sort of a dip, which Jamie felt meant that they ought to be able to see it, but they couldn't.

They knew that the dip led down to the river. They knew that the various customs and immigration controls were in buildings on this side of the river. The river itself was the border between the two countries, but the bridge, apparently, was Poland. So they had to get right across to the other side.

They didn't know what additional buildings or defences had been put into place since the second turn, but the old man had been able to tell them what it had looked like a few years back. In essence, there had been very little to prevent a determined driver from barging through apart from the enormous crush of people and vehicles. At the other end, well past the custom and immigration sheds, just this side of the bridge, there had been a solitary soldier in a pillbox controlling a light barrier. However, this alone would not have stopped a car; it was merely used to control the flow of traffic. Also, every official had seemed to have a gun. That was all that he had been able to tell them. Not much.

"Well," he said, looking at Anita, "I guess it's now or never." She nodded, reached across and gave him a light kiss on his cheek.

"Got the passport?"

He patted his chest.

"Yep," incredibly, the old man had provided them with a British passport. He'd said that he'd found it in the abandoned house in which the Mercedes was stored. It was some years out of date, but it was ideal for waving at people. Which people? Jamie had wondered. Those shooting at us or those welcoming us? And would they welcome us, anyway?

There was so much that they didn't know. He put the car into first gear and pulled onto the road.

+

Fifty miles an hour. That was about eighty kilometres an hour. Fuel was good, one quarter left. Engine temperature was good. Everything looked okay. His hands grasped the wheel with a claw-like strength, his knuckles white.

Two hundred metres ahead were the sheds, immigration and customs. "Think we'll skip those, today," he murmured almost audibly. The smile on his face was old and frightened.

They were seconds from death. On the floor, to his left, Anita was curled somehow onto her legs. Her head was level with the seat she had been sitting in until a few moments ago. In her hand she held the end of a piece of orange string.

Seconds from death.

The Mercedes was travelling across a wide expanse of brightly lit tarmac, perhaps a hundred metres wide, that narrowed into a half dozen channels between the customs and immigration sheds. These channels were designed to allow two cars to pass side by side at a walking pace.

Jamie noted with astonishment that there seemed to be no one in sight. He could see everything clearly. The whole area was lit by enormous arc lamps. He put his foot down.

They'd be through in moments. Or dead.

He found that he was praying.

A uniformed figure emerged from a door in a shed to the left. For a moment he seemed to be stationary. Then he started to shout, and ran into the path of the Mercedes waving wildly. It crossed Jamie's mind that perhaps the man didn't understand exactly what was happening. It was rather as though he thought that perhaps Jamie simply hadn't realised that he ought to stop.

Jamie kept his foot on the throttle. If it was him or them then he was afraid that it would have to be him. He was horrified to realise that he was mouthing 'Die you dog, die.' Where had that thought come from?

Oh shit!

His hands gripped the wheel. His foot stayed on the throttle.

And suddenly the man seemed to understand...with moments to spare he leapt to one side, still shouting.

'Oh God, thank God', Jamie found himself thinking. He didn't want to kill anyone. He just wanted to live.

Figures seemed to be springing out of most of the doors now, but it was almost too late. They all seemed to be wearing hand guns as a part of their uniform, but none of them seemed prepared for a situation where they might be required to use them.

The Mercedes shot through channel 4. It was still labelled for non-Polish cars and campers. The correct channel, anyway, he thought.

As he passed the uniformed figures he could see the astonishment on their faces. He almost grinned. Then he saw the man with the light machine gun emerging from the right.

"Down," he screamed at Anita, who was already as low as she could get. He hunched his shoulders—it felt like it might help.

He dropped the Merc into third and put his foot down. He could feel a slight surge as she pulled away, but she was old and tired. His eyes flicked back and forth from the tarmac to the speedo.

They came out of the sheds into another wide space of tarmac. Close to their left were a row of buildings that seemed to have no windows. To their right, there was a large area of tarmac bordered by some serious looking fencing. About a hundred metres ahead, up a slight slope, the tarmac narrowed and curved to the left.

The space between his shoulders squirmed. Would he feel anything? Would he know what had happened if he was shot? Was the guy shooting already? Would he hear it? Crazy thoughts bounced around inside his head. He squeezed his shoulders tighter together.

Yes, the answer was yes. He could hear the rattle of shots. It didn't sound much like a gun to him, it wasn't what he'd imagined, but he could hear it. He could also hear some dull noises at the back of the Merc which he assumed meant that the guy was doing fairly well.

He swung the wheel over to the right for a moment, and then back. He'd seen enough films to know that that was what you were supposed to do. The Merc didn't like it, though. Swerving violently at over eighty kilometres an hour obviously wasn't its forte. It was a bit of a struggle to point it back in the correct direction. It was just as well that this section of road was so wide.

"What are you doing?" Anita hissed.

"Zig zagging," he yelled back. This didn't seem to be the moment for whispering. If he was going to speak, might as well make sure that he was understood. He might not get a second chance.

"Why?" she hissed.

"Why??" he yelled back.

"Why?" she hissed.

"Because," he began at a yell, when a row of shots hit the steel plate behind the front seats with a sudden clatter.

"Shit!" she screamed, ramming her head down out of sight in the footwell.

They were almost there, but he had give the Merc another wobble to put the guy off. This time he was a lot more gentle, easing the wheel slightly to the right and then back again. The car swung sedately back and forth.

A slight swing to the left as the tarmac narrowed, straighten out to the right and they were on what one might call a normal road. Normal except for the enormous steel barrier that was closing across their path and the last building that made up the checkpoint on this side of the brightly lit bridge.

He could see clear across it. At the other end of the bridge there was a lot of bright light, lots of vehicles, tarmac and buildings.

Freedom.

And freedom.

Freedom was there.

He plunged his foot flat on the throttle, gripped the wheel and found that he was praying again. Or was he still praying?

The barrier was creeping across the road. It looked too heavy to move fast. It seemed to be an enormous rigid steel girder, maybe a metre high and heaven knew how thick, sliding across the road. It was coming from a large concrete structure to the right and was obviously designed to lock into the similar structure to the left. It looked pretty solid.

There'd be no chance, absolutely no chance of driving the Merc through it once it was closed. It'd be like having a head-on with a forty tonner.

310

It looked very solid. A moment's hesitation. Just for a moment.

But what choice did they have?

None.

To fail now was to die.

He kept his foot on the floor. Flat. With his right hand he flicked on all the lights. All of them. Might as well.

The barrier was almost halfway across.

The gap was getting very narrow.

As they powered towards the barrier it seemed to speed up.

Who, he found himself thinking, in their right minds would fit a barrier that couldn't be closed in the time that it took to drive from the sheds to the barrier itself?

No one, that's who.

It must have been designed to close in time. Otherwise it was pointless.

They were dead.

Oh, Jesus!

Suddenly everything ahead seemed even brighter than a moment ago. What had they done?

Just metres...

A heavily amplified voice started to say something. It didn't seem to make any sense. Anyway, he had more important things to think about.

The gap was very small!

Would this be it?

Oh, Jesus, he was still praying. He could feel his lips moving.

There wasn't room!

It couldn't work!

They were dead!

Jesus, Jesus...was he yelling?

They were so close.

The gap was so small.

He took the car as far to the left as possible. Did it matter? If there wasn't space, there wasn't space. His hands were gripping the wheel...gripping...Of course it mattered!

With a sudden thump, and a scream of tearing metal the Merc slammed into a gap that simply wasn't wide enough. Still, he gripped the wheel, his foot flat on the gas...

...Jesus, dear Jesus...

He could feel the right hand side of the car being torn apart by the steel of the closing barrier, as the opposite side of the car folded up against the concrete...

"What's happening," Anita was screaming, her face white and terrified. She began to pull herself out of the footwell. The Merc was dead, they could feel that. They'd just hit steel and concrete at eighty kph, fifty mph.

Even as she screamed the car seemed to scramble through the barrier, and they were on the bridge. Three hundred metres to go.

Battered, broken and horribly misshapen the Merc was still moving in the right direction. The bonnet seemed to have got higher, the doors somehow tighter and closer and the steering was complete chaos. Desperately, he tried to steer the car across the bridge, but it had developed a mind of its own together with a sort of a looseness that felt most unhealthy.

There was something horribly wrong with the front end of the car. He clung desperately to the wheel, willing the Merc to cover the last three hundred metres, his foot still flat on the throttle. Everything felt wrong. The pedals seemed disconnected, parts of the car seemed to be scraping the ground, he could hardly see out of the windscreen because the bonnet seemed unnaturally high, the driver's door was hard up against his arm and the floor felt buckled. Was that possible?

And still they were moving forwards. Against all odds the Merc hadn't died.

Shooting!

They were shooting!

"The string," he yelled, "pull the string!" And Anita started scrabbling about on the floor looking for the piece of orange string.

"Pull it," he kept yelling.

"Yes, yes, all right," she found that she had time to answer. Where was the bloody thing? She'd had it a moment ago!

"Pull it," he screamed. He couldn't see what she was doing, but he knew that she hadn't pulled it. He was desperate.

Only the Good Lord knew how fast they were moving, but it wasn't fast. The Merc was giving up and he was barely able to keep her from running off the side of the bridge.

Jesus, oh Jesus...

They wouldn't go off the side, he could see that. The sides of the bridge were solid. It looked like wrought iron, it could have been anything, but it looked solid. If they hit the side they'd stop.

They didn't want to stop.

Please, please...he urged the car, or was he praying? Anything! Just keep going.

The rear of the car erupted! It sounded as though the boot had exploded.

Fantastic! He almost yelled. She'd found the piece of string. It had been one of the old man's crazy ideas, along with the sheet of steel. Make a smoke screen; they won't be able to see you. So they'd built a sort of oily bonfire in the boot out of oil soaked rags, an old tyre and a little petrol.

Amazing! The smoke was pouring out.

Fantastic!

She hauled herself back into position, a wide grin across her face.

About two hundred metres to go!

Two hundred metres to life!

Life!

"Fantastic, eh?" she yelled at him. He suddenly realised how very noisy everything was. The sound of screaming steel being dragged along tarmac was the most prominent sound, but somewhere a horn seemed to be sounding, and there was the sound of the engine roaring - they must have lost their exhaust, they sounded like a tank. And shooting.

So much noise.

He grinned in response.

The wheel was shaking really badly, and pulling hard to the left. He seemed to have to correct each lurch to the left with an ever increasing wrench to the right. It was only a matter of time.

He'd lose her soon.

But on she went.

About a hundred metres to go.

Two thirds across the bridge.

Not bad for a tramp and a whore, he found himself thinking. The two of us against the whole world. Well, half the world, anyway.

Not bad. His grin stayed.

And suddenly he'd lost it! The Merc lurched once more to the left and he couldn't hold her.

It all happened so fast!

And yet it seemed to take a lifetime...

The left hand front wing caught the bridge and the car started to swing. He tried to turn into the skid, but this was no skid, this was chaos. The car was practically in pieces. Using all his strength he couldn't haul the wheel around to the right.

He could feel the back of the car swinging in an arc...beside him Anita was screaming an obscenity...his hands gripped the useless wheel...his right foot was still rammed down flat on the throttle...the engine was screaming...he'd lost it...

He'd lost it!

He was screaming! Was he screaming?

He opened his eyes...he couldn't remember closing them!...the world was spinning...all around him all he seemed to see was steel bridge walls...moving walls...

Steel!

With a sudden thump he was slammed against the driver's door. Every bone in his body, every muscle, every organ, each ounce of flesh on his body crashed into the door as the car completed a 180 degree spin, its right hand side crashing into the bridge.

Anita seemed to be on his lap, limbs waving like a rag dolls. There was dust and smoke everywhere. The steel of the bridge was tearing away at the side of the car.

The noise was incredible.

For a moment, for just a moment as the car spun, they were face on to the way they'd come.

How much more of this could the Merc take?

Remind me to buy German, next time, he found himself thinking, they know how to build them.

They were moving...they must be!

Backwards?

No, he realised as he tried to see around Anita, they were still spinning, but slowly. The thump against the bridge that had knocked the stuffing out of him had slowed her down a lot.

The Merc was dead now, really. Really. She'd sunk real low, he could feel that she was dragging the whole of her belly on the tarmac. The bonnet seemed even higher. The whole thing had been knocked apart.

Finished.

She was finished.

But still sliding, still spinning.

Slowly.

What a noise! Screaming steel on tarmac. And the smell! The smell of heat, flame, burnt out power and death.

Death.

Were they shooting? He wasn't sure. Too much noise, too little time.

And still the Merc was moving, sliding slowly, spinning slowly.

And suddenly, she was stopped.

He breathed.

They were broadside on. Blocking the bridge. A perfect target.

To their left, freedom. To their right, death. Behind them, he realised that the boot was still alight. Of course, it was only moments since Anita had ignited it.

Anita was ramming her body against the front passenger door. He didn't suppose that any of the doors would open, not now. She was screaming. He didn't recognise her words, but her meaning was clear.

The car was burning and she couldn't open the door.

For a moment he sat, motionless, not really thinking, just trying to gather his thoughts together. He was aware that every thought that he had might be his last conscious thought.

A sudden burst of heavy gun fire startled him into activity. He unclipped his seat belt and clambered into the back. It wasn't so easy. Every bone in his body ached and the wretched headrests got in the way.

He landed with one knee on the edge of the steel plate, and screamed in pain as it cut through to the bone, but he didn't stop moving. He found himself scrambling through piles of cardboard towards the rear left hand door.

He pushed it, hard. Very hard. Expecting it to resist, but it must have been half open already, because it swung open and he found himself tumbling out onto the tarmac.

"Anita," he yelled even before he'd hit the ground, "Anita, Anita," he was screaming as he picked himself up. Ahead, he could see Nato army personnel and vehicles.

About a hundred metres away.

The Merc really was on fire. It wasn't just the bonfire in the boot! He leaned in, still yelling her name, and hauled her scrabbling body through the gap between the front seats.

Suddenly, she was on the tarmac beside him.

"Oh, God!"

They were both coughing. Everything seemed to be covered in smoke or dust. Or maybe both. For a moment they crouched, coughing, each of them alone with their own thoughts. He noticed how dirty she was. Her face and hands were black. Her clothes were a mess; torn and stained. Her hair seemed a different colour.

He realised that he must be in a similar state. He began to cough, again.

Two shots rang out.

Shit!

She caught his eye. She almost smiled. Almost. She couldn't quite make it.

"Thanks," she murmured. For what, he thought, tearing at his jacket.

"For what?" he asked.

"For the rest of my life." He smiled, nearly.

From inside his jacket he produced the passport. He held it above his head for a moment, before sticking it back into a pocket.

"C'mon," he half stood and offered her his hand.

It was about one hundred metres. Freedom was about one hundred metres away. They could see the Nato military. Just one hundred metres away. All they had to do was to run that one hundred metres.

When he was a kid he could have run it in moments. Tonight it might take them the rest of their lives. She took his hand, and without looking back they started to run...

+

The lieutenant watched the two figures moving away from the burning Merc at a run. Camera three showed him every detail under the powerful flood-lights. Closer to the line, Sergeant Horne had the night glasses screwed tight to his eyes, his mutterings occasionally breaking through on his throat mike.

The female runner had taken the male runner's hand and they had started an uncomfortable run away from the Merc, bent low and crouching at the knee. The male figure was wearing trousers and jacket, but the female was wearing a calf length coat that hindered her movements as she tried to keep her body low and to run at the same time. For a few metres the thick smoke from the burning car offered them some protection, but within moments they were in the open. The heavy machine gun to the south of the bridge would have a clear line of fire.

"Move, move," Peters and the lieutenant could hear John Horne's muttering, "move!"

"Kill the floods," the lieutenant's voice in Horne's ear.

"Done," the floods were gone. The bridge was thrown into comparative darkness, although still lit.

There was a sudden flare from the Merc as the fuel tank ignited. A moment later, the woosh of the exploding fuel swept across the bridge.

"Ah, shit!"

And the two runners were flung to the ground by the explosion. They clawed themselves onto their hands and knees, scrambled back to their feet, and ran on, still bent uncomfortably.

Eighty metres to go.

With a vicious crackle the heavy machine gun opened up from the south of the bridge, shooting wide of the runners, and spraying the western end of the bridge with a wave of death.

"Jesus, Jesus," Peters yelled as the ground crew pressed themselves deeper into the dirt, "Too close, too close".

There were rules. A vicious game, but there were rules, and they were supposed to be followed. No fire should cross the line.

"Where are those medics?" Peters yelled into his handset.

"They're in the snake pit. East end," Horne's calm voice. Well, he would be calm, wouldn't he, Peters thought, because he wasn't trying to dig himself a hole with his finger nails while NRC machine gun fire whistled through his hair. What hair he had! Peters smiled.

The machine gun fire stopped. Blessed silence.

Fifty metres to go.

"Go, go, go."

Peters wondered what the hell was going on, that both heavy machine guns should be silent. Jammed, or what? Someone would be getting a bollocking.

There was still a steady stream of hand weapon fire from directly across the bridge, but with the burning Merc, the plumes of thick, black smoke, right in the line of fire they were unlikely to do any damage.

Thirty metres to go. Mere seconds, now.

Twenty metres. Almost home.

With a sudden clatter, the northern machine gun post opened up. Instinctively, the ground crew ducked their heads back into the dirt. The angle of fire was now so acute that the ground crew were almost directly in the line of fire.

"Second man down. Second man down," Waugh yelled.

"Shit!" Peters raised his head. There was one runner up, about eight metres away— just eight metres away—and one down. They weren't far from where Groupie was lying, unmoving.

On camera three, the male runner—running slightly ahead of the female—had run into the fire of the northern machine gun. He had simply been blown away. One moment running, the next moment straightening for a moment as the bullets tore into him, taking another couple of paces, and collapsing in a pile.

"Shit, oh shit," this was looking bad.

A couple more paces, and the female runner was slowing to a stop, stooping lower over the downed runner, feeling, touching, shouting. Her long hair all over the place, her coat in the way.

"Come on, come on," the ground crew were yelling at her, "Come on!"

"Jesus, Jesus!" she wasn't moving. She was kneeling over the downed man, apparently oblivious to the machine gun fire. Now that she was on her knees she was protected to some extent by the waist high, ornate steel bridge walls.

"Janus," she was screaming, "Janus," she was shaking him. He was still.

Her voice carried clearly beyond the ground crew at the line, back to Sergeant Horn's view point and very possibly right across the bridge. Despite the British passport, she was screaming in Polish, and still apparently oblivious to the gun fire.

"Alfa is opening," Horne's voice. Lieutenant James's eyes flicked briefly from camera three to camera six. Alfa was opening. "Oh, shit," he mouthed.

"Peters, get her in. Alfa is opening."

"Affirmative, sir," Peters responded.

"As soon as you can. We don't want more down."

"No, sir. Affirmative, sir."

She hadn't budged from the spot. She was still kneeling over the downed runner. With one hand she swept her hair back from her face, and screamed, "Help me."

"We can't," Waugh yelled back in perfect Polish.

"Help me!"

"We can't. Get over here. You'll be hit."

"Help me!" she was screaming frantically, "Help me!"

"For Christ's sake, get her out of there," the lieutenant.

"Affirmative, sir."

"Help me!"

"Loot wants her out," Peters said to Waugh. Waugh gave him a very old fashioned look.

"Alfa is opening!"

"Shit!" Waugh turned back to the runner "You must get off that bridge now," he yelled, "They'll get you, if you don't. Now, please!"

"Transport approaching bridge," Horne's voice. Again, the lieutenant's eyes flicked briefly from the action on camera three to camera six. Sure enough, NRC army transport was approaching the bridge.

"Help me, please, please help," she was desperate.

"We can't. You must leave him! You must come here!"

This was unbearable. The men watched, unbelieving, as she continued to kneel, swaying back and forth, over the downed runner, looking no older than a school girl, and apparently oblivious to the gun fire.

They had only moments. Once Alfa was open, NRC transport would come right up to the line. The river and the bridge were theirs. Once the transport was past the Merc the female runner would be dead if she hadn't already crossed the line. They'd have a clear line of fire with a one hundred metre range. She wouldn't have a chance.

The clatter of the northern machine gun paused.

"Peters, there's transport entering the bridge. She's got seconds," the lieutenant, "Tell her she she's going to die!   She must move!"

"Affirmative, sir. Waugh!" Waugh turned, "Transport entering bridge. We've got to get her in".

"Why won't you help me?"   Her blackened face turned to them as she screamed for help. Jesus, Horne thought, getting his first proper look at her through his night glasses, she's barely more than a school girl.

"Get out!   Get out!   You must get out, now!"

"Alfa is open. Transport now on bridge," Horne, again.

It was a covered military jeep with a weapon mounted on the roof behind the driver. A popular border patrol vehicle. It was fast, powerful, and manoeuvrable.

Kneeling over Jamie, Anita was screaming for help from the soldiers lying behind a small protective ridge, but they had refused. She couldn't understand why. For a moment the heavy sound of gun fire seemed to have stopped.

She raised herself to her feet, grabbed Jamie by his hands and pulled his inert body towards the end of the bridge. She imagined, correctly, that the line of green twinkling lights marked the border. She had only seven or eight metres to go. Just a few paces.

His body dragged heavily on the road surface. It was very hard work. Why weren't the soldiers helping?   Again, she screamed for help. Again they shouted for her to come. Jamie's hands held tight in hers, she knew that she

324

would never let him go. Never. She would pull until she died or until they crossed the line together. A man who could offer a whore a home was worth dying for. Every muscle in her body strained as she leaned backwards, pulling him by his hands. She screamed again,

"For Christ's sake help me!" She dug her nails deep into his flesh. She'd get him home, whatever happened, she'd get him home.

One of the soldiers was up on his feet, just three or four metres away.

A sudden clatter of gun fire.

She glanced up to see a jeep racing towards her, maybe only eighty metres away. There was a man shooting from a gun on the roof.

Again, she screamed for help, howling like a wild animal, not understanding why these men wouldn't help pull Jamie to freedom.

But all they would shout was "Get over here, leave him, get over here!"

Behind her, the ground crew had dropped back to the ground, as the gunner in the jeep struggled to shoot the runner without allowing his shots to cross the line. He wasn't very good at it. There was lead flying all over the place.

Two metres to go! If she fell over backwards she would almost be there!

The jeep was barely fifty metres away.

"Jesus, Jesus, will somebody do something!" Horne.

With an extra heave, a heave that took from her everything that she had, she wrenched Jamie backwards, at the same time screaming again in frustration and fear. The jeep was practically on top of her, the man with the gun horribly human.

Possibly less than a metre to the line!

Hands were reaching out to her from over the line. Voices screaming at her to come, to cross the line, to leave Jamie, to run, to save her life, to get safe! The hands reaching for her found her coat, grappling, getting a grip, pulling. And still she clung to Jamie's two hands. She wasn't going anywhere without him. She squeezed tighter, her nails already deeply imbedded in his flesh.

Peters and Waugh, now back on their feet, grabbed handfuls of her coat, their feet firmly on the west side of the line, and wrenched her backwards. And still she gripped Jamie's hands.

The jeep was terribly close, hurtling towards them, the gunner now no longer able to fire; the range and the angle of the target making it impossible from the moving vehicle without the very high probability of killing the soldiers immediately over the line. Two soldiers were steadying themselves, getting ready to leap off the vehicle and retrieve Anita.

One step, two steps and suddenly they were over the line. Another half step and Jamie's whole body was clear.

With a squeal of tyres, the jeep slid to a halt just metres short of the line.

"Bastards!" Anita hissed.

There was a moments silence.

"Medics, on station, now!" Horne's voice.

GREAT BRITAIN

"Granny, Tom's spilt his cereals!" Trix shrieked, wide-eyed.

Again! Helen Ingram smiled. Another Saturday morning. Helen Ingram returned to the table with cloth and sponge. John Ingram was hiding behind his newspaper. When the phone rang, Trix leapt down from her seat, brushing everything aside, and headed into the living room to answer it.

"Shall I?" Helen was about to follow.

"No," John grinned, "I'll do it." Trix had just discovered the telephone as a toy, but had not yet mastered normal telephone etiquette. Callers tended to get cut-off unexpectedly, or simply abandoned mid call.

"Hello," Trix whispered into the mouth piece.

"Hello," said Jamie, from his hospital bed in Berlin.

"Who's that?" Trix whispered.

+

Printed in Great Britain
by Amazon.co.uk, Ltd.,
Marston Gate.